SELECTED WRITINGS OF
BLAISE CENDRARS

SELECTED WRITINGS OF
BLAISE CENDRARS

Edited, with a Critical Introduction, by
Walter Albert

and with a Preface by
Henry Miller

A NEW DIRECTIONS BOOK

CONTENTS

PROSE

PREFACE

BY HENRY MILLER

Cendrars was the first French writer to look me up, during my stay in Paris, and the last-man I saw on leaving Paris. I had just a few minutes before catching the train for Rocamadour and I was having a last drink on the terrasse of my hotel near the Porte d'Orléans when Cendrars hove in sight. Nothing could have given me greater joy than this unexpected last-minute encounter. In a few words I told him of my intention to visit Greece. Then I sat back and drank in the music of his sonorous voice which to me always seemed to come from a sea organ. In those last few minutes Cendrars managed to convey a world of information, and with the same warmth and tenderness which he exudes in his books. Like the very ground under our feet, his thoughts were honeycombed with all manner of subterranean passages. I left him sitting there in shirt sleeves, never dreaming that years would elapse before hearing from him again, never dreaming that I was perhaps taking my last look at Paris.

I had read whatever was translated of Cendrars before arriving in France. That is to say, almost nothing. My first taste of him in his own language came at a time when my French was none too proficient. I began with *Moravagine,* a book by no means easy to read for one who knows little French. It was like reading a phosphorescent text through smoked glasses. I had to divine what he was saying, Cendrars, but I got it. If he had written it in Tegalic I would have gotten it. Everything is written in blood, but a blood that is saturated with starlight. Cendrars is like a transparent fish swimming in a planetary sperm; you can see his backbone, his lungs, his heart, his kidneys, his intestines; you can see the red corpuscles moving in the blood stream. You can look clean through him and see the planets wheeling. The silence he creates is deafening. It takes you back to the beginning of the world, to that hush which is engraved on the face of mystery.

I always see him there in the hub of the universe, slowly revolving with the vortex. I see his slouch hat and battered mug beneath it. I see him "revolutionizing," because there is nothing else to do. Yes, he was a sort of Brahman *à rebours,* as he said of himself, a Brahman who is the envoy plenipotentiary of the active principle itself. He is the man of the dream which he is dreaming, and he will be that until the dream ends. There is no subject and object. *There is.* A transitive mode which is expressed by the intransitive; action which is the negation of activity. Cendrars is the eye of the navel, the face in the mirror which remains after you have turned your back on it.

If he had wanted to be anything he could have been it most successfully. He did not want. He was like the sage in the Chinese story who, when asked why he never performed the miracles attributed to his disciple, replied: "The Master is able to do these things, but he is also able to refrain from doing them." His disinterestedness was always a positive, active quality. He was not inactive — *he refused, he rejected.*

It is this instinctive, ordained defiance in Cendrars which makes the word "rebel" sound ridiculous when applied to him. He was not a rebel, he was an absolute traitor to the race, and as such I salute him. The salute is wasted, of course, because

Cendrars didn't give a damn whether you saluted him or not. Would you salute a tree for spreading its foliage? Whether you are at the bottom or the top was all the same to Cendrars. He didn't care to know what you were trying to do; he was only interested in what you were. He looked you through and through, pitilessly. If you were meat for the gristle, fine! he devoured you. If you were just suet, then down the sewer you went — unless that day he happened to be in need of a little fat. He was the epitome of injustice, which is why he appeared so magnanimous. He did not forgive, or pardon, or condemn, or condone. He put you in the scales and weighed you. He said nothing. He let you do the talking. With himself he was equally rigorous. "Moi, l'homme le plus libre du monde, je reconnais que l'on est toujours lié par quelque chose, et que la liberté, l'indépendance n'existe pas, et je me méprise autant que je peux, tout en rejouissant de mon impuissance."

He has been accused of writing trash. It is true that he did not always write on the same level — but Cendrars never wrote trash. He was incapable of writing trash. His problem was not whether to write well or badly, but whether to write or not to write. Writing was almost a violation of his way of living. He wrote against the grain, more and more so as the years went on. If, on the impulse of the moment, or through dire necessity, he took the notion to do a piece of reportage, he went through with it with good grace. He went about even the most trivial task with pains, because fundamentally he did not recognize that one thing is trivial and another important. If it was not anti-human, his attitude, it was certainly anti-moral. He was as much ashamed of being disgusted or revolted as of being exalted or inspired. He had known what it is to struggle, but he despised struggle, too.

His writing, like his life, was on different levels. It changed color, substance, tempo, just as his life changed rhythm and equilibrium. He went through metamorphoses, without however surrendering his identity. His behavior seemed to be governed not merely by internal changes — psychic, chemical, physiologic — but by external ones also, chiefly by interstellar configurations.

He was tremendously susceptible to changes of weather — the spiritual weather. He experienced in his soul genuine eclipses; he knew what it means to fly off at a tangent, or to sweep across the sky like a flaming comet. He had been put on the rack, drawn and quartered; he had pursued his own shadow, tasted madness. It seems to me that his greatest tribulation was to accept the quality of the grandiose which was written in his destiny. His struggle had been with his own fate, with the grandeur which for some reason he had never wholly accepted. Out of desperation and humility he had created for himself the most human rôle of the antagonist. But his destiny was laid down in royal colors. He did not fit in anywhere because his whole life had been lived in defiance of the pattern which was ordained. And desperate and tragic, even foolish as such a course may seem, it is the very inmost virtue of Cendrars, the link which binds him to the human family, which makes him the wonderful *copain* he is, the marvelous man whom even the unseeing recognize immediately. It was this challenge which he carried around in him, which he hurled now and then in his mad drunken moments; it was this which really sustained those about him, those who had even the least contact with him. It was not the blustering, heroic attitude, but the blind, tragic defiance of the Greeks. It was the resistance to fate which is always aroused by a super-endowment of strength, by a super-wisdom. It was the Dionysian element which is created at the moment of greatest lucidity: the frail, human voice denying the god-impulse because to accept it would mean the death of all that is creative, all that is truly human. It was on this wheel of creation and destruction that Cendrars turned, as the globe itself turns. It was this which isolated him, made him a solitary. He refused to spread himself thin over an illusory pattern of grandeur; he muscled deeper and deeper into the hub, into the everlasting no-principle of the universe.

SELECTED WRITINGS OF
BLAISE CENDRARS

ACKNOWLEDGMENTS

I should like to acknowledge gratefully the interest and assistance of Professors Roger Shattuck, James Duffy, and Eléonore Zimmermann and of Brandeis University, whose generous grant helped make possible the publication of this volume. I should also like to thank Mr. Henry Miller for the permission to use excerpts from *The Henry Miller Reader* and the editors of *Texas Studies in Literature and Language* for graciously consenting to the publication of material which originally appeared in that journal in a somewhat different form. I wish in particular to thank Professor Robert Champigny, who both directed and clarified my initial work, and my wife, whose personal and professional skills brought order out of chaos.

W. A.

INTRODUCTION

I

Cendrars painted by Modigliani in a slightly rumpled Little Lord Fauntleroy suit, his lips primly pursed as if in mockery of the attitude in which the painter saw him; photographed in the heart of the South American jungle, his heavy, worn sailor's face improbably framed by giant, knife-like cacti and elephant-ear ferns; smiling savagely, one eyebrow lifted sardonically as his wife, Raymone, feeds a slant-eyed donkey; cupping his hands to light a cigarette, his collar open to expose a seamed chest; an end of a cigarette limp and wet in a corner of his mouth as he peers off into the distant horizons of his eternal vagabondage: each of these multiple poses defining his image, fixing the private intelligence in a public pose, accessible and yet remote, the landscape as exotic as the Brazilian forests or as homely as a rainswept street in a Paris suburb.

Cendrars presumably had no patience with legends. "They see only a single character in my books: Cendrars! That's not very bright. L'Or is Cendrars. Moravagine is Cendrars. Dan

YACK is Cendrars. I'm fed up with that Cendrars!" Yet the name Blaise Cendrars was itself a fiction, assumed by Frédéric-Louis Sauser in Paris in 1907, at "216 de la rue Saint-Jacques, 'Hôtel des Étrangers,'" the address at which Sauser-Cendrars, in his poem "Au cœur du monde," claimed to have been born. It was not until 1960 that the Parisian birth of Cendrars was shown by the Swiss writer, Jean Buhler, to have been a spiritual and not a physical birth. Frédéric-Louis Sauser was born on September 1, 1887, in La Chaux-de-Fonds, in the Swiss canton of Neuchâtel. The birth of which he spoke in his poem was, as Buhler points out, the moment at which Sauser "changed direction, becoming Blaise Cendrars and being born . . . to poetry." And it was the new French identity which was idealized and canonized by his critics and biographers, in a pose struck as early as 1926 by his first critical admirer, Georges Charles, who saw him "striking out like the leading Racer, in a torn jersey, traveling about the world or meditating in Paris. . . ."

Impatient and restless as he may have been, he lent himself willingly enough to the formation of this kaleidoscopic legend. In April of 1950, he was interviewed in a series of broadcasts over the French radio network. The interviewer, Michel Manoll, a sympathetic, enthusiastic participant in the mosaic-like chain of reminiscences, anticipated Cendrars's answers, led Cendrars into chanting repetitions of Manoll's own suggestions, attempting to maintain the illusion that the poet-novelist was laying bare the intimate secrets of his life:

— In your series of poems that follow the *Elastic Poems*, there is a volume you titled *Kodak*. If you gave it this title, it was because you meant to suggest . . .
— Mental photographs . . .
— They are mental photographs, a kind of film, pictures of your traveling. . . . In *Travel Notes* . . .
— Those are post cards I sent to my friends, that I intended for my friends. . . .
— That's it.
— That I intended for my friends, that's why there are a lot of unpretentious stories, quite intimate, mainly evocations of friends. . . .

— Of countries too.
— Of countries too. . . .

    .   .   .   .   .

— I told you the other day I wasn't writing any more poems.
— It's unbelievable!
— I make up poems, I make up poems for myself, that I recite and digest and enjoy. . . .
— Let's hope that one day . . .

The interviews, published in 1952, extend and codify the legendary aspect of Cendrars's life and work. If the poems, novels, chronicles, and essays all seemed to be imaginative extensions of Cendrars's private life, they were still so many fragmented, detachable episodes. A savagely melancholy, violent temperament linked the works into a continuous affective unit, but the episodes could be considered as mythical formulations of the personality, created by the intelligence rather than creating it. The disparate adventures, the ceaseless traveling, the constant search for new horizons, new experiences, all this might be viewed as the transfiguration of an acutely sensitive and mystical sensibility. Then, the voice — more intimate than written words — confirmed with names, dates, places, the materials of his books. And, with the man and the myth merging into a single personality, the voice faltered, hesitated, and the public oratory, so conclusive, became another function of the imagination. "It's true that here is *my* voice, and that only the voice carries on the radio, whatever it says. But I don't know *my* voice. I find it very moving, but it distracts me . . . It's idiotic. . . ."

This confusion was revelatory of Cendrars's contradictory nature. Although he was by inclination a contemplative, a willing recluse, his sympathy for and dedication to his friends, the physical world, the eccentric and bizarre, precipitated him into the very heart of life. Writing, a solitary act, was a denial, he felt, of the active life he was impelled to lead. "Writing," he said in *Bourlinguer,* "is a kind of abdication." But it was a necessity, an act of self-immolation which exalted and destroyed him, ashes giving birth not to the legendary phoenix but to the legendary poet.

L'écriture est un incendie qui embrase un grand remue-ménage d'idées et qui fait flamboyer des associations d'images avant de les réduire en braises crépitantes et en cendres retombantes. Mais si la flamme déclenche l'alerte, la spontanéité du feu reste mystérieuse. Car écrire, c'est brûler vif, mais c'est aussi renaître de ses cendres.

(L'Homme foudroyé)

Even as he created his name, renewing his person, he was constantly, like the flame, projecting himself from a dead past into an eternal present. Yet his work was built on the past and fed on it. Even the ultimate rejection, in the poem "Le Ventre de ma mère," the final splenetic cry "Shit, I don't want to live!" is perhaps an unwilling acknowledgment of this inheritance, and it is the past that reveals the intimate, sequential nature of his work.

II

Cendrars's father, Georges-Frédéric Sauser, a "fantaisiste et un impatient," in the words of his son, was a brilliant but impractical inventor who refused to concern himself with the exploitation of his inventions. He no sooner finished one than he started another, leaving the development of each (and the profit) in other hands. Cendrars's mother, Marie-Louise Dorner, originally from Zurich, was as impractical as her husband and inhabited increasingly an unreal, dreamlike world to which she was driven by a progressively worsening nervous ailment. His father's wanderlust, his mother's spiritual displacement, the temporary households the family occupied in England, Paris, Montreux, Naples, and — for a longer period — Germany: all this was to mark the work of the mature Cendrars, reflecting the urge of the one to move on, and of the other toward retreat and seclusion.

His education under these circumstances was spotty. Taught for a time by a neurotic English governess, then enrolled in a gymnasium in Germany, he was transferred finally to a commercial school in Neuchâtel, only to accumulate 375 unexcused absences in 1901–1902. Whatever the nature of the studies, he felt keenly their insufficiency as this comment in "Le Panama" shows:

> How can you expect me to bone up for my exams?
> You sent me to all the boardingschools in Europe
> Prepschool
> Highschool
> College
> How can you expect me to bone up for my exams

His sketchy formal training did not, however, keep him from his father's library, or from devouring everything that fell into his hands. "Reading has always been a drug for me," he wrote and his work reflects and incorporates this omnivorous reading.

But he was not lost in his books. When Cendrars was fifteen, his father learned that his son had run up debts in local bars, that he was subscribing to obscene publications (even as he was later to write them), and that he had taken as mistress a properly mysterious South American heiress. His father, moved to desperate means, retaliated by confining the boy to his room and restricting him to bread and water. Cendrars, never one to be unwillingly deprived of his freedom, waited until his parents had gone to mass, and escaped by way of the second-story window, after stuffing his pockets with all the money he could find lying about and carrying away as much of the family silver as he could comfortably manage. He took the first train to Basel, and at Basel, afraid to leave the station, boarded another train, this one destined for Berlin. At Berlin, he took another, and still another, fleeing around Germany in a kind of frenzied nightmare, sleeping in train compartments, on station benches, eating in buffets, knowing neither where he was going nor why. Then, in the Pforzheim station, he was befriended by an itinerant jewel merchant and opportunist, the Varsovian Jew, Rogovine, who offered the boy a job. The job, which he immediately accepted, was apparently that of general factotum, and it led Cendrars, during the next three years, into Russia and as far east as Siberia at the time (1904–1905) of the Russo-Japanese war.

By 1906 his relationship with Rogovine had worn thin. The merchant, angry with Cendrars for getting the better of him in a business deal and even more irritated by his refusal to marry his daughter, dismissed him. Cendrars returned to France and in 1907 settled in the suburbs of Paris, at Multien, where he raised bees and dallied with the daughter of a neighboring farmer. Tiring of these pastoral activities, he embarked for a brief period on medical studies, but he found himself unable to settle down to the demands of his courses and soon abandoned them. It was at this time that he met Remy de Gourmont, a prolific and tragic writer whose passionate devotion to the contemplative life fascinated the young traveler-adventurer and on whose book *Le Latin mystique* he was to draw for the preface to his first long poem, "Les Pâques à New-York." Gourmont was not his only literary friend; as if to counterbalance the influence of this reclusive esthete, he spent long hours with Gustave Le Rouge, writer of popular mysteries and semi-erudite books on such esoteric subjects as love potions and magic among the ancient Aztecs. In 1909 Cendrars, turned juggler, was sharing the bill in a London music hall with Charlie Chaplin and the "world-champion" of Diabolo, Simon Kra, who later became an influential publisher and promoter of young writers.

The next year took him back to Russia and, eventually, to the United States via the West, through Canada. Here, in New York, at Easter of 1912, he wrote in a single night the first and final draft of "Les Pâques à New-York." It was the climax of a period in which he was now a tailor, now a pianist in a Bowery movie and — in a "furie d'apprendre" — spending most of his free time reading at the New York Public Library.

The poem finished, he returned to Paris and to a literary and artistic scene in a period of consolidation and change. The most commanding figure on the poetic horizon was Guillaume Apollinaire, acknowledged leader of the avant-garde and associate editor of the influential new literary review *Soirées de Paris*. Cendrars's relationship with Apollinaire has never been satisfactorily clarified. Cendrars knew the older poet, contributed to his magazine, worked on a series of pornographic novels of which Apollinaire was the general editor, and, like Apollinaire, was himself an editor, art critic, and poet. Cendrars certainly did not consider himself as a poet in any way inferior to Apollinaire, if we may judge from his statement in the poem "Hamac":

> Apollinaire
> 1900–1911
> For 12 years the only poet in France

There is, and this has never been denied by Apollinaire's most ardent supporters, a striking similarity between Apollinaire's poem "Zone" and Cendrars's "Les Pâques à New-York," and dates of composition would seem to suggest that it was Apollinaire who profited from his friend's work. But whatever the relationship, the most influential poet of the era and the most independent shared a common interest in the new spirit, alive to the contemporary world, and to a poetry which would have its roots in this world, the poetry, as Apollinaire put it, "of our epoch."

The events of 1914 put a temporary end to Cendrars's literary activity. Shortly after his hasty marriage to a Russian whom he would divorce soon after the armistice, Cendrars signed a declaration calling upon all poets to enlist and engage actively in the fighting. He followed his own advice by joining the Foreign Legion and fought in some of the hardest earlier campaigns. His military career was abruptly ended in September of 1915 when a wound he received in the Champagne offensive necessitated the amputation of his right arm above the elbow. He said later that he was moved to "learn that Remy de Gourmont died the day [he] was to lose [his] arm" and in a mystic exaltation reminiscent of the older poet saw the hand become a cabalistic configuration in the Orion constellation:

> Today it is above my head
> The great mast pierces the palm of this hand which must suffer
> As my amputated hand, transfixed by a continuous shaft, makes
>   me suffer

> (*Documentaires*)

He was so unwilling to accept the partial disability the loss of his hand imposed on him that, in the hospital, he boxed furiously, his stump bleeding as he pounded it into his pillow. As the amputation healed, he quickly learned to write with his left hand, to work at a typewriter, drive, and, rejecting any artificial help, is said to have purposely left a prosthetic arm in a train station.

Released from the military hospital, he returned to Paris where he dabbled briefly in typographical experiments (in the manner of Apollinaire's *Calligrammes*) in his own "Sonnets dénaturés," and wrote, in "La Guerre au Luxembourg," an ironic parody of war seen through the eyes of children. In 1917, having written "Au cœur du monde," a poem so antipoetical it overwhelmed even Cendrars, he decided to give up both poetry and Paris and let them, as he said, get along as best they could without him.

This departure from the Parisian poetic scene was not as drastic as he intended it to be. He was back in Paris in 1918 and on the day of Apollinaire's burial, trying to find the trench which was to hold the poet's body, Cendrars noticed a clump of earth in a gaping hole: "The earth had the very shape of Apollinaire's head and grass was planted just as his hair had grown when he was alive, around his trepanation scar. You didn't have to delude yourself to notice the resemblance." (*Blaise Cendrars vous parle . . .*) Cendrars was not alone at that moment. He was accompanied by the painter Fernand Léger and by Raymone Duchâteau, the talented young actress who — as his constant companion and, after 1946, as his wife — was to share the uncertainties of Cendrars's life until the day of his death. It was as though Cendrars were gathering about him the diverse characters of his own creative impulse — his beloved Raymone to whom marriage a quarter of a century later was to coincide with a great regenerative cycle which produced his crowning works, the autobiographical chronicles; his friend Léger, whose presence signified the union of poet and artist in Cendrars's own temperament; and the psychic manifestation of the poet whose inspiration he had felt so profoundly. In the death of Apollinaire, Cendrars, it would seem, found a rededication to his own life.

Apparently free for the moment of any commitment to his own writing, Cendrars served as editor for the Éditions de la Sirène, publishing his own *Anthologie nègre* and the first edition of Lautréamont's *Les Chants de Maldoror* to appear since the original edition of 1868. He also continued an interest in movie-making which had been manifested as early as 1914 when he filmed documentaries for Pathé. The wealth of possibilities of the moving image seemed the perfect complement for his own terse, image-oriented style, and in 1921 he collaborated with the noted French director Abel Gance in the filming of *The Wheel,* with its celebrated montage sequence of a moving train, which seemed to draw on Cendrars's "Prose du Transsibérien," and for which Arthur Honnegger wrote his modernistic tone-poem "Pacific 231." Cendrars formed his own film company but lost it, and a fortune, in a financial debacle in Italy. He worked for a time in London and then returned to Rome, where in October of 1923 he filmed *The Black Venus* with the Hindu dancer Durga and a menagerie gathered from a local zoo. His last cinema undertaking was a documentary on the elephant, filmed in Africa. Then he was off for Brazil, entering upon the period of his great wanderings. From 1924 until the beginning of World War II, as he said, "not a year went by without my spending one, three, or nine months in America, especially in South America, I was that tired of old Europe."

For a time, at the very beginning of the war, he served as correspondent. After the armistice of 1940, he went into isolation in Provence, at Villefranche-sur-Mer. For three years, Louis Parrot, one of his biographers, informs us, "Cendrars writes nothing. He lives in absolute solitude, in an apartment that is frigid in winter and where he takes refuge in his kitchen with a type-writer he does not open and books he never looks at." In 1943, he was visited by his friend, the novelist Edouard Peisson. The two men began to talk of writing, of writers, and of Cendrars's long inactivity. Then, as if the visit were a catalyst, Cendrars began to write the first lines of *L'Homme foudroyé.* It was the beginning of a flaming-up of activity, as he published, in what was to be the final great creative cycle, the four chronicles, a novel, reportage, descriptive commentary for a series of photographs of Paris. His poetry? As he said in his interviews with Manoll, he now wrote only poems for himself and, perhaps, for Raymone. Death came to Cendrars in Paris, at number 5, rue José-Maria de Heredia, in the house where Renoir painted "La Balançoire," on January 21, 1961. This was only four days after he had received the only literary prize of his career, the Grand Prix Littéraire de la Ville de Paris. Cendrars never esteemed awards of any kind, and it was fitting that his death came as a kind of reproach to the city that had waited until the eve of his death to recognize him.

III

Cendrars, in the series of radio interviews conducted by Michel Manoll, may have shown considerable reticence about the significance of his role in the formation of a new poetic voice in France, but he was never hesitant about proclaiming the necessity for an esthetic revolution. His most direct and outspoken formulation of such an esthetic is contained in the slender volume of essays and prose poems, *Aujourd'hui,* published by Grasset in 1931. The earliest of the essays, an appreciation of Marc Chagall, was written in 1912. The most recent in date of publication, a short article on the French novel, appeared in 1929, but all of the essays, originally published over a fifteen-year period, show an intense preoccupation with the changing face of the contemporary landscape, the profound effect of this transformation on the modern sensibility, on language — spoken and written — and ultimately on the literature of the present and future.

The essays, dealing variously with poetry, painters and painting, the novel, advertising, the movies, and the contemporary world, are all very much concerned with the implications of the title. "The poet has become aware of his era," he writes in one essay. "He is this era's conscience." The poet, or artist, is alive to the nature of the world about him; his poems, paintings, novels must testify to this awareness of its physical and spiritual aspects. This consciousness is not, however, simply a perception of forms and shapes. Cendrars reproaches the Cubist painters for their failure to study their models in depth and for reproducing only still lifes in their analytic pursuit of dimensions. *Conscience,* the constantly recurring key word in his manifestos, is not a matter of participating in an involved readjustment of physical form to present the world from new, startling angles. It is most essentially a private and spiritual involvement in the nature of life, its metaphysical meanings, "life in all its manifestations . . . the continuous activity of the mind."

Three long compositions serve as focal points for the book. They are the prose poem "Profound Today" ("Profond Aujourd'hui"), a lyrical evocation of the machine age; "The Principle of Utility" ("Le Principe de l'utilité"), an essay dedicated to the genius of the age, Henry Ford; and a two-part transcription of a lecture delivered in São Paulo in 1924, "Modern Poets in the Totality of Contemporary Life" ("Les poètes modernes dans l'ensemble de la vie contemporaine"), and "Today's Poets Confronted by the Science of Modern Linguistics" ("Les poètes d'aujourd'hui devant la science de la linguistique moderne"). Each of the essay-poems seeks to present the world in depth. The earliest of them, "Profond Aujourd'hui," is the most successful in its refusal to be anything more than a fragmented poem, composed of short, bewildering perspectives of plant, mineral, and animal life, rising to an ecstatic affirmation of the integrity of existence and the poet's identification with its pulse and beat. "The Principle of Utility" — a mixture of lyrical prose poetry and visionary interpretations of history, prehistory, and the future possibilities of the human race — concludes with a portentous repetition of the title "Profond Aujourd'hui" to reaffirm the earlier feeling. And the lecture-essay, buttressed by lengthy quotations from J. Vendryes's work, *Le Langage, introduction linguistique à l'histoire,* and with examples from Reverdy, Apollinaire, Rimbaud, Cocteau, Desnos, and, not illogically, Cendrars's own verse, is a gigantic pseudointellectual attempt to justify modern poetry in the light of linguistic science.

It is "The Principle of Utility" which provides the clearest exposition of Cendrars's esthetic. The principle, which might also be called the principle of functional esthetics, concerns the coincidence between esthetic and utilitarian values in the construction of tools.

11

> The caveman, who halved his stone axe, curved the handle to fit his hand, polished it with loving care, gave it a line pleasing to the eye, was obeying the principle of utility in the same way the modern engineer who carves the hull of a 40,000-ton transatlantic steamer is guided by it. . . .

This creation of a functional beauty is reflected not only in machines but in the accessories of modern life, the "highways, canals, train networks, ports . . . which dominate the contemporary landscape and impose on it their own grandiose geometry." This subjugation of the means of transportation results in a kind of "monoculture" as it operates in all parts of the earth, in all climates, without respect for the limitations of a particular environment. Man has imposed this new geometry, and it shows his ability to transcend boundaries, natural and national, to subordinate the face of the earth to a man-made beauty. It is a sign of man's greatness, as his will, like that of the artist, controls the materials at hand and works them into an artistic harmony, yet retains, at the same time, a functional utility.

This transformation also extends to those domains of activity which attempt to escape utility and mechanism. It affects the language and, through the language, all forms of expression.

> . . . the language — of words and things, of disks and runes, of the Portuguese and the Chinese, of numbers and trademarks, of industrial patents, postal stamps, travel tickets, bills of lading, signal codes, the French National Network — this language is remade and reformed, this language which is the reflection of the human conscience, the poetry which reveals the images of the mind that conceives, the lyricism that is a way of being and feeling, the demotic, live script of the movies that speaks to the impatient crowd of untutored folk, newspapers that ignore grammar and syntax to make a quicker impression with inset typographical announcements, the price warm with feeling under a tie in a shop window, the multicolored banners and gigantic letters that shore up the hybrid architecture of cities and jostle one another in the streets, the new electric constellations that rise each evening into the sky, the abacus of smoke in the morning wind.
> Today.
> Profound today.

This expression of utility, at first defined functionally, now enters another dimension. It changes the shape of the language, makes this language synonymous with the visual telegraphy of the movies, the slogans of advertising, the electric signs on buildings. This extension of the frontiers of language is a movement away from the traditions imposed by the past. Grammar and syntax are jettisoned by newspaper advertising and this observation fore-shadows Cendrars's own admission, some twenty-five years later, that he is "ignorant of and scorn[s] grammar which is a dead issue." Struck by the color and drama of signs, advertising, the skyline of the modern city, he finds the traditional language inca-pable of transmitting the new impressions it is receiving, and a new tongue (which he does not define precisely) is forged.

There is one section of this program to which, through repetition, Cendrars gives a significant value: ". . . this language which is the reflection of the human conscience, the poetry that reveals the image of the mind that conceives it, the lyricism that is a way of being and feeling. . . ." It appears in an essay called "Publicité = Poésie" with only a slight variation: "Lyricism is a way of being and feeling, language is the reflection of human awareness, poetry illuminates (as advertising does a product) the image of the mind that conceives it." And in the introductory remarks to "Modern Poets in the Totality of Contemporary Life," this language takes on a Claudelian, Old Testament verse move-ment, as if to emphasize its relation to Holy Writ in Cendrars's critical canon:

> Ce qui caractérise l'ensemble de la jeune poésie française est son lyrisme.
> Le lyrisme est une façon d'être et de sentir.
> Nous savons bien que la langue est le reflet de la con-science humaine, la poésie fait connaître l'image de l'esprit qui la conçoit.

In Cendrars's insistence upon *esprit, conscience,* and feeling, and in his view of language, the exterior shape of thought, as the reflection or the end product of an interior work, seems to lie his idea of depth. The São Paulo lecture represents his most ambitious attempt to define the exact nature of this new kind of language.

It is significant that the lecture is posited on an admission of inadequacy. In the first section he points out that there is, in the spoken language, a spontaneity which "envelops and colors" the expression of the thought and makes grammar unstable. In the second part, he attempts to indicate the modifying influences at work in the language which transform thought as it is articulated or written. He says that he would like to go into the science of grammar as it develops from "the study of comparative languages" but that, unfortunately, he does not have the time. His authority, then, will be the work of J. Vendryes on language, and his exposition will simply be an illustration of Vendryes's principles. Science, maintains Cendrars, has already done the essential preparation. Poetry will develop and extend it. The body of the essay is a citing of poetry, and the incantatory qualities of verse must carry the burden of the argument Cendrars refuses to define. He is not a definer of principles, except in the most visionary sense, but a chanter of facts, the fact of the work of art, experience restated and reshaped to go beyond principle into the sensory meaning behind statement. "Life," he says in one of his poems, "is the simple fact of existing," and this "fact" is not ascertainable by logic or reason. It is an experience of the total being, with the intelligence become an immediate emotion. Here, for Cendrars, is the disparity between thought and language, and it is in this unconscious area of the creative mind, moving free of traditional restraints, that the modern artist must seek his guiding inspiration. The exterior world provides the impetus, but the interior world re-creates and extends.

> It is the great privilege of modern poets and poetry to have descended to such a depth in the conscious and the unconscious and to want to annex this still virgin region of the human being where the most acute forms of civilization and the most ancient terrors of life thunder like the voice of God in the desert.
>
> ("Today's Poets Confronted by the
> Science of Modern Linguistics")

The prophet in Cendrars speaks and the visionary in him rejects the purely functional esthetic he himself has proposed. A deeper sense of responsibility moves him than a duty to a contemporary spirit. In his voice, reject tradition as he will, the Hebrew prophets echo Yahweh's will, and the poet, prophet of the heart and mind, asserts the supremacy of the eternal soul.

The essays, then, are all chiefly important in their portrayal of an attitude. This attitude has multiple facets, but its main aspect is a belief in the esthetic significance of the material world. The belief may be subordinated to the mystic in Cendrars, but it affects the range of his subjects and the nature of his imagery. The attempt to be modern is a deliberate one, the *conscient,* but its deepest implications are in the *inconscient,* in areas plumbed not only by Cendrars but by a whole generation of postwar Surrealist poets. He dissociated himself from that generation but, in effect, he had already preceded them and he was impatient to be moving on. The implications of the essays foreshadow his whole artistic development, which was away from the manifesto, from even poetry itself, toward a more expansive and less restricted form. It was a spiritual odyssey, as he was the greatest of modern travelers, but the outlines were evident in his earliest poetry, continued in his mid-period essays, and prolonged into a forty-year period of sustained prose writing, so that the reading and study of his work becomes of itself a voyage.

IV

"Les Pâques à New-York," in spite of its very free use of the Alexandrine and its suggestions of an effort to break away from traditional poetics, still remains linked to that tradition. It is in "Prose du Transsibérien et de la petite Jeanne de France" that Cendrars makes a deliberate effort to renovate form and substance. "Prose du Transsibérien" is in intent and in declaration a poetic manifesto, the proclamation of a new esthetic.

> I have deciphered all the confused texts of the wheels and I have
> assembled the scattered elements of a most violent beauty
> That I control
> And which compels me.

The earlier poem translated a physical and moral dislocation verbally but "Prose du Transsibérien" — at the same time that it exhibits a preoccupation with visual and rhythmical effects — is also the record of a different kind of experience. It is an admitted esthetic departure in an attempt to break through the tradition-imposed boundaries of vocabulary and form and create a new kind of expression.

"Prose du Transsibérien," abandoning the dependence on the Alexandrine, is written in free verse. Cendrars, however, does not use free verse as Jules Laforgue and the Symbolists used it. In the earlier poets, the line still retains its metrical cadence, and poetry is reinforced by end-rhymes, occasional strophes in regular verse, and a unity of tone and movement. Cendrars, dedicated to the new, rejects these props as unnecessary to the structure of the poem. The poetic line may consist of two words thrown out like a cry ("O Paris") or, like the Biblical verset, may draw itself out in a long, almost chanting statement.

> Great smoldering hearth with the intersecting embers of your
> streets and your old houses which bend over them and warm
> one another

The movement determines the line, and the poet is free to concentrate on the image and the feeling that forces him into the composition of the poem.

The very designation of the text as "prose" points up the departure from traditional versification. If, in his essay on "The Principle of Utility," he saw the materials of poetry everywhere about him in the modern world, this extension of the nature of poetry could also remove the boundaries between poetry and prose. As we shall observe in his novels and reminiscences, longer prose works may be simply an extension of the techniques of poetry, and the use of the word "prose" in the title of this early poem may already prefigure his own re-evaluation of the traditional formal limitations.

It is also possible that Cendrars was thinking of the prose sequences of the medieval Latin church, psalms of ten to thirty versets to which, as Remy de Gourmont, Cendrars's acknowledged mentor, points out in his book *Le Latin mystique,* "only occasional

rhymes and final or interior assonances give the look of a poem."
These hymns, in irregularly cadenced lines, could be considered
a precedent for the irregular line lengths of the poem. Cendrars
had already used a quotation from the Gourmont book to preface
"Les Pâques à New-York." The unmistakable title reference to
Jeanne d'Arc in the title of "Prose du Transsibérien" gives a
frame of medieval reference to the poem, and the dedication of
the text "to the musicians" might very reasonably be considered
an allusion to the musical settings of the medieval hymns. There
is also in the opening verse of "Prose du Transsibérien" the use of
end-rhymes and initial "head-rhymes" ("j'étais" — "j'avais") to
carry the somewhat prosy nature of their statements.

> En ce temps-là j'étais en mon adolescence
> J'avais à peine seize ans et je ne me souvenais déjà plus de mon
>   enfance
> J'étais à 16.000 lieues du lieu de ma naissance
>
>   . . . . .
>
> Car mon adolescence était alors si ardente et si folle
> Que mon cœur, tour à tour, brûlait comme le temple d'Éphèse ou
>   comme la Place Rouge de Moscou

Thus, in these initial end-rhymes, in the assonance of "Moscou" —
"rouge" in the succeeding lines, the repetition of introductory
phrases, one could see an effort to utilize the free techniques of
the hymns. These techniques, in their reference to a much earlier
poetry, could inject a "new" note in the poetry of the period and
bring a new expressive range to it. And some thirty years later, in
his prose work, L'Homme foudroyé, Cendrars acknowledges an
implicit debt to the "sequences of the Stammerer of the Abbey of
Saint Gall, the greatest of the medieval Christian poets and the
father of modern poetry." Cendrars's voyage is not only through
space but through time, and if he is a man of a new century, he
is also aware of a heritage to which he feels himself eternally in
debt.

   For a poet so concerned with the present implications of his
work, so involved with the material world of the day, Cendrars's

poetry and much of his prose exhibit a marked preoccupation with the past. His motivating force is that of memory, suffused with anguish and melancholy, and if there are idyllic moments of delight, the dominating feeling is of sadness, which becomes at times so violent as to destroy the present-past boundary and propel him into a timeless void. In "Les Pâques à New-York" the initial and dominating tense is the present. In "Prose du Transsibérien," on the other hand, from the opening lines we are thrown into the past ("It was in the time of my adolescence / I was scarcely sixteen . . ."), and it is not until the final lines that Cendrars consistently uses the present tense. But within the poem, shifts in tense — as the present and its demands intrude upon the poet's reverie — reveal much of his intentions and impart a temporal tension which reflects Cendrars's conscious attempt to write a new poetry.

The first incursion of the present occurs in an early section in which he is describing the rhythm of the train and his experiences and feelings during the trip.

> The rustling of women
> And the steam engine's whistle
> And the everlasting sound of wheels whirling madly along in
>   their ruts in the sky
> The windows are frosted over
> No view!

The adjective "everlasting" (*éternel*) prepares the shift to the present tense and defines its quality: it is an eternal rather than momentary present that is suggested. The shifts in tenses correspond to shifts in feeling. The use of the present tense continues to recur through all the sections of the poem in which the train pursues its relentless forward movement. The poet only reverts to a consistent use of the past when he reminds himself that it is memory on which the poem feeds and that the present offers no haven.

> What's the use of documenting myself
> I give myself over
> To the bounds of memory . . .

18

> At Irkutsk the trip became much too slow
> Much too long

The past-present tension is reflected not only in tense shifts but also in the choice of imagery. If the image of the train, in its savage, brutal flight, provides the principal rhythmical pulse, the overwhelming feeling of sadness is also associated with the poet's traveling companion, Jeanne, the little Montmartre prostitute. The one section of the poem in which the lines achieve any sort of regular metrical length is in the introduction of Jeanne.

> She is only a child, blond, laughing . . . and sad,
> She does not smile and she never cries;
> But deep in her eyes, when she lets you drink there,
> Trembles a gentle silver lily, the poet's flower.

This lyrical description, five stanzas long, is marked by the grace of the movement, a slow, reflective evocation with traditional imagery, the woman as a gentle flower, the poet's homage to his beloved as a fragile, delicate being, separate and apart.

> For she is my love, and the other women
> Have only dresses of gold on tall bodies of flame,
> My poor friend is so lonely,
> She is quite naked, has no body — she is too poor.

The women with bodies of flame recall the women, like "flowers of blood" in "Les Pâques à New-York," and their vividness contrasts strikingly with Jeanne's pallor. The other women are more evocative of the creative fire consuming the poet, but it is ironic that it is Jeanne, paler than a thought but strong with the suggestive power of emotion, who breaks through the poem's striving for novelty, provides it with its dominating melancholy accent, and returns the poet to a permanent present in the closing lines of the poem. Jeanne becomes an implied admission of failure, as this one memory, more relentless than the train, destroys the past and prolongs itself into the present.

After this lengthy description she becomes nothing more than the constantly repeated question, again breaking through the fabric of the poem, "Tell me, Blaise, are we very far from

Montmartre?" This simple question also counteracts the fleeting, incisive image-associations that move bewilderingly in a frenzy that would assimilate a world of experience into the poem.

> The trainmasters play chess
> Backgammon
> Pool
> Pool balls
> Parabolas
> The railroad is a new geometry

The associative jump from pool balls to parabolas, from the language of the game to the precise designation of mathematics, is both a visual and an aural movement, developing out of rhyme ("caramboles" — "paraboles") and out of the visual reference of the images. The materials of the game, the billiard balls, in their movement, suggest a geometrical arrangement implemented by the relationship in the construction of the two words. The short, hard-sounding lines, instead of being simply words thrown out at random in the poem, lead to a global conclusion. The "new geometry" refers not only to the material elements in the world but to the construction of the poem itself, which is equally a new geometry, demonstrating new arrangements and new relationships.

The sadness motif, associated with Jeanne, is first aroused by the train rhythms.

> And yet . . . and yet . . .
> I was as sad as a child
> The rhythms of the train

It is then absorbed into his feeling for Jeanne and extended to merge with the travel motif and ultimately with the landscapes seen through the train windows.

> And beyond, the Siberian plains the lowering sky and the tall
>   shapes of the Silent Mountains that rise and fall

In none of this does the traveler find escape and oblivion. Sorrow and love are also awareness and obsessive reminders that there is disease and corruption even at the heart of beauty.

On Fiji it's always spring
Drowsiness
Love makes the lovers swoon in the tall grass and syphilis in heat
    prowls under the banana trees

Jeanne and his melancholy are cold feelings, not illustrative of renewal or rebirth. But there is another side of love, warm and passionate, and this is the important motif of poetic creation. In "Les Pâques à New-York," fire and blood were more the color and materials of hallucination and anguish. In "Prose du Transsibérien," fire is creation, and it is the creative act which partakes of the nature of fire. ("I was in Moscow, where I was trying to nourish myself with flames . . .") It is a process in which the entire being is engaged.

    Because my adolescence was so intense and so insane
    That my heat, in its turn, burned like the temple at Ephesus or
        like the Red Square of Moscow
    When the sun is setting.
    And my eyes were lighting ancient paths.

The setting sun implies the death of this creative fire, as does the destruction of the temple at Ephesus; but the poet's eyes, lighting ancient ways, are already recreating. The sun, consumed by its own heat, disappears, but the light of the intelligence remains, suggestive of a more permanent illumination.

    References to the creative act are numerous in the poem.

    On the escarpments the tulip trees are in bloom
    Riotous vines are the sun's tresses
    They seem a painter's palette and brushes
    Colors booming like gongs,
    Rousseau was there
    His life was dazzled

         . . . . .

    So many associative images I can't develop in my verse
    Because I'm still a very bad poet

         . . . . .

    Because I'm not capable of going to the end
    And I'm afraid.

. . . . .

> I have deciphered all the confused texts of the wheels and I have
> assembled the scattered elements of a most violent beauty
> That I control
> And which compels me.

Even so, Cendrars is not proclaiming a precise, definite program.
These outbursts are the comments made during creation, the
doubts that trouble every artist at work. He may, as he claims,
be in possession of the elements of this new poetry, but he is not
in complete control of them: they are working through him,
imposing themselves upon him. The inspiration of Cendrars's
poetry is emotional. Thus, the references to violence, the obsession
with the color red, with fire, the idea of destruction and regenera-
tion, are all various manifestations of the poem as a Dionysian
act, the poet inspired by a creative frenzy. And uncertain of the
direction the frenzy may take, unable to control the materials, he
fears the exhaustion of the source.

"Prose du Transsibérien" was written in 1913. It is the second
of his long poems ("Le Panama," of 1913–1914, was the last), the
finest, and, in many respects, the most significant of all his output.
Here the themes of memory, sadness, the preoccupation with his
own past, the obsession with fire and violence, the quick associative leaps in imagery, all the motivating impulses of his creative
work are present. The conclusion of the poem, like that of
"Les Pâques à New-York," depicts the poet exhausted, the main
themes (as in a musical coda) reappearing. The tone is more of
resignation and, perhaps, of regret than of hallucination.

> I will go to the Lapin Agile to recall my lost youth
> And drink a few glasses
> Then I'll return home alone

Such a conclusion, gathering into its compass the residue of
genuine emotion felt by the poet, is a reminder that the poem is not
a thing of joy, flushed with the delight of creation and illustrative
of renewed vitality and energy. The work was born of desperation,
of sorrow. It imposed itself upon the poet, as it imposes itself upon

the reader, and the lack of logical, sequential development, the vast complex of emotions and memories, all proceed out of an undefined emotional reservoir. The poem, lacking any definite statement of an esthetic, becomes its own end and esthetic, as it grows out of the debilitating forces of fire and blood, of death and destruction.

* * *

One cannot help being struck by the fact that Cendrars, from 1912 to 1924, published principally poetry and, from 1924 until his death, published almost exclusively prose. In fact, all of the major poetic works — "Les Pâques à New-York," "Prose du Transsibérien et de la petite Jeanne de France," and *Dix-Neuf poèmes élastiques* — were composed prior to the outbreak of World War I in an astonishingly short period of three years. It was in 1917, as he tells Michel Manoll in the radio interviews, that he quit Paris, and poetry, definitively. This was the year before Apollinaire's death and the era of the first tentative efforts of the Surrealists in their initial Dadaist phase. He has said of the Surrealists that "there is not a single one of these kids or daddy's boys who produced something new. It's a poetic flea market." In 1913 he was complaining that he was a young poet among the old; only four years later, dissatisfied with the newer generation, he criticizes them for writing for the sake of novelty, for employing the shock tactics of a group of children, and withdraws from their contaminating presence.

This is not, then, merely a fact of biography. Indeed, the rupture with Paris was by no means complete. Paris remained his home port, to which he returned after his numerous trips around the world, and it was in Paris that he died in 1961. The physical break was a temporary retreat to mark his own displeasure, and even anger. The spiritual separation was the more lasting, and this disaffection is evident in his poetry after "Prose du Transsibérien" until, in his final volumes of verse — *Documentaires* (1924) and *Feuilles de route* (1924–1928) — there is a complete disavowal of his earlier techniques and subject matter and an almost total disintegration of the power, vigor, and beauty of his best verse. It is only in his volumes of prose that he recaptures the intensity of the poetry and his creative work enters a transformed, if not an entirely new, plane.

The transitional and crucial poem in this progression is "Le Panama ou les aventures de mes sept oncles," written in 1913–1914, published in 1918, and the longest of the three major postwar poems. ("Le Panama" has 516 lines as compared with 446 lines in "Prose du Transsibérien" and 205 lines in "Les Pâques à New-York.") It is the least satisfying poetically of the three, but it is also the most revelatory of the direction Cendrars's work was taking. Sprawling, flawed, imperfect, its very imperfections serve to accent the nature of Cendrars's method, its limitations and its possibilities.

The trend toward autobiography was already evident in the two earlier poems. The major *persona* was Cendrars, with autobiography as emotional reportage dominating in "Les Pâques à New-York," and precise detail combining with emotion to produce a more direct and more savage expression in "Prose du Transsibérien." "Le Panama" provides a more varied cast of characters, with the significant events in the life of each of the seven uncles documented in some detail, but the emotional level is reduced as a minimum of intensity is supplemented by a maximum of incident.

The most immediate result is to diminish the effectiveness of the verse form. Free verse, at best, is difficult to sustain poetically, to keep from falling into the less stringent rhythms of prose. The difficulties are already great in a short poem, but to maintain the drive of a poem as long as "Le Panama" without a dominating, forceful meter is to ask almost the impossible. "Prose du Transsibérien" was impelled by the relentless drive of the train and colored by the power of the emotional impulse. The train gave a formal unity to the less formalized technique, unifying and strengthening the poem's structure. In "Le Panama" the unifying element is the thread of anecdote evoked by letters from each of the uncles. It is discursive rather than descriptive, and a less impelling sense of urgency relaxes and weakens the poem's fabric. This disintegrating element was further emphasized in the original edition by the train-map tracings that separated various sections of the poem, dividing it into so many chapters. The train, once the vehicle of the verse, is now a map to chart the poem's references and no longer the poem's pulse.

The lower intensity is also emphasized by the inverse emotional structure of the strophes. Cendrars will begin a strophe with a phrase or a statement of high emotional pitch, but the pitch will diminish within the strophe and end on a less emotionally charged note. Thus a strophe beginning "Oh my uncle, mother told me the whole story" finishes with the absurdly flat declaration, "Since then your wife has married again, a wealthy jam manufacturer this time." The same diminution is evident in the following selection of first and final strophic lines:

I'm thirsty
Damn it
. . . . .
I'm on my way back from America on the *Volturno* for 35
  francs from New York to Rotterdam.

There's no such thing as hope
You've got to work
. . . . .
Be sure to note my new address,
Biarritz etc.

Oh my uncle, I waited a year for you and you never came
. . . . .
200 black bulls bellowing
Argentine tango.

This release within the strophe gives the poem, at times, a rising and falling motion, passing from the low level of the end of one strophe to the higher emotional pitch of the beginning of the next. It becomes in itself a rhythm, lulling and monotonous.

On reading the poem, it becomes increasingly evident that the words are the poem, the imagery being called upon to supply the tension and impetus the rhythms do not establish. This is true of much of Cendrars's work. He was, as he often said, a passionate reader of dictionaries, and the *word* (*le verbe*) is as central in his poetry as it was in that of the Symbolists. At its most disastrous this can lead to a mere enumeration, as in the poem in *Documentaires* titled simply "Menus."

> Green tortoise paste with truffles
> Lobster à la mexicaine
> Florida pheasant
> Iguana with caraibe sauce
> Gumbo and palm cabbages

"Your menucards," he says in "Le Panama" of his chef-uncle, "are the new prosody." At first glance a willful extravagance, this perspective on closer examination proves to be closely allied to his (and Apollinaire's) conviction that advertising is one of the poet's most fruitful sources of artistic materials. ("Yes, truly," Cendrars wrote in "Advertising = Poetry," "advertising is the finest expression of our time, the greatest novelty of the day, an Art.") This also causes him, in "Le Panama," to insert as an illustration an announcement of the Denver Chamber of Commerce. (See page 127.) Not only is this document an example of the "new lyricism" of advertising, but it is also — in the precision of its numerical detail (i.e., "Denver has 810 factories, in which 16,251 wage earners were employed during 1911") — an imaginative extension of the magical properties of words in poetry to figures and ciphers, re-establishing in a new context the metaphysical significance numbers had in medieval literature. Now, however, it is not that *3, 7,* or *13* are endowed with magic properties. Cendrars is concerned with size, with conveying by numbers the same multi-dimensional attempt to encompass the earth that the poems demonstrate by their varied imagery. Dictionaries, menus, numerals, telegraphic signals convey both the extent and the variety of contemporary life.

Menus, signs, brochures, advertisements, these all partake of distinctive arrangements of words and numbers. The words, often incomplete phrases, slogans, catchwords, are designed to touch the reader's sensibility through brevity or novelty. In "Le Panama" the reiterated phrase, "en route," like a slogan, forces the poem along by its reference to movement and travel.

Consider this technique at work in the following lines:

> Moi aussi j'aime les animaux
> Sous la table
> Seul
> Je joue déjà avec les chaises
> Armoires portes
> Fenêtres
> Mobilier modern-style
> Animaux préconçus
> Qui trônent dans les maisons
> Comme le reconstitution des bêtes antédiluviennes dans les
>   musées
> Le premier escabeau est un aurochs!

Words here are thrown out like advertising designations. The poem moves by fits and starts, and it is only on reaching "Animaux préconçus" and moving through to the exclamatory final line that "Armoires portes/Fenêtres" lose their enumerative value as objects and become metaphors, drawing and reflecting meaning. The poem grows not so much through the accumulation of lines of equivalent poetic weight, emotionally and rhythmically charged, as through the growth of blocks of images, thrown out at first as if they were separate messages and communicating a total message only when the passage or the section as a whole has been read. The poet reacts to a whole world of objects, a world whose elements all seem equally new and fresh to him, immediate and very much present. For him, the world is an object or a series of objects, which — like the furniture he played with as a child — can be grouped together and given a poetic life of its own.

This insistence on technique tends to fragment the long poem and to break it up into a series of shorter poems. The same telegraphic technique is used in the *Dix-Neuf poèmes élastiques,* written between 1913 and 1918, but here the brevity makes for greater effectiveness. The short, pungent image seems to demand a shorter compass. And, almost as if he were aware of this limitation, Cendrars — in the final section of "Le Panama" — passes from a description of the decaying machines of the Panama Company, abandoned in the Panamanian jungles, to an ecstatic and apocalyptic vision of the poet, dizzied by his traveling, seeking to involve the whole universe in his frenzied pace. ("Suns moons stars/Apocalyptic worlds/All of you have still your parts to play.") The savage abandoning of the rusting machines arouses an equally savage disregard in the poet for the boundaries of his global enterprise, and the poem ends in a mystic suspension, the sage lost in his own contemplative world.

> I'm waiting.

> I want to be the fifth wheel of the juggernaut
> Thunderstorm
> Noon at fourteen o'clock
> Nothing and everywhere.

If "Le Panama" is a failure as a long poem, it shows Cendrars moving into a new country. The evocative power of anecdote, the exhilaration of casting off the bonds of space and time, the trend toward a telescopic, highly charged prose style — all this foreshadows the movement from poetry into prose. "Le Panama" is a last prolonged attempt to fix his literary talents in a verse form. The very insufficiency of that attempt suggests a new direction to his sensibility. There will be years of trial and error: the flat, undemanding prosy poetry of *Documentaires* and *Feuilles de route;* the spare, direct prose style of his novel *L'Or;* the mystical, apocalyptic prose poem "La Fin du monde." But all these efforts will be crystallized in a freer form, a more expansive medium that still has its sources deep in the early poetry and shows not a rejection of it but a utilization of its materials in a new medium, the biographical chronicle.

V

"Writing is a kind of abdication. . . ." Cendrars, whose vocation as a writer always seemed torn out of him, produced in spite of himself. Yet it was in the early years, the years of his poetry, that he was, perhaps, closest to abdicating. The concision, precision, terseness of poetry, its attention to silences between strophes — all this is as much a dedication to contemplation as it is to the business of putting words on paper in an orderly fashion. Good poetry, by suggestion and allusion, moves as much in a nonverbal medium as in a verbal one. His renunciation of Paris and of poetry, then, would seem to have indicated a desire to give himself up completely to the solitude he had felt imposed upon him when he lost his arm in the war: "The man experienced the need to lie fallow, and the poet to retreat into solitude." Yet this "demon of writing," as he characterized it, would not permit him a retreat, and the flow of books was never greater than in the years after his withdrawal.

What is thus intriguing in Cendrars's dilemma is that, instead of diminishing, his output became a flood, diffuse in structure, torrential in composition, and bewildering in its variety. Prose poems, essays, novels, short stories, autobiographical chronicles, historico-religious essays: the range was as restless and wide as his experience of life. And his art, born unwillingly (if we are to believe his protestations of boredom and dissatisfaction), paralleled his traveling and experimentation abundantly and richly. Vigorous and reluctant, his very nature expressive of the extremes he saw in the face of the earth, he commented upon, expanded, and elaborated his astonishing career in his work.

The most significant development of this work is evident in the four volumes of autobiography, *L'Homme foudroyé, La Main coupée, Bourlinguer,* and *Le Lotissement du ciel,* all published between 1945 and 1949, but its essential structure can be observed taking shape in three novels published in 1925, 1926, and 1929 — *L'Or, Moravagine,* and *Dan Yack.* In each of these groups the work seems once again to fall into a cyclical pattern, recalling the intense period of poetic activity that produced the three long poems in 1912, 1913, and 1914. It is not difficult to see in his work a rhythmical pattern that corresponds to his characterization of writing as a fire rising up spontaneously and consuming the writer, then disappearing as mysteriously as it had come. Such a rhythm argues a strongly emotional basis for the works and yet in the coherent nature of the results, widely separated in time though they may be, there is an indication of the strength of the writer's control, and the unity of intent in his creative impulse. The last group of prose works marks a return to the intensely personal nature of his early poetry, and yet the style, more complex and diffuse, is a progression from the quick, spare telegraphic imagery of the poetry and a continuation of the longer, more crowded line noted in sections of "Prose du Transsibérien." The prose is like a gloss of the poetry, spinning out its implications in a loose web of almost infinite variety and design.

The poetry treated Cendrars's emotional crises, weaving in anecdotes of his family, his own life, his friends, his travels. The poetic "I" was the directing force, consolidating and ordering the diverse materials. In the three novels, Cendrars attempted to submerge this personal character and to maintain his artistic detachment from the narrative. He was markedly unsuccessful. The only novel to maintain the fiction of the novelist's nonintervention is the earliest, *L'Or,* the most popular of Cendrars's works, translated into ten languages and twice filmed.

The popularity of this single work is not difficult to explain. It treats, in a sober, classically restricted focus the life of California cattle baron General August Sutter. The swift rise to fortune of the destitute German immigrant (one of the most attractive real-life legends of the American frontier), the feverish excitement of the Gold Rush, and the tragic, relentless destruction of Sutter's properties and spirit — these are elements universal and yet sufficiently colorful and particular to stimulate any reader's imagination. The style is of the utmost simplicity, direct, straightforward; the point of view is consistent; there is a grain of commentary on the merciless passions of men inflamed by their greed; and there is pathos. The simplicity is totally unlike Cendrars, stripping his style of its complexities and his thought of its myriad digressive detours. In its spareness it reads like a digest's condensation of Cendrars, and it is certainly the most accessible of his prose writings. There is only one reference that might suggest the intrusion of a character resembling Cendrars into the frame of the novel — one Judge Thompson, "un esprit, juste, pondéré, éclairé, qui remplit ses fonctions en toute independence. . . . Une propension naturelle de son esprit l'entraîne à la contemplation."

Here, then, are the two poles of Cendrars's existence: the active, productive man of the world and the ascetic, meditating in solitude. "In general," Cendrars told the interviewer Manoll, "the writer is a recluse." And in "Le Panama" he observed that "hemmed-in lives grow densest." The active life, suggests *L'Or*, leads to ultimate destruction, and the failure of Sutter is the failure of the man who thinks he can control his material existence. The primary function of *L'Or* can thus be seen as the description of an amoral universe, with the only possible morality that of the individual who mistrusts the world's morality and creates his own within him, inaccessible and carefully guarded.

Moravagine and *Dan Yack* contrast markedly with *L'Or* but are ramifications of its moral lesson. *Moravagine* is the episodic history of a genius-madman liberated, a completely amoral spirit whose story is told in the first person by his doctor and friend, prefaced and postfaced by extensive, apologetic notes of Cendrars, maintaining the fiction of Moravagine as a man of letters whose complete works are entrusted to Cendrars for editing and publication. The portrait of Moravagine is only a pretext for the narrator who takes over, dominating the narrative and recounting anecdotes of Cendrars's experiences in Russia, Brazil, Paris, and on the great trains that cross Europe by night. This consolidation is evident quite early in the book as Moravagine begins to merge with the narrator-Cendrars. When Moravagine describes his feelings of violence and destruction ("I would have liked to kill them, I would have liked to gouge out their eyes"), the lines — in tense and mood — recall these from "Prose du Transsibérien":

> And all the days and all the women in the cafés and all the
> glasses
> I should have liked to drink them and break them
> And all the shopwindows and all the streets

Moravagine rebels against a senseless society, matching its insanity
with his own meaningless destructive acts. The patient, suffering
Christlike figure of *L'Or* has become the destroying angel, and
the artist — no longer content to conceal himself behind the
work — becomes the creator-destroyer, the amoral act providing
the genesis of the work of art.

Dan Yack, the third in this series of spiritual odysseys, is
the most conclusive. Dan Yack, explorer, inventor, architect of
a new society and civilization, a mystic who cannot content himself
with solitude, finds a redemption which neither Sutter nor Moravagine had considered: the saving grace of a woman's love. Love
for Sutter was a comfortable, bourgeois existence. Like Job, he was
struck down and his family dispersed; unlike Job, he did not have
his world rebuilt for him. Moravagine finds in love a destructive
force that compels him to kill the women he feels himself drawn
to. Moravagine is a sadist, a masochist (as love itself, the narrator
claims, is masochistic), and a murderer: Moravagine is the English
assassin Jack-the-Ripper, only one of the disguises he assumes in
his travels. For Dan Yack, love is the ultimate solution and the
ultimate mystery, and it is interesting that the two women he
loves are, in a sense, phantoms: the one, Hedwiga, a memory from
his past; the other, Mireille, a young girl whom he loves platon-
cally and who dies tragically sending Dan Yack once again into
solitude. This is, possibly, a banal conclusion to the cycle, but it
expresses one of the major sources of Cendrars's work, evident
from the first lines of "Les Pâques à New-York": his sympathy,
understanding, and love for the weak, the misfit, the displaced.
Hedwiga is Woman — pure, remote, serene, a northern goddess
smiling from the remote past upon her lover. Mireille — sick,
dying, incapable of returning physically the love of Dan Yack —
is the creature for whom he can feel pity, whom he can cherish,
and yet from whom he can remain detached.

It is obvious that with the possible exception of Sutter, who is more a puppet manipulated by external forces, these characters are both involved and detached. Moravagine is basically a force unto himself, and his involvement — brief and violent — takes the form of destruction and annihilation. Dan Yack, now working to create, now withdrawing into painful isolation, seems rhythmically motivated to seek and to flee. It is a dilemma unresolved in the two later works, as Moravagine retreats into madness and death, and Dan Yack, seeking to perpetuate himself, adopts a child whom he calls Dan Yack, seeing in the child the eyes of the remote Hedwiga, an implicit admission of his own essential detachment.

This detachment is also emphasized by the inordinate attention given in all of Cendrars's work to the world of artifacts and objects. If, in each of the novels, there is a single well-defined character, he moves in a world of oversized things. Moravagine speaks of the "violent passion" that overcame him for objects, inanimate things, as he becomes aware of the "formidable mass of permanent energy that each inanimate object contains." This was already suggested by a passage in the poem "Le Panama." ("I'm already playing with chairs/Wardrobes doors/Windows . . .") It is evident in Cendrars's attachment for the world of advertising, slogans, machines as he imposes on the reader an overpowering sense of mechanistic presence as man — artifact among other artifacts — differs only in his power to give and receive warmth and love. The artist (and the man) is as much a creation as the world he moves in, and the literary biography Cendrars fashions for himself is a composite mass of gestures, movements, animosities — all directed toward the physical world, burdening his sentences with masses of lengthy descriptions and prefiguring the enumerations and "thingness" of the anti-novelists.

Yes, in this prodigious activity, in the midst of all this cotton, this rubber, this coffee, this rice, this cork, these groundnuts, these Pustet litanies, these cast-iron salmon, this iron thread of two-tenths of an inch in diameter, these sheep, these lambs . . .

(*Moravagine*)

He spins out his lists, forcing us through his insistence on the reiterated "this" to take note of them, item by item, thickening the word texture of the novel and, by his repetitions, making them as prominent as any of the characters.

This mass of words, dizzying and cloying in the novels, becomes the very fabric and structure of the four biographical chronicles. Cendrars's language, taking shape by fits and starts in the earlier works, codifies, assumes at times an almost over-powering weight, and becomes the most distinctive feature of the chronicles. A commentary by Cendrars in the radio interview series points up and illuminates the quality of his style.

> Language is a thing that seduced me. Language is a thing that perverted me. Language is a thing that deformed me. . . . I am ignorant of and scorn grammar which is a dead issue, but I am a great reader of dictionaries. . . . At the origin is not the word but the sentence, a modulation. Listen to the song of the birds!

And it is the sentence, longer even than the Proustian phrase, that is the heart of his narratives.

> Dans cet immense jardin, touffu comme un parc et tout planté d'arbres des différentes essences du pays et que prolongeait en bordure du funiculaire un verger rempli de toutes les variétés des arbres à fruit, dont les étages en talus étaient marqués par des rangées de figuiers centenaires et les terrasse-ments servaient de maçonnerie à des canaux, des rigoles, des petites écluses, des fontaines aboutissant, tout au bas de la propriété, à un grand bassin rectangulaire avec, aux quatre coins, des néfliers tordus, sis au milieu d'un quinconce ombragé de mûriers blancs dont les baies étaient douces comme fraises écra-sées, ce qui faisait que nous nous y attardions gourmands, Élena et moi, assourdis par les grenouilles, et d'où partait un mauvais chemin tout encombré de grosses pierres rondes qui menait à un fonds perdu, à une maisonnette enfouie sous le jasmin et l'hélio-trope qui retombaient du toit, s'agrippant aux volet toujours clos, derrière lesquels brûlait une lampe en plein jour, s'entendait la musique d'un piano furibond, passait de temps en temps une ombre entre les lamelles disjointes, une camisole blanche, un madras, *zia* Régula, une folle, qui vivait là, enfermée, et que

personne ne visitait jamais et qu'Élena et moi, qui étions in-
séparables, allions surveiller de loin, en loin avec le secret espoir
de la surprendre, un jour qu'elle sortirait de son alcôve pour se
mettre à sa fenêtre et fumer le cigare, un long toscan, ou qu'elle
ferait taire son piano pour faire quelques pas dehors comme
Benjamin, le vieux jardinier, nous avait dit que cela arrivait
parfois, et nous nous tenions en embuscade dans ce coin le plus
abandonné de la propriété, un véritable maquis, à contrebas, à
l'extrême droite, faisant corne, Benjamin y cultivant un carré
en potager séparé du fouillis des mauvaises herbes par une
barrière vétuste et branlante dont nous arrachions les lattes pour
nous faire sabres et poignards de bois et pouvoir tailler en pièces
les chardons, les orties, les longues herbes gommeuses et collantes
dont nous avions du mal à nous dépêtrer quand nous nous
cachions là-dedans, Élena et moi, de l'autre côté de la barrière,
parce que cela était défendu — il y avait même un poteau dans
ce fonds portant le mot DANGER et, en effet, il y avait quelque
part un puisard dans l'emméli-mélo des tiges poilues et des
grandes feuilles rugueuses et déchiquetées par les chenilles des
courges et des potirons et des candélabres poussiéreux des belles-
de-nuit dont la fleur comme en papier mâché a une odeur de
beurre rance au soleil — et aussi pour faire enrager l'Anglaise
armée d'un alpenstock . . .

(*Bourlinguer;* see p. 253 for translation.)

The sentence continues torrentially for another twenty-five lines,
sketching a new sequence — the English governess searching
wildly for her charges — and ends, comically, only when the
children innocently appear on the patio and the governess, breathless, drops her alpenstock, crying, "Ah, mon Dieu, mon lorgnon!"

The complexity of this sentence is not caused by the complexity of the narrative matter. There are three narrative-descriptive
sequences. The first is the description of the garden which shades
into the description of the house of *zia* Regula. The surveillance
of the house is the second and central sequence (the mid-point
of the movement in time and space), and the camera — at first
focusing on the immense garden, bushy and wild — moves in
closer to catch movement and sound. The children, like the
cameraman hidden behind his camera, wait unseen, concealed
in high grasses, a jungle safari waiting for the prey to show itself

at the waterhole. (And this image is ironically continued by the old woman making water when she finally appears.) But the watchers themselves are pursued, and the third — and final — episode, moving into bumbling comedy, concludes with the cry of the nurse, an unconscious comment on her own blindness. She never saw the children (as the children had not yet seen the madwoman), and the entire passage, a series of attempts at discovery, closes on blindness, underscored by the bushiness of the park and the clouded vision.

This formal, three-part structure — description (suspended time), the waiting (expectant time), and the flight (irruption of time) — is deceptive in its apparent orderliness. The passage is extraordinarily dense ("touffu"), and the prolixity and profusion of detail correspond to the density of the scene, so that there is an intimate relation between the syntactical ordering of clauses and the close, taut, confusing nature of the garden itself. The caginess of the children, the confusion of the governess, the secretive, hidden life of the madwoman — these are extended and implemented by the sequence of details. It is extremely difficult to construct an order of importance. The passage may fall into three larger divisions, but within the sequences the details are on the same level of emphasis so that the gardener, Benjamin, is as lifelike and insistent in his presence as are the children or the governess. The reader is asked to be aware simultaneously of the garden, the house with the madwoman, the children watching, the gardener working, so that a rapid series of snapshots dazzles the eye and the mind.

The movement is not long and unhurried but quick and breathless. Cendrars, if he is addicted to the long sentence, constructs it in innumerable small units, staccato-like in their effect ("une camisole blanche, un madras, *zia* Regula, une folle, qui vivait là, enfermée"). The author's voice seems to punctuate and arrest the reader, and it is this quality of *insistence* — the author pointing with his finger, gesturing with his voice, demanding with the impressive presence of his style that the reader see and consider — that is most characteristic of his prose. This is not a seductive, lyrical voice, insinuating its vision in subtle harmonies. It is the voice of the orator, the preacher driving home his points with a fist pounding on the pulpit, quotation from the sacred text supplementing his main argument. The whole is bound loosely together by words like *and, when,* and *where* — words of little intensity that act as momentary breathing pauses before the next descriptive sequence is spat out. It is a violent movement whose force leaves the reader, like the governess, out of breath, and her cry, "Mon lorgnon!" is the cry of the reader trapped in the passage, following its long contours until he stumbles into the final punctuation, an exclamation point. Cendrars has captured the attention in prose of overwhelming concentration and minuteness of detail, and it is an attention which can be ruptured only with a brutal outcry.

This vision is basically a fragmented one, broken up into so many small parts. And the fragmentation is characteristic even of his poetry. The nineteen "elastic" poems are like so many cryptic notes for a more complex detailing.

> The Cross opens
> Dances
> There's no parish hall
> There's no airport
> There's no holy pyramid
> I'm not too clear about the meaning of the word "Imperialism"
>   ("Mardi Gras")

And in "Prose du Transsibérien" there is the same listing of details, tied together by conjunctions, which imparts a jerky, halting motion to much of the poem.

> Et je n'avais pas assez des sept gares et des mille et trois tours
> Car mon adolescence était alors si ardente et si folle
> Que mon cœur, tour à tour, brûlait comme le temple d'Éphèse
>   ou comme la Place Rouge de Moscou
> Quand le soleil se couche.
> Et mes yeux éclairaient des voies anciennes.
> Et j'étais déjà si mauvais poète
> Que je ne savais pas aller jusqu'au bout.

Instead of concealing the contours of his thought, he displays them publicly, as the work appears to spring spontaneously from the mind's working. You may call it conversational, didactic, hortatory, epic (the bard spinning out his tales for a captive audience), but it is the voice of the writer — not muted or hidden but public and involved.

If, however, it is here the voice of the teller of tales, it is often also the voice of the lay mystic, a poet "without faith" who is, nevertheless, the "lover of the secret part of things."

> . . . I removed myself in order to expand and strengthen myself in Love, on a level where everything — acts, thoughts, feelings, words — is a universal communion after which (something I was not then aware of myself) just as one enters into a religion and comes into the cloister whose grills close silently after you, without having pronounced any vows, one is in complete solitude. In a cage. But with God. It is a great strength. And you become silent through desire for the Word . . ."
>
> (*L'Homme foudroyé*)

Cendrars uses "Verbe" for "the Word," the same essence the Symbolist poets were trying to communicate in their verse, and this most "modern" of poets, the most avowedly anti-traditional, proclaims his kinship with both the Christian mystics (in spite of his professed faithlessness) and the most significant current in modern French poetry. The relationship between "Prose du Transsibérien" and the medieval Christian hymns, his own instinct for contemplation and solitude, his attempt to link the world of secret essences and the world of things, can all demonstrate that Cendrars is distinctive not so much for his novelty as for his absorption of the very past he claims to have rejected. "Les Pâques à New-York," so much a part of a metrical tradition, bridges Cendrars's modernism without detaching it from the past. Modernity may be an awareness of the shapes and contours of the contemporary world, but it sees them in molds dictated by older experiences.

If one were to cite one figure to whom Cendrars is most drawn and with whom he seems to feel a most intimate relation, it might very well be the levitating saint, Joseph of Cupertino, the subject of an extensive treatment by Cendrars in the last of his biographical chronicles, *Le Lotissement du ciel*. He devotes almost two hundred pages to this saint and other manifesters of the power to fly, using as his point of departure the text of Oliver Leroy, *La Levitation,* published in 1928. He finds in the simple-hearted naïveté of this sixteenth-century man of God a profound awareness of the "secret part of things," and in the section, "The Ecstasy of Love," the saint and the writer Cendrars, entering into ecstatic communion with God, become one, and the language of the writer parallels the transport of the saint.

> Immolation.
> Ecstasy.
> The flame of the holocaust sparks and rises straight up. The sacrifice is consummated. All the sins of the world depart in smoke. Abel and Cain. Again. Enough. The flocks bleat on the outskirts. Adam readies his flute. No shepherdess Eve. A turtledove coos in the gorge. In the wood, the sound of running water . . .

The text is stuffed with Latin citations, classical precedents, and the entire section is titled "The New Patron of Aviation." The title is suggestive of the nature of Cendrars's interest. The traditional saint — modern, in Cendrars's conception, in his ability to transcend the material world — is a symbol for that same world. And in *L'Homme foudroyé,* Cendrars describes a film he hopes to make, the life of Mary Magdalene, to be climaxed by the woman mounting into the skies, "in the very heavens. . . . Shall I descend again . . . ? . . . I think I shall return . . . Yes . . . Live, first of all, live. I am of the earth." The mystic's transport will pass, and the man will participate in the rites of the earth, not scriptural but the communion of man with man.

VI

Diverse as Cendrars's prose writings may be, it is more probably as a poet that his reputation will endure. The very range and vigor of his vision that fragment the prose compositions, making of them striking vignettes and absorbing personal anecdotes rather than a compelling, coherent body of closely textured and ordered work, make of the poetry a rich and varied canvas which forces its attention upon the reader. We may read the prose works with interest and curiosity, but we do not read them with the same impelling sense of urgency communicated in the poetry. The four biographical chronicles are recondite, colorful, and evocative of the man and his travels and reminiscences. But they are extensions — not transformations — of the vein he was working in 1912, and the poems have a more than personal significance. "Prose du Transsibérien" is the finest of these, a long and successful poem written in an era that prefers the writing, and reading, of shorter, more intimate verse forms. We have taken to heart Poe's belief in the ultimate validity and the superiority of the short poem over the long one. "Prose du Transsibérien" is a long poem, but its length is sustained by an emotional drive, immediate and intense, a range of emotional coloring responding now to the impulsive movement of the train, now to his feeling of kinship with Jeanne and the humble creatures of this world. It is an impressive achievement, and an isolated one, even in his own work.

Alfred de Vigny, in his poem "La Maison du Berger," published in 1844, could not have foreseen that in his criticism of man's adoption of the productions of modern technology (typified by the image of the train, a roaring monster with "teeth of iron") he was anticipating the revolution in time and space from which Cendrars, and many other twentieth-century writers, have profited.

> La distance et le temps sont vaincus. La science
> Trace autour de la terre un chemin triste et droit.
> Le monde est rétréci par notre expérience,
> Et l'équateur n'est plus qu'un anneau trop étroit.

For Vigny, this speed and blind pursuit of the "moment and the end" were inimical to true poetic and philosophical beauty and thought.

> Jamais la Rêverie amoureuse et paisible
> N'y verra sans horreur son pied blanc attaché;

Car il faut que ses yeux sur chaque objet visible
Versent un long regard, comme un fleuve épanché. . . .

Yet, in that paradox in which writers so often fix themselves, Vigny took the thing he criticized and made it the material of poetry. A lengthy section describing the ferocious, blind movement of the train is central to the development of the poem and contrasts with the crystallization of poetic beauty in the form of Woman, Eva, whose dreamy look everywhere spreads "ses flammes colorées / Son repos gracieux, sa magique saveur."

In *Dan Yack,* Eva is Hedwiga, the remote, inaccessible woman who, by her very absence, controls the direction of Dan Yack's search for meaning, and in Vigny the train's movement is ultimately subordinated to the "enthousiasme pur" which Eva generates. In "Prose du Transsibérien" the sections concerning Jeanne are quiet lyrical pauses in the relentless onrush of the train. The poem can thus be seen as a kind of poetic inversion of "La Maison du Berger," with the modern world's ferocity and power, captured in the train, dominating the mood of nostalgic reverie and contemplation to which the woman invites the poet. But, as in *Dan Yack* and "La Maison du Berger," it is finally the woman whose tone dominates, and the slow measured cadences of the finale of "Prose du Transsibérien" attest to her ability, like that of the train, to break through time and space and impose herself on the poet.

If Cendrars is torn between contemplation and action, the two poles of his travels, he is also uncertain in his defense of modernity and the contemporary world. The reliance on memory is already a remove from that contemporary world, and the final conviction in the novels that his own spiritual essence is as much related to that of the saint and mystic as to the creator of the modern society attests to his increasing reliance on the past. Yet the two strains, the modern and the traditional, are both dominating elements in his work, and in this variety of inspiration, the very tension of his sources and feelings dictates the richness of the texture of his poetry and his prose.

Cendrars's vision is rooted in an absorption of his own experiences into a loose poetic or prose framework. Like the Romantic writers, he incorporates the personal ego, the intense physical or spiritual life, into a poetic context, deepening and diffusing it. However, where Victor Hugo in "La tristesse d'Olympio," Alfred de Musset in "Souvenir," and Alphonse de Lamartine in "Le Lac" attempt to recall a time that was happy, to capture the intensity of a privileged experience, isolating certain moments and giving them a special value, Cendrars gathers together in a single context an often bewildering variety of experiences. He gives to them not the aura of a nostalgic happiness and beauty but the record of memories intense and vivid enough to impose themselves upon him. These memories possess sufficient force to break through the traditional limits of poetry or the novel. After a single poem, "Les Pâques à New-York," and a single novel, *L'Or,* in which he attempted to contain his vision within a formal framework, he moved away, in poetry, from the restraining Alexandrine and, in prose, from the classically sober and spare novel. As he poignantly states in "Prose du Transsibérien," he is incapable any longer of "going to the end." Formal content, for him, cannot be restricted to a tight formal structure. This metrical and structural liberation permits him a spatial freedom, and as Vigny has pointed out, the world has "narrowed." It is not, as it was with the Romantics, Man and Nature, or Man and the Universe, but man and world about him, distance conquered by science and the modern imagination.

L'heure de Paris l'heure de Berlin l'heure de Saint-Pétersbourg
   et l'heure de toutes les gares

Thus, Cendrars stands, at the same time, in a Romantic tradition, personal experience furnishing the material of the poem, and departs from it by refusing to find an ultimate relationship between structure and experience. Where the Romantic poets sought to deepen the experience in a temporal relationship, Cendrars insisted upon a spatial relationship.

The spatial and structural distension express a permanent dislocation, and the Romantic contemplation of a past experience is uprooted by fusion with the Rimbaud poet-traveler in revolt, the vagabond in time and space, amassing a bewildering array of experiences. Cendrars's poetry, like that of Rimbaud in *Saison en enfer*, is the lyrical biography of a vagabond in flight, but instead of using the prose poem, Cendrars preferred to use free verse, with its more formal poetic grouping into strophes rather than the paragraphs of the prose poem. The semimystical exaltation of Rimbaud is only suggested in the poetry, but in the prose writings Cendrars develops and exploits his mystical leanings. Here too the style, at times, merges with the prose poem, and the boundaries between prose and poetry — often tenuous in Cendrars's work — become even less clear.

Cendrars's poetry assumes a constant poetic attitude, based on the importance of the personal experience, from the most banal to the most intense, and this attitude extends to the novel and biographical chronicle. The poetry admits a wider range of experience than its predecessors, both in vocabulary and in spatial extension, but it seems to awaken only a muted echo in the poems following it. The interior landscape with only faint imprints of the exterior world, rather than the exterior landscape heightened by an expressive lyricism, is more characteristic of the Surrealists and their successors. The Surrealists, in their dredging up from the well of the unconscious, were responding to a real need of poets, a need expressed by Cendrars in his two poetry lectures, to tap a deeper inspiration. Cendrars's vigor, his range of imagery, and his humanitarian feeling, were either beyond or beneath these poets. His separation from poetic schools has perhaps resulted from a very real lack of identification with their aims and methods, and his vision, sounding a recognizably personal note, has been perhaps too distinctive a pattern for other poets to attempt to reproduce or to incorporate into their own poetry.

As Cendrars turned from poetry to the movies to the novel to the biographical chronicle, it might be argued that instead of enriching and developing his talent, he simply recast it into different molds. Rather than creating a distinct form which would be detached and dependent on its own merits, he projected so many extensions of his own biography, writing and rewriting his emotional and physical life, his feeling for the outsiders, and his distinctness from any school or camp, into a lengthy autobiography, now in terms of poetry, now in terms of the camera, now in terms of prose. He always remained faithful to his ideal and refused to subordinate his personal impulses to any poetic hierarchy or trend. Yet it was only at sixty, as he was in the midst of the composition of the four chronicles, that (as he tells us) he finally believed in his vocation as a writer. These four works, then, become the spiritual and literary testament of that faith. They are heterogeneous collections of anecdotes, glosses of texts, lyrical effusions of his deepest, most private feelings buttressed by footnotes and asides. And in these footnotes, directed to the "unknown reader," the voice cries out, the man and the writer asking to be heard, its accents, like Cendrars himself, in varied tones expressive of his diverse and complex nature.

VERSE

LES PÂQUES À NEW-YORK

A Agnès

Flecte ramos, arbor alta, tensa laxa viscera
Et rigor lentescat ille quem dedit nativitas
Ut superni membra Regis miti tendas stipite . . .
FORTUNAT, *Pange lingua*

Fléchis tes branches, arbre géant, relâche un
    peu la tension des viscères,
Et que ta rigueur naturelle s'alentisse,
N'écartèle pas si rudement les membres du
    Roi supérieur . . .
REMY DE GOURMONT, *Le Latin mystique*.

Seigneur, c'est aujourd'hui le jour de votre Nom,
J'ai lu dans un vieux livre la geste de votre Passion,

Et votre angoisse et vos efforts et vos bonnes paroles
Qui pleurent dans le livre, doucement monotones.

Un moine d'un vieux temps me parle de votre mort.
Il traçait votre histoire avec des lettres d'or

Dans un missel, posé sur ses genoux.
Il travaillait pieusement en s'inspirant de Vous.

A l'abri de l'autel, assis dans sa robe blanche,
Il travaillait lentement du lundi au dimanche.

Les heures s'arrêtaient au seuil de son retrait.
Lui, s'oubliait, penché sur votre portrait.

46

EASTER IN NEW YORK

To Agnès

Flecte ramos, arbor alta, tensa laxa viscera
Et rigor lentescat ille quem dedit nativitas
Ut superni membra Regis miti tendas stipite . . .
FORTUNAT, *Pange lingua*

Flex your limbs, giant tree, relax a bit
  your viscera,
Unbend your natural rigidity,
Do not pull so roughly the members of the
  supreme King . . .
REMY DE GOURMONT, *Le Latin mystique*

Lord, this day is dedicated to You,
I read about your Passion in an old book I once knew,

And about your torments and your struggles and the good
  things You said
Crying softly in the book, monotonous and sad.

There your death is described by a monk of old.
He traced out your story in letters of gold

In a missal perched on his knee.
Inspired by You he worked piously.

In the shelter of the altar, dressed in white,
From Monday morning until Sunday night.

The hours would pause at the door of his nook.
He forgot himself bending over your book.

A vêpres, quand les cloches psalmodiaient dans la tour,
Le bon frère ne savait si c'était son amour

Ou si c'était le Vôtre, Seigneur, ou votre Père
Qui battait à grands coups les portes du monastère.

Je suis comme ce bon moine, ce soir, je suis inquiet.
Dans le chambre à côté, un être triste et muet

Attend derrière la porte, attend que je l'appelle!
C'est Vous, c'est Dieu, c'est moi, — c'est l'Éternel.

Je ne Vous ai pas connu alors, — ni maintenant.
Je n'ai jamais prié quand j'étais un petit enfant.

Ce soir pourtant je pense à Vous avec effroi.
Mon âme est une veuve en deuil au pied de votre Croix;

Mon âme est une veuve en noir, — c'est votre Mère
Sans larme et sans espoir, comme l'a peinte Carrière.

Je connais tous les Christs qui pendent dans les musées;
Mais Vous marchez, Seigneur, ce soir à mes côtés.

Je descends à grands pas vers le bas de la ville,
Le dos voûté, le cœur ridé, l'esprit fébrile.

Votre flanc grand-ouvert est comme un grand soleil
Et vos mains tout autour palpitent d'étincelles.

Les vitres des maisons sont toutes pleines de sang
Et les femmes, derrière, sont comme des fleurs de sang,

When the bells sang at vespers from the tower above,
The good brother did not know whether it was his love

Or yours, or whether it was your Father, Lord,
Beating with great blows on the monastery door.

I am like that good monk, I am restless tonight.
A sad and silent presence is waiting outside,

Standing behind the door, waiting for me to call!
It is You, it is God, it is I — it is the Eternal.

Tonight I think of You: I am afraid.
When I was a child I never prayed.

I didn't know You then — or now, I guess.
My soul is a widow in mourning at the foot of your cross;

My soul is a widow in black — my soul is your Mother,
Dry-eyed and hopeless as Carrière painted her.

In the museums I know every Christ crucified;
But tonight You are walking, O Lord, at my side.

My soul in hunger, I am striding down
With quickening steps toward the lower town.

Your side wide open is a sun in the dark
And your hands everywhere are flickering with sparks.

The windows of the buildings are shining with blood
And the women behind are like flowers of blood,

D'étranges mauvaises fleurs flétries, des orchidées,
Calices renversés ouverts sous vos trois plaies.

Votre sang recueilli, elles ne l'ont jamais bu.
Elles ont du rouge aux lèvres et des dentelles au cul.

Les fleurs de la Passion sont blanches, comme des cierges,
Ce sont les plus douces fleurs au Jardin de la Bonne Vierge.

C'est à cette heure-ci, c'est vers la neuvième heure,
Que votre Tête, Seigneur, tomba sur votre Cœur.

Je suis assis au bord de l'océan
Et je me remémore un cantique allemand,

Où il est dit, avec des mots très doux, très simples, très purs,
La beauté de votre Face dans la torture.

Dans une église, à Sienne, dans un caveau,
J'ai vu la même Face, au mur, sous un rideau.

Et dans un ermitage, à Bourrié-Wladislasz,
Elle est bossuée d'or dans une châsse.

De troubles cabochons sont à la place des yeux
Et des paysans baisent à genoux Vos yeux.

Sur le mouchoir de Véronique Elle est empreinte
Et c'est pourquoi Sainte Véronique est Votre sainte.

C'est la meilleure relique promenée par les champs,
Elle guérit tous les malades, tous les méchants.

Elle fait encore mille et mille autres miracles,
Mais je n'ai jamais assisté à ce spectacle.

Strange flowers like orchids evil and dried,
Open overturned chalices under your side.

Your blood in a cup; they never drank from that glass.
They have rouge on their lips and lace on their ass.

White as a candle is the passion flower,
It is the most beautiful in the Virgin's bower.

It was at this hour, about nine o'clock,
That your head, O Lord, finally fell on your heart.

I am sitting by the edge of the sea,
A German hymn comes back to me,

Where in words very simple, very soft and pure,
The beauty of your face is described in torture.

In a church in Siena, in a sepulchral vault,
I have seen the same face under a curtain on the wall.

At Bourria-Wladislasz I have seen it shine,
Inlaid with gold in a holy shrine.

Worn murky holes take the place of your eyes
And peasants come to kiss them on their knees.

On Veronica's handkerchief there is its print
And that is why Veronica is your saint.

That is the best relic they have ever found,
It cures all the sick, all the sinners around.

It accomplishes thousands and thousands of miracles,
But I never was there at those spectacles.

Peut-être que la foi me manque, Seigneur, et la bonté
Pour voir ce rayonnement de votre Beauté.

Pourtant, Seigneur, j'ai fait un périlleux voyage
Pour contempler dans un béryl l'intaille de votre image.

Faites, Seigneur, que mon visage appuyé dans les mains
Y laisse tomber le masque d'angoisse qui m'étreint.

Faites, Seigneur, que mes deux mains appuyées sur ma bouche
N'y lèchent pas l'écume d'un désespoir farouche.

Je suis triste et malade. Peut-être à cause de Vous,
Peut-être à cause d'un autre. Peut-être à cause de Vous.

Seigneur, la foule des pauvres pour qui vous fîtes le Sacrifice
Est ici, parquée, tassée, comme du bétail, dans les hospices.

D'immenses bateaux noirs viennent des horizons
Et les débarquent, pêle-mêle, sur les pontons.

Il y a des Italiens, des Grecs, des Espagnols,
Des Russes, des Bulgares, des Persans, des Mongols.

Ce sont des bêtes de cirque qui sautent les méridiens.
On leur jette un morceau de viande noire, comme à des chiens.

C'est leur bonheur à eux que cette sale pitance.
Seigneur, ayez pitié des peuples en souffrance.

Seigneur dans les ghettos grouille la tourbe des Juifs
Ils viennent de Pologne et sont tous fugitifs.

Maybe I lack faith, Lord, I lack the goodness
To move in the light of your loveliness.

Yet once, Lord, I went to a dangerous place
Just to look at a beryl intaglio of your face.

O Lord, let the face in my hands You see,
Let fall there the mask that is stifling me.

O Lord, let my hands on my mouth not leave there
The treacherous foam of a savage despair.

I am tired and sick; perhaps because of You,
Perhaps because of another. Perhaps because of You.

Lord, here are the poor for whom You died,
At the flophouses, crowded like cattle inside.

Enormous black liners from across the sea
Arrive and discharge them pell-mell on the quay.

They are Spaniards, Italians, Persians, and Poles,
Russians, Bulgarians, Greeks, Mongols.

They leap the meridians, they land on their feet,
Like dogs they are thrown rotten pieces of meat.

This is prosperity, this dirty spoor,
Lord, take pity on the suffering poor.

Lord, the ghetto tonight is swarming with Jews.
They come from Poland, are all refugees.

Je le sais bien, ils t'ont fait ton Procès;
Mais je t'assure, ils ne sont pas tout à fait mauvais.

Ils sont dans des boutiques sous des lampes de cuivre,
Vendent des vieux habits, des armes et des livres.

Rembrandt aimait beaucoup les peindre dans leurs défroques.
Moi, j'ai, ce soir, marchandé un microscope.

Hélas! Seigneur, Vous ne serez plus là, après Pâques!
Seigneur, ayez pitié des Juifs dans les baraques.

Seigneur, les humbles femmes qui vous accompagnèrent à
    Golgotha,
Se cachent. Au fond des bouges, sur d'immondes sophas,

Elles sont polluées par la misère des hommes.
Des chiens leur ont rongé les os, et dans le rhum

Elles cachent leur vice endurci qui s'écaille.
Seigneur, quand une de ces femmes me parle, je défaille.

Je voudrais être Vous pour aimer les prostituées.
Seigneur, ayez pitié des prostituées.

Seigneur, je suis dans le quartier des bons voleurs,
Des vagabonds, des va-nu-pied, des recéleurs.

Je pense aux deux larrons qui étaient avec vous à la Potence,
Je sais que vous daignez sourire à leur malchance.

Seigneur, l'un voudrait une corde avec un nœud au bout,
Mais ça n'est pas gratis, la corde, ça coûte vingt sous.

I know all about that trial You had;
But I tell You, Lord, they are not all bad.

They sit in their shops under copper lamps
Selling old clothes, weapons, books, and stamps.

Rembrandt loved to paint them in their grimy coats;
This evening I bartered a microscope.

After Easter You won't be around anymore;
Lord, take pity on the Jew at his door.

Lord, the humble women who were with You at Golgotha
Are in hiding; back of bars, on scrofulous sofas

They pollute themselves with the misery of men;
Dogs gnaw at their bones, they hide in gin

Their vice-encrusted soul — and bone-thick.
Lord, when one of them talks to me I feel sick.

Lord, I'd like to be You to love the whores.
Lord, take pity on the whores.

Lord, this is the district of the good thieves' slums,
The fences, the hustlers, the beggars, the bums.

I think of the thieves You were with at the dock,
I know that You deigned to smile at their bad luck.

Lord, one wants a rope with a knot on the end,
But rope isn't free, it costs fifty cents.

Il raisonnait comme un philosophe, ce vieux bandit.
Je lui ai donné le l'opium pour qu'il aille plus vite en paradis.

Je pense aussi aux musiciens des rues,
Au violoniste aveugle, au manchot qui tourne l'orgue de
      Barbarie,

A la chanteuse au chapeau de paille avec des roses de papier;
Je sais que ce sont eux qui chantent durant l'éternité.

Seigneur, faites-leur l'aumône, autre que de la lueur des becs
      de gaz,
Seigneur, faites-leur l'aumône de gros sous ici-bas.

Seigneur, quand vous mourûtes, le rideau se fendit,
Ce que l'on vit derrière, personne ne l'a dit.

La rue est dans la nuit comme une déchirure,
Pleine d'or et de sang, de feu et d'épluchures.

Ceux que vous aviez chassés du temple avec votre fouet,
Flagellent les passants d'une poignée de méfaits.

L'Étoile qui disparut alors du tabernacle,
Brûle sur les murs dans la lumière crue des spectacles.

Seigneur, la Banque illuminée est comme un coffre-fort,
Où s'est coagulé le Sang de votre mort.

Les rues se font désertes et deviennent plus noires.
Je chancelle comme un homme ivre sur les trottoirs.

That old bum was a philosopher, how he could bicker.
I gave him some opium so he'd get to Paradise quicker.

Lord, keep every street musician from harm,
The blind violinist, the organ grinder with one arm,

The girl with the paper roses on her straw hat;
They sing through eternity who sing like that.

Lord, a little charity besides the gas jet's glow,
Lord, a little charity of fat pennies down here below.

Lord, when You died the curtain split wide,
No one has said what he saw on the other side.

The street in the night cuts like a long gash
Full of fire and blood, orange peels and hard cash.

Those You drove from the temple of God with your thongs
Here flog passersby with fistfuls of wrongs.

Then the star disappeared from the tabernacle,
Now it burns in raw light on the theater wall.

Lord, the bank lighted up is a safe locked and sealed
Where the Blood of your dying is lying congealed.

The streets are empty. They are getting dark.
On the pavement I stagger like a drunk.

J'ai peur des grands pans d'ombre que les maisons projettent.
J'ai peur. Quelqu'un me suit. Je n'ose tourner la tête.

Un pas clopin-clopant saute de plus en plus près.
J'ai peur. J'ai le vertige. Et je m'arrête exprès.

Un effroyable drôle m'a jeté un regard.
Aigu, puis a passé, mauvais, comme un poignard.

Seigneur, rien n'a changé depuis que vous n'êtes plus Roi.
Le Mal s'est fait une béquille de votre Croix.

Je descends les mauvaises marches d'un café
Et me voici, assis, devant un verre de thé.

Je suis chez des Chinois, qui comme avec le dos
Sourient, se penchent et sont polis comme des magots.

La boutique est petite, badigeonnée de rouge
Et de curieux chromos sont encadrés dans du bambou.

Ho-Kousaï a peint les cent aspects d'une montagne.
Que serait votre Face peinte par un Chinois ? . . .

Cette dernière idée, Seigneur, m'a d'abord fait sourire.
Je vous voyais en raccourci dans votre martyre.

Mais le peintre, pourtant, aurait peint votre tourment
Avec plus de cruauté que nos peintres d'Occident.

Des lames contournées auraient scié vos chairs,
Des pinces et des peignes auraient strié vos nerfs,

I am afraid of those shadows the buildings project.
I am afraid. Someone's there. I don't dare turn my head.

A step coming closer leaps clippety-clop.
I am afraid. I am dizzy. I finally stop.

A hideous old beggar gives me the cold eye
And wicked as a knife goes clip-clopping on by.

Lord, since You aren't King anymore nothing's changed very
    much.
Evil has turned your cross into a crutch.

I go down the rickety steps of a café;
I am sitting in front of a cup of tea.

I am with the Chinese who smile with their spines.
Bending over as polished as figurines.

Their shop is small, touched up in red,
With curious chromos in bamboo overhead.

Hokusai has painted a mountain face
A hundred ways. What would he have done with your face?

Lord, that last idea at first made me smile,
I saw You on the cross in a shrunken-up style.

Yet one of their painters would have done
Your torment more cruelly than a western one.

Your body sawed through by the curving scythes,
Your nerves striated by pincers and knives,

On vous aurait passé le col dans un carcan,
On vous aurait arraché les ongles et les dents,

D'immenses dragons noirs se seraient jetés sur Vous,
Et vous auraient soufflé des flammes dans le cou,

On vous aurait arraché la langue et les yeux,
On vous aurait empalé sur un pieu.

Ainsi, Seigneur, vous auriez souffert toute l'infamie,
Car il n'y a pas de plus cruelle posture.

Ensuite, on vous aurait forjeté aux pourceaux
Qui vous auraient rongé le ventre et les boyaux.

Je suis seul à présent, les autres sont sortis,
Je me suis étendu sur un banc contre le mur.

J'aurais voulu entrer, Seigneur, dans une église;
Mais il n'y a pas de cloches, Seigneur, dans cette ville.

Je pense aux cloches tues: — où sont les cloches anciennes?
Où sont les litanies et les douces antiennes?

Où sont les longs offices et où les beaux cantiques?
Où sont les liturgies et les musiques?

Où sont tes fiers prélats, Seigneur, où tes nonnains?
Où l'aube blanche, l'amict des Saintes et des Saints?

La joie du Paradis se noie dans la poussière,
Les feux mystiques ne rutilent plus dans les verrières.

Your neck stuck into a carcanet,
Your fingernails and your teeth torn out,

Immense black dragons leaping on your back,
Black poisonous fumes whistling down your neck,

Your tongue torn out and your eyes and your soul,
Your body impaled upon a pole.

Thus You'd have suffered the worst infamy
For that is the cruelest position there is.

Then they'd have thrown You to the hogs,
Your belly and bowels eaten by the hogs.

I am alone now, the others have gone;
There's a bench by the wall; I lie down.

I would have liked to go into a church;
But there are no bells in this city, Lord.

I think of their silence: where are the old bells?
Where are the litanies where the music swells?

Where are the long offices, the beautiful hymns?
Where are the liturgies, the sweet anthems?

Where are your proud prelates, where your little nuns?
Where are those friends of the saints, the white dawns?

Drowned in the dust are the joys of Paradise,
The mystic fires have gone out in the glass.

L'aube tarde à venir, et dans le bouge étroit
Des ombres crucifiées agonisent aux parois.

C'est comme un Golgotha de nuit dans un miroir
Que l'on voit trembloter en rouge sur du noir.

La fumée, sous la lampe, est comme un linge déteint
Qui tourne, entortillé, tout autour de vos reins.

Par au-dessus, la lampe pâle est suspendue,
Comme votre Tête, triste et morte et exsangue.

Des reflets insolites palpitent sur les vitres . . .
J'ai peur, — et je suis triste, Seigneur, d'être si triste.

"Dic nobis, Maria, quid vidisti in via?"
— La lumière frissonner, humble dans le matin.

"Dic nobis, Maria, quid vidisti in via?"
— Des blancheurs éperdues palpiter comme des mains.

"Dic nobis, Maria, quid vidisti in via?"
— L'augure du printemps tressaillir dans mon sein.

Seigneur, l'aube a glissé froide comme un suaire
Et a mis tout à nu les gratte-ciel dans les airs.

Déjà un bruit immense retentit sur la ville.
Déjà les trains bondissent, grondent et défilent.

Les métropolitains roulent et tonnent sous terre.
Les ponts sont secoués par les chemins de fer.

Dawn is slow to break. In the narrow room
Crucified shadows writhe in the gloom.

It is like a dark Golgotha in a mirror at the back,
I can see it shimmering in crimson on black.

Smoke under the lamp is a faded rag
Turning, twisted around your leg.

The pale lamp is hanging overhead
Like your head, bloodless, sorrowing, and dead.

Strange reflections flicker on the windowpane ...
I am afraid, and sad, Lord, to be so sad.

Dic nobis, Maria, quid vidisti in via?
— The light trembling, pale and humble in the East.

Dic nobis, Maria, quid vidisti in via?
— Faint whitenesses flickering like hands in the mist

Dic nobis, Maria, quid vidisti in via?
— The augury of spring shivering in my breast.

O Lord, dawn has slipped in cold as a shroud
Stripping skyscrapers naked under a thin cloud.

Already the city is bursting with sound.
The subways are rolling and thundering underground.

The elevated grumbles, leaps, sways, and strains.
The bridges shake with the railway trains.

La cité tremble. Des cris, du feu et des fumées,
Des sirènes à vapeur rauquent comme des huées.

Une foule enfiévrée par les sueurs de l'or
Se bouscule et s'engouffre dans de longs corridors.

Trouble, dans le fouillis empanaché des toits,
Le soleil, c'est votre Face souillée par les crachats.

Seigneur, je rentre fatigué, seul et très morne . . .
Ma chambre est nue comme un tombeau . . .

Seigneur, je suis tout seul et j'ai la fièvre . . .
Mon lit est froid comme un cercueil . . .

Seigneur, je ferme les yeux et je claque des dents . . .
Je suis trop seul. J'ai froid. Je vous appelle . . .

Cent mille toupies tournoient devant mes yeux . . .
Non, cent mille femmes . . . Non, cent mille violoncelles . . .

Je pense, Seigneur, à mes heures malheureuses . . .
Je pense, Seigneur, à mes heures en allées . . .

Je ne pense plus à Vous. Je ne pense plus à Vous.

New York, avril 1912.

The steam whistles raucously jeer and choke.
The city trembles. Fire, cries, and smoke.

The crowd sweat-stained with the fever of gold
Is engulfing itself, jostling in the cold.

And in the jumble of roofs in the smoky half-light,
The sun is your face all sullied with spit.

Lord, I have come back, tired, alone, and cast down . . .
My room is naked as a tomb . . .

Lord, I am feverish, I am alone . . .
My bed is cold as a coffin . . .

Lord, I close my eyes, my teeth are chattering . . .
I am too much alone. I am cold. I cry out to You . . .

A hundred thousand tops are turning in front of my eyes . . .
No, a hundred thousand women . . . No, a hundred thousand
    violins . . .

I am thinking, Lord, of my wretched hours . . .
I am thinking, Lord, of my passing hours . . .

I think no more of You. I think no more of You.

New York, April 1912.

Translated by Scott Bates

PROSE DU TRANSSIBÉRIEN ET DE LA PETITE JEANNE DE FRANCE

Dédiée aux musiciens

En ce temps-là jétais en mon adolescence
J'avais à peine seize ans et je ne me souvenais déjà plus de
    mon enfance
J'étais à 16.000 lieues du lieu de ma naissance
J'étais à Moscou, dans la ville des mille et trois clochers et des
    sept gares
Et je n'avais pas assez des sept gares et des mille et trois
    tours
Car mon adolescence était alors si ardente et si folle
Que mon cœur, tour à tour, brûlait comme le temple d'Éphèse
    ou comme la Place Rouge de Moscou
Quand le soleil se couche.
Et mes yeux éclairaient des voies anciennes.
Et j'étais déjà si mauvais poète
Que je ne savais pas aller jusqu'au bout.

Le Kremlin était comme un immense gâteau tartare
Croustillé d'or,

PROSE OF THE TRANSSIBERIAN AND OF LITTLE JEANNE OF FRANCE

Dedicated to the musicians

It was in the time of my adolescence
I was scarcely sixteen and I had already forgotten my child-
   hood
I was 16,000 leagues from the place of my birth
I was in Moscow, city of the one thousand and three bell
   towers and the seven stations
And I was not satisfied with the seven stations and the one
   thousand and three bell towers
Because my adolescence was so intense and so insane
That my heart, in turn, burned like the temple at Ephesus or
   like the Red Square of Moscow
When the sun is setting.
And my eyes were lighting ancient paths.
And I was already such a bad poet
That I couldn't go to the end.

The Kremlin was like an immense Tartar cake
Frosted in gold,

Avec les grandes amandes des cathédrales toutes blanches
Et l'or mielleux des cloches . . .
Un vieux moine lisait la légende de Novgorode
J'avais soif
Et je déchiffrais des caractères cunéiformes
Puis, tout à coup, les pigeons du Saint-Esprit s'envolaient sur
    la place
Et mes mains s'envolaient aussi, avec des bruissements d'alba-
    tros
Et ceci, c'était les dernières réminiscences du dernier jour
Du tout dernier voyage
Et de la mer.

Pourtant, j'étais fort mauvais poète.
Je ne savais pas aller jusqu'au bout.
J'avais faim
Et tous les jours et toutes les femmes dans les cafés et tous
    les verres
J'aurais voulu les boire et les casser
Et toutes les vitrines et toutes les rues
Et toutes les maisons et toutes les vies
Et toutes les roues des fiacres qui tournaient en tourbillon sur
    les mauvais pavés
J'aurais voulu les plonger dans une fournaise de glaives
Et j'aurais voulu broyer tous les os
Et arracher toutes les langues
Et liquéfier tous ces grands corps étranges et nus sous les
    vêtements qui m'affolent . . .
Je pressentais la venue du grand Christ rouge de la révolu-
    tion russe . . .
Et le soleil était une mauvaise plaie
Qui s'ouvrait comme un brasier.

En ce temps-là j'étais en mon adolescence
J'avais à peine seize ans et je ne me souvenais déjà plus de ma
    naissance

The great almonds of the cathedrals all in white
And the honeyed gold of the bells ...
An old monk was reading me the legend of Nizhni Novgorod
I was thirsty
And I was deciphering runic letters
When, all at once, the pigeons of the Holy Ghost flew up from
     the square
And my hands took flight too, with the rustling of albatross
     wings
And those were the last reminiscences of the last day
Of the very last voyage
And of the sea.

Still, I was a very bad poet.
I couldn't go to the end.
I was hungry
And all the days and all the women in the cafés and all the
     glasses
I should have liked to drink them and break them
And all the shopwindows and all the streets
And all the houses and all those lives
And all the wheels of cabs turning like whirlwinds over broken
     pavements
I should have liked to plunge them into a furnace of swords
And I should have liked to grind up all the bones
And tear out all the tongues
And dissolve all those tall bodies, naked and strange under
     garments that enrage me ...
I could sense the coming of the great red Christ of the Russian
     Revolution ...
And the sun was a fierce wound
That burned like live coals.

It was in the time of my adolescence
I was scarcely sixteen and I had already forgotten my birth

J'étais à Moscou, où je voulais me nourrir de flammes

Et je n'avais pas assez des tours et des gares que constellaient
 mes yeux

En Sibérie tonnait le canon, c'était la guerre

La faim le froid la peste le choléra

Et les eaux limoneuses de l'Amour charriaient des millions de
 charognes

Dans toutes les gares je voyais partir tous les derniers trains

Personne ne pouvait plus partir car on ne délivrait plus de
 billets

Et les soldats qui s'en allaient auraient bien voulu rester ...

Un vieux moine me chantait la légende de Novgorode.

Moi, le mauvais poète qui ne voulais aller nulle part, je pouvais aller partout

Et aussi les marchands avaient encore assez d'argent

Pour aller tenter faire fortune.

Leur train partait tous les vendredis matin.

On disait qu'il y avait beaucoup de morts.

L'un emportait cent caisses de réveils et de coucous de la
 Forêt-Noire

Un autre, des boîtes à chapeaux, des cylindres et un assorti-
 ment de tire-bouchon de Sheffield

Un autre, des cercueils de Malmoë remplis de boîtes de con-
 serve et de sardines à l'huile

Puis il y avait beaucoup de femmes

Des femmes des entre-jambes à louer qui pouvaient aussi
 servir

Des cercueils

Elles étaient toutes patentées

On disait qu'il y avait beaucoup de morts là-bas

Elles voyageaient à prix réduits

Et avaient toutes un compte-courant à la banque.

I was in Moscow, where I was trying to nourish myself with
     flames
And I was not satisfied with the bell towers and the stations
     that my eyes turned to stars
In Siberia cannon were thundering, it was war
Hunger cold plague cholera
And the muddy waters of Love carted away millions of corpses
In all the stations I saw all the last trains leaving
Nobody could leave anymore because they weren't selling any
     more tickets
And the soldiers who were going away would have liked to
     stay . . .
An old monk was singing to me the legend of Nizhni
     Novgorod.

And I, the bad poet who didn't want to go anywhere, could go
     everywhere
And also merchants still had enough money
To go make their fortunes.
Their train left every Friday morning.
It was rumored there were many dead.
One took along a hundred boxes of alarm clocks and cuckoo
     clocks from the Black Forest
Another, hatboxes, cylinders, and an assortment of Sheffield
     corkscrews
Still another, coffins from Malmö filled with tin cans and cans
     of sardines in oil
Then there were many women
Women with crotches for hire which could also be useful
Coffins
They were all patented
It was rumored there were many dead out there
They traveled at reduced rates
And they all had savings accounts in the bank.

Or, un vendredi matin, ce fut enfin mon tour
On était en décembre
Et je partis moi aussi pour accompagner le voyageur en bijou-
terie qui se rendait à Kharbine
Nous avions deux coupés dans l'express et 34 coffres de joail-
lerie de Pforzheim
De la camelote allemande "Made in Germany"
Il m'avait habillé de neuf, et en montant dans le train, j'avais
perdu un bouton
— Je m'en souviens, je m'en souviens, j'y ai souvent pensé
depuis —
Je couchais sur les coffres et j'étais tout heureux de pouvoir
jouer avec le browning nickelé qu'il m'avait aussi donné

J'étais très heureux insouciant
Je croyais jouer aux brigands
Nous avions volé le trésor de Golconde
Et nous allions, grâce au transsibérien, le cacher de l'autre
côté du monde
Je devais le défendre contre les voleurs de l'Oural qui avaient
attaqué les saltimbanques de Jules Verne
Contre les Khoungouzes, les boxers de la Chine
Et les enragés petits mongols du Grand-Lama
Alibaba et les quarante voleurs
Et les fidèles du terrible Vieux de la montagne
Et surtout, contre les plus modernes
Les rats d'hôtel
Et les spécialistes des express internationaux.

Et pourtant, et pourtant
J'étais triste comme un enfant
Les rythmes du train
La "moëlle chemin-de-fer" des psychiatres américains
Le bruit des portes des voix des essieux grinçant sur les rails
congelés
Le ferlin d'or de mon avenir

Finally, one Friday morning, it was my turn
It was in December
And I left accompanying the jewel merchant who was going to
  Harbin
We had two compartments in the Express and 34 coffers of
  jewelry from Pforzheim
German junk "Made in Germany"
He had bought me a new outfit, and getting on the train, I had
  lost a button
— I remember, I remember, I've often thought of it since —
I slept on the coffers and I was happy to be able to play with
  the nickel-plated Browning he had also given me

I was very happy carefree
I thought it was a game of cops and robbers
We had stolen the Golconda treasure
And we were going, thanks to the Transsiberian, to hide it on
  the other side of the world
I was supposed to defend it against robbers from the Ural who
  had attacked the mountebanks out of Jules Verne
Against the Koungouzes, the Chinese Boxers
And the fierce little Mongol hordes of the Grand Lama
Ali Baba and the forty thieves
And the cohorts of the terrible Old Man of the Mountain
And especially the most up-to-date brigands
Hotel thieves
And crooks operating on the International Express.

And yet ... and yet ...
I was as sad as a child
The rhythms of the train
The trainlike medulla of American psychiatrists
The noise of doors voices wheels grinding over the frozen
  tracks
The golden thread of my future

Mon browning le piano et les jurons des joueurs de cartes dans
    le compartiment d'à côté
L'épatante présence de Jeanne
L'homme aux lunettes bleues qui se promenait nerveusement
    dans le couloir et qui me regardait en passant
Froissis de femmes
Et le sifflement de la vapeur
Et le bruit éternel des roues en folie dans les ornières du ciel
Les vitres sont givrées
Pas de nature!
Et derrière, les plaines sibériennes le ciel bas et les grandes
    ombres des Taciturnes qui montent et qui descendent
Je suis couché dans un plaid
Bariolé
Comme ma vie
Et ma vie ne me tient pas plus chaud que ce châle
Écossais
Et l'Europe tout entière aperçue au coupe-vent d'un express
    à toute vapeur
N'est pas plus riche que ma vie
Ma pauvre vie
Ce châle
Effiloché sur des coffres remplis d'or
Avec lesquels je roule
Que je rêve
Que je fume
Et la seule flamme de l'univers
Est une pauvre pensée ...

Du fond de mon cœur des larmes me viennent
Si je pense, Amour, à ma maîtresse;
Elle n'est qu'une enfant, que je trouvai ainsi
Pâle, immaculée, au fond d'un bordel.

My Browning the piano and the oaths of the cardplayers in the
    next compartment
The fantastic presence of Jeanne
The man with the blue spectacles who paced nervously up and
    down in the corridor and looked at me as he passed
The rustling of women
And the steam engine's whistle
And the everlasting sound of wheels whirling madly along in
    their ruts in the sky
The windows are frosted over
No view!
And beyond, the Siberian plains the lowering sky and the tall
    shapes of the Silent Mountains that rise and fall
I am curled up in a plaid shawl
Motley
Like my life
And my life doesn't keep me any warmer than this Scotch
Shawl
And the whole of Europe seen through the windcutter of an
    Express racing ahead at full speed
Is no richer than my life
My poor life
This frayed
Shawl on the coffers filled with gold
With which I'm traveling
And which I dream
And which I smoke
And the only fire in the universe
Is a shabby thought . . .

From the depths of my heart tears rise
If I think, Love, of my mistress . . .
She is only a child I found,
Pale, immaculate, in the depths of a bordello.

Ce n'est qu'une enfant, blonde, rieuse et triste,
Elle ne sourit pas et ne pleure jamais;
Mais au fond de ses yeux, quand elle vous y laisse boire,
Tremble un doux lys d'argent, la fleur du poète.

Elle est douce et muette, sans aucun reproche,
Avec un long tressaillement à votre approche;
Mais quand moi je lui viens, de-ci, de-là, de fête,
Elle fait un pas, puis ferme les yeux — et fait un pas.

Car elle est mon amour, et les autres femmes
N'ont que des robes d'or sur de grands corps de flammes,
Ma pauvre amie est si esseulée,
Elle est toute nue, n'a pas de corps — elle est trop pauvre.

Elle n'est qu'une fleur candide, fluette,
La fleur du poète, un pauvre lys d'argent,
Tout froid, tout seul, et déjà si fané
Que les larmes me viennent si je pense à son cœur.

Et cette nuit est pareille à cent mille autres quand un train file
        dans la nuit
— Les comètes tombent —
Et que l'homme et la femme, même jeunes, s'amusent à faire
        l'amour.

Le ciel est comme la tente déchirée d'un cirque pauvre dans
        un petit village de pêcheurs
En Flandres
Le soleil est un fumeux quinquet
Et tout au haut d'un trapèze une femme fait la lune.
La clarinette le piston une flûte aigre et un mauvais tambour
Et voici mon berceau
Mon berceau
Il était toujours près du piano quand ma mère comme
        Madame Bovary jouait les sonates de Beethoven

She is only a child, blond, laughing . . . and sad,
She does not smile and she never cries;
But deep in her eyes, when she lets you drink there,
Trembles a gentle silver lily, the poet's flower.

She is gentle and mute, makes no reproach,
With a slow trembling at your approach;
But when I come to her, no fuss, no fret,
She takes one step, closes her eyes — and takes one step.

For she is my love, and the other women
Have only dresses of gold on tall bodies of flame,
My poor friend is so lonely,
She is quite naked, has no body — she is too poor.

She is only a slender white flower,
The poet's flower, a poor silver lily,
So cold, so alone, and already so wilted
That tears rise to my eyes if I think of her heart.

And tonight is like a thousand other nights when a train
    rushes into the dark
— Comets fall —
And men and women, even though young, play at making
    love.

The sky is like the torn tent of a wretched circus in a little
    fishing village
In Flanders
The sun is a smoky lamp
And on a high trapeze a woman does a half-moon bend.
Clarinet trumpet a harsh flute and a dissonant drum
And now here's my cradle
My cradle
It was always near the piano when my mother, like Madame
    Bovary, was playing Beethoven sonatas

J'ai passé mon enfance dans les jardins suspendus de Babylone

Et l'école buissonnière, dans les gares devant les trains en
partance

Maintenant, j'ai fait courir tous les trains derrière moi

Bâle-Tombouctou

J'ai aussi joué aux courses à Auteuil et à Longchamp

Paris-New York

Maintenant, j'ai fait courir tous les trains tout le long de ma
vie

Madrid-Stockholm

Et j'ai perdu tous mes paris

Il n'y a plus que la Patagonie, la Patagonie, qui convienne à
mon immense tristesse, la Patagonie, et un voyage dans
les mers du Sud

Je suis en route

J'ai toujours été en route

Je suis en route avec la petite Jehanne de France

Le train fait un saut périlleux et retombe sur toutes ses roues

Le train retombe sur ses roues

Le train retombe toujours sur toutes ses roues

"Blaise, dis, sommes-nous bien loin de Montmartre?"

Nous sommes loin, Jeanne, tu roules depuis sept jours

Tu es loin de Montmartre, de la Butte qui t'a nourrie du
Sacré-Cœur contre lequel tu t'es blottie

Paris a disparu et son énorme flambée

Il n'y a plus que les cendres continues

La pluie qui tombe

La tourbe qui se gonfle

La Sibérie qui tourne

Les lourdes nappes de neige qui remontent

Et le grelot de la folie qui grelotte comme un dernier désir
dans l'air bleu

Le train palpite au cœur des horizons plombés

Et ton chagrin ricane ...

I spent my childhood in the hanging gardens of Babylon
Playing hooky in stations before departing trains
Now I've made all the trains run after me
Basel–Timbuktu
I've also played the horses at Auteuil and at Longchamps
Paris–New York
Now I've made all the trains run alongside my life
Madrid–Stockholm
And I've lost all my bets
There's nothing left except Patagonia, Patagonia, which suits
    my overwhelming sadness, Patagonia, and a trip on
    Southern Seas
I'm on my way
I've always been on my way
I'm on my way with little Jehanne of France
The train makes a risky leap and lands on all fours
The train lands on all fours
The train always lands on all fours

"Blaise, tell me, are we very far from Montmartre?"

We are quite far, Jeanne, you have been riding for seven days
You are a long way from Montmartre, from the Butte that
    nourished you, from the Sacré-Cœur you cuddled up to
Paris has disappeared and its enormous blazing
There's nothing left except trailing ashes
The rain falling
The landscape swelling
Siberia turning
Heavy flakes of snow rising
And the resounding bell of madness that rings like desire dying
    in the frostbitten air
The train throbs at the heart of leaden horizons
And your despair grins . . .

"Dis, Blaise, sommes-nous bien loin de Montmartre?"

Les inquiétudes
Oublie les inquiétudes
Toutes les gares lézardées obliques sur la route
Les fils télégraphiques auxquels elles pendent
Les poteaux grimaçants qui gesticulent et les étranglent
Le monde s'étire s'allonge et se retire comme un accordéon
     qu'une main sadique tourmente
Dans les déchirures du ciel, les locomotives en furie
S'enfuient
Et dans les trous,
Les roues vertigineuses les bouches les voix
Et les chiens du malheur qui aboient à nos trousses
Les démons sont déchaînés
Ferrailles
Tout est un faux accord
"Le broun-roun-roun" des roues
Chocs
Rebondissements
Nous sommes un orage sous le crâne d'un sourd . . .

"Dis, Blaise, sommes-nous bien loin de Montmartre?"

Mais oui, tu m'énerves, tu le sais bien, nous sommes bien loin
La folie surchauffée beugle dans la locomotive
La peste le choléra se lèvent comme des braises ardentes sur
     notre route
Nous disparaissons dans la guerre en plein dans un tunnel
La faim, la putain, se cramponne aux nuages en débandade
Et fiente des batailles en tas puants de morts
Fais comme elle, fais ton métier . . .

"Dis, Blaise, sommes-nous bien loin de Montmartre?"

"Tell me, Blaise, are we very far from Montmartre?"

Uneasiness
Forget your uneasiness
All the stations, their walls cracked, slanted along the route
The telegraph lines they hang from
The grimacing poles which grope for and strangle them
The world stretches lengthens and retracts like an accordion
      tormented by a sadistic player
In the rents in the sky, the engines furiously
Flee
And in the gaps,
The dizzying wheels the mouths the voices
And the dogs of misfortune barking at our heels
All Hell has broken loose
Rails
Everything is out of tune
The "broun-roun-roun" of the wheels
Shocks
Shattering leaps
We are all a storm in the skull of a deaf man . . .

"Tell me, Blaise, are we very far from Montmartre?"

Of course, you're driving me crazy, can't you see we're quite
      far
Madness boiling-over bellows in the engine
Plague cholera rise around us like burning coals along the
      route
We are disappearing into war drawn into a tunnel
Hunger, that whore, clings to the clouds in flight
And spawns battles in stinking heaps of corpses
Do like her, do your job . . .

"Tell me, Blaise, are we very far from Montmartre?"

Oui, nous le sommes, nous le sommes
Tous les boucs émissaires ont crevé dans ce désert
Entends les sonnailles de ce troupeau galeux Tomsk
Tchéliabinsk Kainsk Obi Taïchet Verkné Oudinsk Kourgane
      Samara Pensa-Touloune
La mort en Mandchourie
Est notre débarcadère est notre dernier repaire
Ce voyage est terrible
Hier matin
Ivan Oulitch avait les cheveux blancs
Et Kolia Nicolaï Ivanovitch se ronge les doigts depuis quinze
      jours . . .
Fais comme elles la Mort la Famine fais ton métier
Ça coûte cent sous, en transsibérien, ça coûte cent roubles
Enfièvre les banquettes et rougeoie sous la table
Le diable est au piano
Ses doigts noueux excitent toutes les femmes
La Nature
Les Gouges
Fais ton métier
Jusqu'à Kharbine . . .

"Dis, Blaise, sommes-nous bien loin de Montmartre?"

Non mais . . . fiche-moi la paix . . . laisse-moi tranquille
Tu as les hanches angulaires
Ton ventre est aigre et tu as la chaude-pisse
C'est tout ce que Paris a mis dans ton giron
C'est aussi un peu d'âme . . . car tu es malheureuse
J'ai pitié j'ai pitié viens vers moi sur mon cœur
Les roues sont les moulins à vent du pays de Cocagne
Et les moulins à vent sont les béquilles qu'un mendiant fait
      tournoyer
Nous sommes les culs-de-jatte de l'espace
Nous roulons sur nos quatre plaies
On nous a rogné les ailes

Yes, we are, we are
All the scapegoats have croaked in the desert
Listen to the trumpeting of this mangy troop Tomsk
Chelyabinsk Kansu Ob Tai Shan Verkhneudinsk Kurgan
     Samara Penza–Tulun
Death in Manchuria
Is our debarkation point is our last lair
God what a terrible trip
Yesterday morning
Ivan Oulitch had white hair
And Kolia Nicolai Ivanovitch has been biting his nails for two
     weeks . . .
Imitate them Death Famine do your job
On the Transsiberian it costs 100 rubles
Excite the train seats and blaze up under the table
The devil is at the piano
His gnarled hands arouse all the women
Human nature
Whores
Do your job
Until we get to Harbin . . .

"Tell me, Blaise, are we very far from Montmartre?"

No but . . . get the hell out . . . leave me in peace
You have angular hips
Your belly is bitter and you have the clap
That's all Paris has put in your crotch
There's also a bit of soul . . . for you are unhappy
I'm sorry I'm sorry come to me come to my heart
The wheels are windmills from the land of Cocaigne
The windmills are crutches a beggar's shaking
We're the cripples of space
We roll along on our four wounds
Our wings are clipped

Les ailes de nos sept péchés
Et tous les trains sont les bilboquets du diable
Basse-cour
Le monde moderne
La vitesse n'y peut mais
Le monde moderne
Les lointains sont par trop loin
Et au bout du voyage c'est terrible d'être un homme avec une
    femme . . .

"Blaise, dis, sommes-nous bien loin de Montmartre?"

J'ai pitié j'ai pitié viens vers moi je vais te conter une histoire
Viens dans mon lit
Viens sur mon cœur
Je vais te conter une histoire . . .

Oh viens! viens!

Aux Fidji règne l'éternel printemps
La paresse
L'amour pâme les couples dans l'herbe haute et la chaude
    syphilis rôde sous les bananiers
Viens dans les îles perdues du Pacifique!
Elles ont nom du Phénix, des Marquises
Bornéo et Java
Et Célèbes à la forme d'un chat.

Nous ne pouvons pas aller au Japon
Viens au Mexique!
Sur ses hauts plateaux les tulipiers fleurissent
Les lianes tentaculaires sont la chevelure du soleil
On dirait la palette et les pinceaux d'un peintre
Des couleurs étourdissantes comme des gongs,
Rousseau y a été
Il y a ébloui sa vie

The wings of our seven sins
And all the trains are the devil's cup and ball
The poultry yard
The modern world
Speed is useless
In the modern world
Distances are too great
And at the end of the trip it's terrible to be a man with a
    woman . . .

"Tell me, Blaise, are we very far from Montmartre?"

I'm sorry I'm sorry come to me I'll tell you a story
Come into my bed
Come into my heart
I will tell you a story . . .

Oh come! come!

On Fiji it's always spring
Drowsiness
Love makes the lovers swoon in the tall grass and syphilis in
    heat prowls under the banana trees
Come to the lost islands of the Pacific!
They have names like Phoenix, the Marquesas
Borneo and Java
And Sulawesi shaped like a cat.

We can't go to Japan
Come to Mexico!
On the escarpments the tulip trees are in bloom
Riotous vines are the sun's tresses
They seem a painter's palette and brushes
Colors booming like gongs
Rousseau was there
His life was dazzled

C'est le pays des oiseaux
L'oiseau du paradis, l'oiseau-lyre
Le toucan, l'oiseau moqueur
Et le colibri niche au cœur des lys noirs
Viens!
Nous nous aimerons dans les ruines majestueuses d'un temple
    aztèque
Tu seras mon idole
Une idole bariolée enfantine un peu laide et bizarrement
    étrange
Oh viens!

Si tu veux nous irons en aéroplane et nous survolerons le pays
    des mille lacs,
Les nuits y sont démesurément longues
L'ancêtre préhistorique aura peur de mon moteur
J'atterrirai
Et je construirai un hangar pour mon avion avec les os fossiles
    de mammouth
Le feu primitif réchauffera notre pauvre amour
Samowar
Et nous nous aimerons bien bourgeoisement près du pôle
Oh viens!

Jeanne Jeannette Ninette nini ninon nichon
Mimi mamour ma poupoule mon Pérou
Dodo dondon
Carotte ma crotte
Chouchou p'tit-cœur
Cocotte
Chérie p'tite chèvre
Mon p'tit-péché mignon
Concon
Coucou
Elle dort.

It's the country of birds
The bird of paradise, the lyrebird
The toucan, the mockingbird
And the hummingbird nests in the heart of black lilies
Come!
We will make love in the majestic ruins of an Aztec temple
You will be my idol
A childish, multicolored idol somewhat ugly and curiously
    strange
Oh come!

If you like we'll go by plane and fly over the land of the
    thousand lakes
The nights are fantastically long
The prehistoric ancestor will be afraid of my motor
I'll land
And I'll build a hangar for my airplane out of fossilized mam-
    moth bones
The ancient fire will warm our meager love
Samovar
And we will make love like a good bourgeois couple near the
    pole
Oh come!

Jean Jeanette Naureen Nanette Nounou Mitsou
Mimi my love my delight my Peru
To sleep sweet teat
Turd my bird
Shush-shush my thrush
To sleep
My pear my lamb
My peach
Humhum
Coocoo
She sleeps.

Elle dort

Et de toutes les heures du monde elle n'en a pas gobé une
     seule

Tous les visages entrevus dans les gares

Toutes les horloges

L'heure de Paris l'heure de Berlin l'heure de Saint-Péters-
     bourg et l'heure de toutes les gares

Et à Oufa, le visage ensanglanté du canonnier

Et le cadran bêtement lumineux de Grodno

Et l'avance perpétuelle du train

Tous les matins on met les montres à l'heure

Le train avance et le soleil retarde

Rien n'y fait, j'entends les cloches sonores

Le gros bourdon de Notre-Dame

La cloche aigrelette du Louvre qui sonna la Barthélémy

Les carillons rouillés de Bruges-la-Morte

Les sonneries électriques de la bibliothèque de New-York

Les campanes de Venise

Et les cloches de Moscou, l'horloge de la Porte-Rouge qui me
     comptait les heures quand j'étais dans un bureau

Et mes souvenirs

Le train tonne sur les plaques tournantes

Le train roule

Un gramophone grasseye une marche tzigane

Et le monde, comme l'horloge du quartier juif de Prague,
     tourne éperdument à rebours.

Effeuille la rose des vents

Voici que bruissent les orages déchaînés

Les trains roulent en tourbillon sur les réseaux enchevêtrés

Bilboquets diaboliques

Il y a des trains qui ne se rencontrent jamais

D'autres se perdent en route

Les chefs de gare jouent aux échecs

Tric-trac

She sleeps
And she hasn't gobbled up a single minute of all the hours in
    the world
All the faces glimpsed in stations
All the clocks
The time in Paris the time in Berlin the time in Saint Peters-
    burg and the time in all the stations
And at Ufa, the bloodied face of the cannoneer
And the stupidly luminous face of Grodno
And the continuous rushing of the train
Every morning all the clocks are set
The train is set forward and the sun is set back
Nothing can be done, I hear the sonorous bells
The big clapper of Notre Dame
The shrill ringing of the Louvre announcing Saint Bartholo-
    mew
The rusted bells of Bruges-la-Morte
The electric bells of the New York Public Library
The city bells of Venice
And the bells of Moscow, the clock at the Red Gate which
    kept time for me when I was in an office
And my memories
The train rumbles on revolving plates
The train rolls
A phonograph grinds out a gypsy march
And the world, like the clock in the Jewish quarter in Prague,
    turns desperately counterclockwise.

Strip the compass card
How the unleashed storms rage!
The trains roll like whirlwinds over tangled tracks
Insane cups-and-balls
There are trains which never meet
Others are lost on the way
The trainmasters play chess
Backgammon

Billard
Caramboles
Paraboles
La voie ferrée est une nouvelle géométrie
Syracuse
Archimède
Et les soldats qui l'égorgèrent
Et les galères
Et les vaisseaux
Et les engins prodigieux qu'il inventa
Et toutes les tueries
L'histoire antique
L'histoire moderne
Les tourbillons
Les naufrages
Même celui du Titanic que j'ai lu dans le journal
Autant d'images-associations que je ne peux pas développer
    dans mes vers
Car je suis encore fort mauvais poète
Car l'univers me déborde
Car j'ai négligé de m'assurer contre les accidents de chemin
    de fer
Car je ne sais pas aller jusqu'au bout
Et j'ai peur.

J'ai peur
Je ne sais pas aller jusqu'au bout
Comme mon ami Chagall je pourrais faire une série de tab-
    leaux déments
Mais je n'ai pas pris de notes en voyage
"Pardonnez-moi mon ignorance
"Pardonnez-moi de ne plus connaître l'ancien jeu des vers"
Comme dit Guillaume Apollinaire
Tout ce qui concerne la guerre on peut le lire dans les
    "Mémoires" de Kouropatkine

90

Pool
Pool balls
Parabolas
The railroad is a new geometry
Syracuse
Archimedes
And the soldiers who butchered him
And the galleys
And the ships
And the prodigious machines he invented
And all the ways of killing
Ancient history
Modern history
Whirlwinds
Shipwrecks
Even that of the Titanic I read about in the paper
So many associative images I can't develop in my verse
Because I'm still a very bad poet
Because the universe overwhelms me
Because I neglected to insure myself against train accidents
Because I'm not capable of going to the end
And I'm afraid.

I'm afraid
I'm not capable of going to the end
I could make a series of hallucinatory paintings like my friend
    Chagall
But I didn't take any notes on my trip
"Forgive me my ignorance
Forgive me for no longer knowing the old game of writing
    poetry"
As Guillaume Apollinaire says
Everything about war can be found in the *Memoirs* of Kropot-
    kin

Ou dans les journaux japonais qui sont aussi cruellement
    illustrés
A quoi bon me documenter
Je m'abandonne
Aux sursauts de ma mémoire . . .

A partir d'Irkoutsk le voyage devint beaucoup trop lent
Beaucoup trop long
Nous étions dans le premier train qui contournait le lac
    Baïkal
On avait orné la locomotive de drapeaux et de lampions
Et nous avions quitté la gare aux accents tristes de l'hymne
    au Tzar.
Si j'étais peintre je déverserais beaucoup de rouge, beaucoup
    de jaune sur la fin de ce voyage
Car je crois bien que nous étions tous un peu fous
Et qu'un délire immense ensanglantait les faces énervées de
    mes compagnons de voyage
Comme nous approchions de la Mongolie
Qui ronflait comme un incendie.
Le train avait ralenti son allure
Et je percevais dans le grincement perpétuel des roues
Les accents fous et les sanglots
D'une éternelle liturgie

J'ai vu
J'ai vu les trains silencieux les trains noirs qui revenaient de
    l'Extrême-Orient et qui passaient en fantômes
Et mon œil, comme le fanal d'arrière, court encore derrière
    ces trains
A Talga 100.000 blessés agonisaient faute de soins
J'ai visité les hôpitaux de Krasnoïarsk
Et à Khilok nous avons croisé un long convoi de soldats fous
J'ai vu dans les lazarets des plaies béantes des blessures qui
    saignaient à pleines orgues

92

Or in the Japanese newspapers which are also cruelly illus-
trated
What's the use of documenting myself
I give myself over
To the bounds of memory . . .

At Irkutsk the trip became much too slow
Much too long
We were in the first train which wound around Baikal Lake
The engine was decorated with flags and Venetian lamps
And we had left the station to the sad harmonies of the Czarist
hymn.
If I were a painter I would spill great splashes of yellow and
red over the end of this trip
Because I am quite sure we were all a little mad
And that a raging delirium was bloodying the lifeless faces
of my traveling companions
As we approached Mongolia
Which roared like a bonfire.
The train had slowed its pace
And I perceived in the continuous groaning of the wheels
The insane howling and sobbing
Of an eternal liturgy

I saw
I saw the silent trains the black trains returning from the Far
East and passing like phantoms
And my eye, like a rear signal light, is still running along
behind those trains
At Talga 100,000 wounded were dying for lack of care
I visited the hospitals of Krasnoyarsk
And at Khilok we encountered a long convoy of soldiers who
had lost their minds
In the pesthouses I saw gaping wounds bleeding full blast

Et les membres amputés dansaient autour ou s'envolaient
   dans l'air rauque
L'incendie était sur toutes les faces dans tous les cœurs
Des doigts idiots tambourinaient sur toutes les vitres
Et sous la pression de la peur les regards crevaient comme
   des abcès
Dans toutes les gares on brûlait tous les wagons
Et j'ai vu
J'ai vu des trains de 60 locomotives qui s'enfuyaient à toute
   vapeur pourchassées par les horizons en rut et des bandes
   de corbeaux qui s'envolaient désespérément après
Disparaïtre
Dans la direction de Port-Arthur.

A Tchita nous eûmes quelques jours de répit
Arrêt de cinq jours vu l'encombrement de la voie
Nous le passâmes chez Monsieur Iankéléwitch qui voulait me
   donner sa fille unique en mariage
Puis le train repartit.
Maintenant c'était moi qui avais pris place au piano et
   j'avais mal aux dents
Je revois quand je veux cet intérieur si calme le magasin du
   père et les yeux de la fille qui venait le soir dans mon lit
Moussorgsky
Et les lieder de Hugo Wolf
Et les sables du Gobi
Et à Khaïlar une caravane de chameaux blancs
Je crois bien que j'étais ivre durant plus de 500 kilomètres
Mais j'étais au piano et c'est tout ce que je vis
Quand on voyage on devrait fermer les yeux
Dormir
J'aurais tant voulu dormir
Je reconnais tous les pays les yeux fermés à leur odeur
Et je reconnais tous les trains au bruit qu'ils font

And amputated limbs danced about or took flight into the
   raucous air
Fire was on all the faces in all the hearts
Idiot fingers rapped on all the windowpanes
And in the press of fear glances burst open like abscesses
In all the stations where all the cars were burning
And I saw
I saw trains with 60 engines fleeing at top speed pursued by
   flaming horizons and by flocks of crows flying desperately
   after them
Disappearing
In the direction of Port Arthur.

At Chita we had a few days' rest
Five days stopover because of blocked tracks
We spent it with Monsieur Iankelevitch who wanted to give
   me his only daughter in marriage
Then the train took off again.
Now it was I who was at the piano and I had a raging
   toothache
When I want to I can still see that calm interior the father's
   store and the eyes of the daughter who would come each
   evening into my bed
Moussorgsky
And Hugo Wolf *lieder*
And Gobi sand dunes
And at Kailar a caravan of white camels
I'm quite sure I was drunk for more than 500 kilometers
But I was at the piano and that's all I saw
When you travel you should close your eyes
Sleep
I would so have liked to sleep
I can identify all the countries by their smell with my eyes
   closed
And I can identify all the trains by the noise they make

Les trains d'Europe sont à quatre temps tandis que ceux d'Asie
sont à cinq ou sept temps
D'autres vont en sourdine sont des berceuses
Et il y en a qui dans le bruit monotone des roues me rappel-
lent la prose lourde de Maeterlinck
J'ai déchiffré tous les textes confus des roues et j'ai rassemblé
les éléments épars d'une violente beauté
Que je possède
Et qui me force.
Tsitsikar et Kharbine
Je ne vais pas plus loin
C'est la dernière station
Je débarquai à Kharbine comme on venait de mettre le feu
aux bureaux de la Croix-Rouge.

O Paris
Grand foyer chaleureux avec les tisons entrecroisés de tes rues
et tes vieilles maisons qui se penchent au-dessus et se
réchauffent
Comme des aïeules
Et voici des affiches, du rouge du vert multicolores comme
mon passé bref du jaune
Jaune la fière couleur des romans de la France à l'étranger.
J'aime me frotter dans les grandes villes aux autobus en marche
Ceux de la ligne Saint-Germain-Montmartre m'emportent à
l'assaut de la Butte
Les moteurs beuglent comme les taureaux d'or
Les vaches du crépuscule broutent le Sacré-Cœur
O Paris
Gare centrale débarcadère des volontés carrefour des inquié-
tudes
Seuls les marchands de couleur ont encore un peu de lumière
sur leur porte
La Compagnie Internationale des Wagons-Lits et des Grands
Express Européens m'a envoyé son prospectus

European trains move to measured beats while Asian trains
     move to broken rhythms
Others move to muted sounds these are cradle songs
And there are those which in the monotonous noise of their
     wheels make me think of Maeterlinck's heavy prose
I have deciphered all the confused texts of the wheels and I
     have assembled the scattered elements of a most violent
     beauty
That I control
And which compels me.
Tsitsihar and Harbin
I'm not going any further
It's the last station
I got off at Harbin just as they set fire to the offices of the Red
     Cross.

O Paris
Great smoldering hearth with the intersecting embers of your
     streets and your old houses which bend over them and
     warm one another
Like grandmothers
And here are signs red green gaily colored like my past in
     short yellow
Yellow the proud color of French novels sold abroad.
I like to rub up against moving buses in the big cities
Those of the Saint Germain–Montmartre line carry me to my
     assault of the Butte
The engines bellow like golden bulls
The bovine dusk grazes on the Sacré-Cœur
O Paris
Central Station last stop of desire crossroads of unrest
Only the hardware and paint stores still have a bit of light
     on their doors
The "Compagnie Internationale des Wagons-Lits et des
     Grands Express Européens" has sent me its prospectus

C'est la plus belle église du monde
J'ai des amis qui m'entourent comme des garde-fous
Ils ont peur quand je pars que je ne revienne plus
Toutes les femmes que j'ai rencontrées se dressent aux hori-
zons
Avec les gestes piteux et les regards tristes des sémaphores
sous la pluie
Bella, Agnès, Catherine et la mère de mon fils en Italie
Et celle, la mère de mon amour en Amérique
Il y a des cris de sirène qui me déchirent l'âme
Là-bas en Mandchourie un ventre tressaille encore comme
dans un accouchement
Je voudrais
Je voudrais n'avoir jamais fait mes voyages
Ce soir un grand amour me tourmente
Et malgré moi je pense à la petite Jehanne de France.
C'est par un soir de tristesse que j'ai écrit ce poème en son
honneur
Jeanne
La petite prostituée
Je suis triste je suis triste
J'irai au "Lapin agile" me ressouvenir de ma jeunesse perdue
Et boire des petits verres
Puis je rentrerai seul

Paris

Ville de la Tour unique du grand Gibet et de la Roue

Paris, 1913.

It's the most beautiful church in the world
I have friends who surround me like guardrails
They are afraid when I leave that I won't return
All the women I've met rise up on the horizon
With pitiful gestures and the sad looks of lighthouses in the
      rain
Bella, Agnes, Catherine, and the mother of my son in Italy
And she, mother of my love in America
There are siren blasts that tear at my soul
Over in Manchuria a belly still heaves as if it were giving
      birth
I would like
I would like never to have taken my trips
This evening an intense love torments me
And in spite of myself I think of little Jehanne of France
It was on an evening filled with sadness that I wrote this poem
      in her honor
Jeanne
The little prostitute
I am sad I am sad
I will go to the Lapin Agile to recall my lost youth
And drink a few glasses
Then I'll return home alone

Paris

City of the incomparable Tower of the Rack and the Wheel

                                        Paris, 1913.

LE PANAMA OU LES AVENTURES DE MES SEPT ONCLES

A Edmond Bertrand
Barman au Matachine

Des livres
Il y a des livres qui parlent du Canal de Panama
Je ne sais pas ce que disent les catalogues des bibliothèques
Et je n'écoute pas les journaux financiers
Quoique les bulletins de la Bourse soient notre prière quo-
tidienne

Le Canal de Panama est intimement lié à mon enfance . . .
Je jouais sous la table
Je disséquais les mouches
Ma mère me racontait les aventures de ses sept frères
De mes sept oncles
Et quand elle recevait des lettres
Éblouissement!
Ces lettres avec les beaux timbres exotiques qui portent les
vers de Rimbaud en exergue
Elle ne me racontait rien ce jour-là
Et je restais triste sous ma table

PANAMA OR THE ADVENTURES OF MY SEVEN UNCLES

To Edmond Bertrand
barman at Matachinos

Books
There are books about the Panama Canal;
I don't know what the library catalogues say
I don't pay much attention to the financial journals
In spite of the fact that the stock reports are our daily prayer.

The Panama Canal is intimately bound up with my child-
    hood . . .
I used to play under the table
Dissecting flies
And mother used to tell me the adventures of her seven
    brothers
And when she got letters
I was hornswoggled,
Those letters with handsome exotic stamps that might have
    verses of Rimbaud on the label,
That day she wouldn't tell me any stories
And I was blue under my table.

C'est aussi vers cette époque que j'ai lu l'histoire du tremble-
    ment de terre de Lisbonne
Mais je crois bien
Que le crach du Panama est d'une importance plus universelle
Car il a bouleversé mon enfance.
J'avais un beau livre d'images
Et je voyais pour la première fois
La baleine
Le gros nuage
Le morse
Le soleil
Le grand morse
L'ours le lion le chimpanzé le serpent à sonnette et la mouche
La mouche
La terrible mouche
— Maman, les mouches! les mouches! et les troncs d'arbres!
— Dors, dors, mon enfant.
Ahasvérus est idiot

J'avais un beau livre d'images
Un grand lévrier qui s'appelait Dourak
Une bonne anglaise
Banquier
Mon père perdit les trois-quarts de sa fortune
Comme nombre d'honnêtes gens qui perdirent leur argent
    dans ce crach,
Mon père
Moins bête
Perdait celui des autres,
Coups de revolver.
Ma mère pleurait.
Et ce soir-là on m'envoya coucher avec la bonne anglaise

Puis au bout d'un nombre de jours bien long . . .
Nous avions dû déménager

It's about this time too that I read the history of the earth-
        quake at Lisbon
But I think
That the Panama panic has a more universal importance
Because it turned my childhood topsyturvy.

I had a fine picturebook
And I was seeing for the first time
The whale
The big cloud
The walrus
The sun
The great walrus
The bear the lion the chimpanzee the rattlesnake and the fly
The fly
The terrible fly
— Mummy, the flies! the flies! and the trunks of trees!
— Go to sleep my child go to sleep
Ahazuerus is an idiot.

I had a fine picturebook
And a big beagle named Durak,
An English maid.
A banker
My father lost three-fourths of his fortune
Like a number of good people who lost their money in this
        panic;
My father
Not so silly
Lost other people's money.
Revolver shots,
My mother crying;
That night they sent me off to sleep with the English maid;

Then at the end of a very great number of days . . .
We'd had to move

Et les quelques chambres de notre petit appartement étaient
    bourrées de meubles
Nous n'étions plus dans notre villa de la côte
J'étais seul des jours entiers
Parmi les meubles entassés
Je pouvais même casser de la vaisselle
Fendre les fauteuils
Démolir le piano . . .
Puis au bout d'un nombre de jours bien long
Vint une lettre d'un de mes oncles

C'est le crach du Panama qui fit de moi un poète!
C'est épatant
Tous ceux de ma génération sont ainsi
Jeunes gens
Qui ont subi des ricochets étranges
On ne joue plus avec des meubles
On ne joue plus avec des vieilleries
On casse toujours et partout la vaisselle
On s'embarque
On chasse les baleines
On tue les morses
On a toujours peur de la mouche tsé-tsé
Car nous n'aimons pas dormir.

L'ours le lion le chimpanzé le serpent à sonnette m'avaient
    appris à lire . . .
Oh cette première lettre que je déchiffrai seul et plus grouil-
    lante que toute la création
Mon oncle disait:
Je suis boucher à Galveston
Les abattoirs sont à 6 lieues de la ville
C'est moi qui ramène les bêtes saignantes, le soir, tout le long
    de la mer
Et quand je passe les pieuvres se dessent en l'air
Soleil couchant . . .

104

And the few rooms of our little apartment were jammed up
    with furniture,
We weren't in our villa on the shore any longer;
I was left alone entire days
Among the piledup furniture
They even let me break crockery
Make holes in the chairs
Bust up the piano . . .
Then at the end of a very great number of days
Came the letter of one of my uncles.

It's the Panama panic that made me a poet
Amazing
Everybody in my generation is like that,
Youngsters
Victims of strange ricochets,
We don't play with chairs and tables any more
We don't play with antiques any more
We're always and everywhere breaking crockery
We ship
We go whaling
Hunt walrus
We're always afraid of the tsetse fly
Because we're not fond of being asleep.

The bear the lion the chimpanzee the rattlesnake had taught
    me to read
O that first letter that I made out all alone more teeming
    than all creation
My uncle said:
I am a butcher in Galveston
The stockyards are six leagues from the town
It's me that brings back the bleeding carcasses in the evening
    along the seabeach
When I pass the octopuses rise up on their tentacles
At sundown . . .

Et il y avait encore quelque chose
La tristesse
Et le mal du pays.

Mon oncle, tu as disparu durant le cyclone de 1895
J'ai vu depuis la ville reconstruite et je me suis promené au
    bord de la mer où tu menais les bêtes saignantes
Il y avait une fanfare salutiste qui jouait dans un kiosque en
    treillage
On m'a offert une tasse de thé
On n'a jamais retrouvé ton cadavre
Et à ma vingtième année j'ai hérité de tes 400 dollars d'éco-
    nomie
Je possède aussi la boîte à biscuits qui te servait de reliquaire
Elle est en fer-blanc
Toute ta pauvre religion
Un bouton d'uniforme
Une pipe kabyle
Des graines de cacao
Une dizaine d'aquarelles de ta main
Et les photos des bêtes à prime, les taureaux géants que tu
    tiens en laisse
Tu es en bras de chemise avec un tablier blanc

Moi aussi j'aime les animaux
Sous la table
Seul
Je joue déjà avec les chaises
Armoires portes
Fenêtres
Mobilier modern-style
Animaux préconçus
Qui trônent dans les maisons
Comme la reconstitution des bêtes antédiluviennes dans les
    musées
Le premier escabeau est un aurochs!

There was something else too
Gloom
Homesickness.

Poor uncle, you disappeared in the cyclone of '95
Since then I've seen the rebuilt town and taken a walk along
    the seabeach where you drove home in the evening with
    the bleeding carcasses from the stockyards;
A Salvation Army band was playing in a trellised bandstand,
They set me up to a cup of tea.
They never found your body
And in my twentieth year I inherited the 400 dollars you'd
    saved up
I also possess the crackerbox that was your reliquary
It's a tin box
All the religion of your poor life:
The button off a uniform
A Kabyl pipe
Some cocoa beans
A dozen watercolors you'd painted
Some photographs of prize stock, giant bulls you hold by
    the halter,
You're in your shirtsleeves with a white apron.

Me too I like animals
Under the table
Alone
I'm already playing with chairs
Wardrobes doors
Windows
Art nouveau furniture
Synthetic animals
That lord it over houses
Like the reconstructions of prehistoric beasts in museums of
    natural history.
That stool is an aurochs.

J'enfonce les vitrines
Et j'ai jeté tout cela
La ville, en pâture à mon chien
Les images
Les livres
La bonne
Les visites
Quels rires!

Comment voulez-vous que je prépare des examens?
Vous m'avez envoyé dans tous les pensionnats d'Europe
Lycées
Gymnases
Université
Comment voulez-vous que je prépare des examens
Quand une lettre est sous la porte
J'ai vu
La belle pédagogie!
J'ai vu au cinéma le voyage qu'elle a fait
Elle a mis soixante-huit jours pour venir jusqu'à moi
Chargée de fautes d'orthographe
Mon deuxième oncle:
J'ai marié la femme qui fait le meilleur pain du district
J'habite à trois journées de mon plus proche voisin
Je suis maintenant chercheur d'or à Alaska
Je n'ai jamais trouvé plus de 500 francs d'or dans ma pelle
La vie non plus ne se paye pas à sa valeur!
J'ai eu trois doigts gelés
Il fait froid . . .
Et il y avait encore quelque chose
La tristesse
Et le mal du pays.

Oh mon oncle, ma mère m'a tout dit
Tu as volé des chevaux pour t'enfuir avec tes frères

I busted all the windows
And chucked all that
I fed the town to my dog
Pretty pictures
Books
The maid
Company coming,
A big laugh.

How can you expect me to bone up for my exams?
You sent me to all the boardingschools in Europe
Prepschool
Highschool
College
How can you expect me to bone up for my exams
When there's a letter under the door?
I saw it
Magnificent pedagogy!
In the movies I saw its travels
It took sixty-eight days to reach me
Full of mistakes in spelling.
My second uncle:
I've married the woman who makes the best bread in the
    district
I live three days' journey away from my nearest neighbor
Now I'm a prospector in Alaska after gold
I've never found more than 500 francs' worth of gold in my
    spade
You can't sell your life either for what it's worth
I've had three fingers frozen
It's cold up here
Then there was something else too
Gloom
Homesickness.

Oh my uncle, mother told me the whole story
You stole a pair of horses to run away with your brothers

Tu t'es fait mousse à bord d'un cargo-boat

Tu t'es cassé la jambe en sautant d'un train en marche

Et après l'hôpital, tu as été en prison pour avoir arrêté une
diligence

Et tu faisais des poésies inspirées de Musset

San-Francisco

C'est là que tu lisais l'histoire du général Suter qui a conquis la
Californie aux États-Unis

Et qui, milliardaire, a été ruiné par la découverte des mines
d'or sur ses terres

Tu as longtemps chassé dans la vallée du Sacramento où j'ai
travaillé au défrichement du sol

Mais qu'est-il arrivé

Je comprends ton orgueil

Manger le meilleur pain du district et la rivalité des voisins 12
femmes par 1.000 kilomètres carrés

On t'a trouvé

La tête trouée d'un coup de carabine

Ta femme n'était pas là

Ta femme s'est remariée depuis avec un riche fabricant de
confitures

J'ai soif

Nom de Dieu

De nom de Dieu

De nom de Dieu

Je voudrais lire la "Feuille d'Avis de Neuchâtel" ou "le Cour-
rier de Pampelune"

Au milieu de l'Atlantique on n'est pas plus à l'aise que dans
une salle de rédaction

Je tourne dans la cage des méridiens comme un écureuil dans
la sienne

Tiens voilà un Russe qui a une tête sympathique

Où aller

You got a job as cabinboy on a freighter
You broke a leg jumping from a moving train
When you got out of the hospital you got into jail for holding
     up a stagecoach
And you wrote verses inspired by de Musset.
San Francisco
That's where you were reading the history of General Sutter
     who conquered California for the United States and who
     already a multimillionaire was ruined by the discovery of
     gold on his plantation.
You hunted a long time in the Sacramento Valley where I
     worked clearing farmland,
But what happened?
I can understand your pride
Eating the best bread in the district and the envy of the
     neighbors
12 women per 1,000 square kilometers.
They found you
Daylight shot through your skull by a rifle;
They didn't find your wife
Since then your wife has married again, a wealthy jam manu-
     facturer this time.

I'm thirsty
Damn it
God damn it to hell
I'd like to be reading the *Feuille d'Avis de Neuchâtel* or the
     Pamplona *Correo,*
In the middle of the Atlantic you're no more at home than in
     the pressroom of a newspaper,
I go round and round inside the meridians like a squirrel in a
     squirrelcage.
Why there's a Russian looks like he might be worth talking to;
Where to go?

Lui non plus ne sait où déposer son bagage
A Léopoldville ou à la Sedjérah près Nazareth, chez Mr Junod
    ou chez mon vieil ami Perl
Au Congo en Bessarabie à Samoa
Je connais tous les horaires
Tous les trains et leurs correspondances
L'heure d'arrivée l'heure du départ
Tous les paquebots tous les tarifs et toutes les taxes
Ça m'est égal
J'ai des adresses
Vivre de la tape
Je reviens d'Amérique à bord du "Volturno", pour 35 francs
    de New York à Rotterdam

C'est le baptême de la ligne
Les machines continues s'appliquent de bonnes claques
Boys
Platch
Les baquets d'eau
Un Américain les doigts tachés d'encre bat la mesure
La télégraphie sans fil
On danse avec les genoux dans les pelures d'orange et les
    boîtes de conserve vides
Une délégation est chez le capitaine
Le Russe révolutionnaire expériences érotiques
Gaoupa
Le plus gros mot hongrois
J'accompagne une marquise napolitaine enceinte de 8 mois
C'est moi que mène les émigrants de Kichinef à Hambourg
C'est en 1901 que j'ai vu la première automobile,
En panne,
Au coin d'une rue
Ce petit train que les Soleurois appellent un fer à repasser
Je téléphonerai à mon consul
Délivrez-moi immédiatement un billet de 3ᵉ classe

112

He doesn't know any more than I do where to set down his
    grip
At Leopoldville or at the Sedjerah near Nazareth or at the
    house of my old friend Perl
In the Congo in Bessarabia or Samoa.
I know all the timetables
All the trains and their connections
The time they arrive the time they leave
All the liners all the fares all the taxes.
What the hell
I've got addresses
Live by grafting
I'm on my way back from America on the *Volturno* for 35
    francs from New York to Rotterdam.

It's the baptism of the line
The endless swat thump of the engines
Boys
Splash
Soused in a bucket of seawater
An American with inkstained fingers keeps time
Sparks
You dance up to your knees in orangepeels and old tincans;
A delegation is waiting on the captain,
The Russian revolutionist erotic experiences,
Gaoupa
The worst Hungarian cussword.
I'm the escort of a Neapolitan marquise eight months gone
I'm the one that's arranging for the transportation of the
    emigrants from Kishinev to Hamburg.
It's in 1901 that I saw my first automobile
Broken down
At the corner of a street.
That little train the people of Soleure call the flatiron.
I'll call up the consulate on the telephone
I want to take up that 3rd Class ticket at once

The Uranium Steamship C°
J'en veux pour mon argent
Le navire est à quai
Débraillé
Les sabords grand ouverts
Je quitte le bord comme on quitte une sale putain

En route
Je n'ai pas de papier pour me torcher
Et je sors
Comme le dieu Tangaloa qui en pêchant à la ligne tira le
    monde hors des eaux
La dernière lettre de mon troisième oncle:
Papeete, le 1er septembre 1887.
Ma sœur, ma très chère sœur
Je suis bouddhiste membre d'une secte politique
Je suis ici pour faire des achats de dynamite
On en vend chez les épiciers comme chez vous la chicorée
Par petits paquets
Puis je retournerai à Bombay faire sauter les Anglais
Ça chauffe
Je ne te reverrai jamais plus . . .
Et il y avait encore quelque chose
La tristesse
Et le mal du pays.

Vagabondage
J'ai fait de la prison à Marseille et l'on me ramène de force
    à l'école
Toutes les voix crient ensemble
Les animaux et les pierres
C'est le muet qui a la plus belle parole
J'ai été libertin et je suis permis toutes les privautés avec le
    monde
Vous qui aviez la foi pourquoi n'êtes-vous pas arrivé à temps

The Uranium Steamship Co
I want my money's worth
The ship docked
Dismantled
Holds gaping wide
I went down the gangplank in a hurry like walking out on a
    dirty tart.

All aboard.
I've run out of toiletpaper
And I find in my pocket
Like the god Tangaloa who was bottomfishing and pulled the
    earth up out of the waters
The last letter of my third uncle:
Papeete, September 1st, 1887,
My sister, my very dear sister,
I've become a Buddhist, member of a political sect
I'm here to buy dynamite
They sell it in the grocerystores here like chicory at home
In little packages
Then I'm going back to Bombay to blow up the Britishers
Things are getting pretty hot
I'll never see you again . . .
Then there was something else too
Gloom
Homesickness.

On the bum
I was in jail in Marseilles
And they took me by force back to school
All the voices cry out together
Animals stones
It's the dumbest knows the word of meaning
I've done what I damn pleased I've taken all sorts of liberties
    with the world
You who had faith why didn't you turn up in time?

A votre âge

Mon oncle

Tu étais joli garçon et tu jouais très bien du cornet à pistons

C'est ça qui t'a perdu comme on dit vulgairement

Tu aimais tant la musique que tu préféras le ronflement des
     bombes aux symphonies des habits noirs

Tu as travaillé avec de joyeux Italiens à la construction d'une
     voie ferrée dans les environs de Baghavapour

Boute en train

Tu étais le chef de file de tes compagnons

Ta belle humeur et ton joli talent d'orphéoniste

Tu es la coqueluche des femmes du baraquement

Comme Moïse tu as assommé ton chef d'équipe

Tu t'es enfui

On est resté douze ans sans aucune nouvelle de toi

Et comme Luther un coup de foudre t'a fait croire à Dieu

Dans ta solitude

Tu apprends le bengali et l'urlu pour apprendre à fabriquer
     les bombes

Tu as été en relation avec les comités secrets de Londres

C'est à White-Chapel que j'ai retrouvé ta trace

Tu es convict

Ta vie circoncise

Telle que

J'ai envie d'assassiner quelqu'un au boudin ou à la gaufre
     pour avoir l'occasion de te voir

Car je ne t'ai jamais vu

Tu dois avoir une longue cicatrice au front

Quant à mon quatrième oncle il était le valet de chambre du
     général Robertson qui a fait la guerre aux Boërs

Il écrivait rarement des lettres ainsi conçues

Son Excellence a daigné m'augmenter de 50 £

Ou

Son Excellence emporte 48 paires de chaussures à la guerre

At your age . . .
My uncle
You were a goodlooking boy you really played the trombone
    very well
That was your perdition as the saying is
You were so fond of music that you preferred the snort of
    bombs to the symphonies of the stuffed shirts
You worked with a merry crowd of Italians building the rail-
    road in the outskirts of Baghavapur.
Once underway
You got to be the ringleader
Your goodnature and your knack for chorussinging
You were the squire of dames of the camp
Like Moses you knocked out your foreman
And fled.
We were twelve years without news of you.
Like Luther a thunderbolt made you believe in God.
In your solitude
You learned Bengali and Urlu to find out how to make bombs
You corresponded with secret committees in London
I ran across your tracks in Whitechapel;
Now you're a convict
Your life closed up, completed.
So that
I've half a mind to bump someone off with a sandbag or
    blackjack to get a chance to see you
Because I've never seen you
I imagine you with a long scar on your forehead.

As for my fourth uncle, valet to General Robertson who
    fought the Boer war
He'd write rarely but letters like this:
His Excellency has had the goodness to give me a raise of fifty
    pounds
Or
His Excellency is taking 48 pairs of shoes to war with him

Ou
Je fais les ongles de Son Excellence tous les matins ...
Mais je sais
Qu'il y avait encore quelque chose
La tristesse
Et le mal du pays.

Mon oncle Jean, tu es le seul de mes sept oncles que j'aie
      jamais vu
Tu étais rentré au pays car tu te sentais malade
Tu avais un grand coffre en cuir d'hippopotame qui était tou-
      jours bouclé
Tu t'enfermais dans ta chambre pour te soigner
Quand je t'ai vu pour la première fois, tu dormais
Ton visage était terriblement souffrant
Une longue barbe
Tu dormais depuis quinze jours
Et comme je me penchais sur toi
Tu t'es réveillé
Tu étais fou
Tu as voulu tuer grand'mère
On t'a enfermé à l'hospice
Et c'est là que je t'ai vu pour la deuxième fois
Sanglé
Dans la camisole de force
On t'a empêché de débarquer
Tu faisais de pauvres mouvements avec tes mains
Comme si tu allais ramer
Transvaal
Vous étiez en quarantaine et les horse-guards avaient braqué
      un canon sur votre navire
Prétoria
Un Chinois faillit t'étrangler
Le Tougéla
Lord Robertson est mort
Retour à Londres

Or
I manicure His Excellency's nails every morning
But I know
That there was something else too
Gloom
Homesickness.

My uncle John, you are the only one of my seven uncles I ever
    saw
You came home sick
You had a big chest of hippopotamus hide that was always
    locked
You used to shut yourself up in your room to take medicine,
The first time I saw you you were asleep
Your face was knotted up with pain
Your long beard
You'd been asleep for 15 days
And while I was leaning over you
You woke up
Crazy.
You tried to kill grandmother
And they shut you up in an asylum
That's where I saw you for the second time
Strapped down
In a straitjacket:
They wouldn't let you land,
You made helpless motions with your hands
As if you were rowing,
Transvaal:
You were in quarantine and the horseguards had trained a
    gun on your ship,
Pretoria:
A Chinaman nearly strangled you
Tugela:
Lord Robertson died there,
Return to London:

La garde-robe de Son Excellence tombe à l'eau ce qui te va
   droit au cœur
Tu es mort en Suisse à l'asile d'aliénés de Saint-Aubain
Ton entendement
Ton enterrement
Et c'est là que je t'ai vu pour la troisième fois
Il neigeait
Moi, derrière ton corbillard, je me disputais avec les croque-
   morts à propos de leur pourboire
Tu n'as aimé que deux choses au monde
Un cacatoès
Et les ongles roses de Son Excellence

Il n'y a pas d'espérance
Et il faut travailler
Les vies encloses sont les plus denses
Tissus stéganiques
Remy de Gourmont habite au 71 de la rue des Saints-Pères
Filagore ou seizaine
"Séparés un homme rencontre un homme mais une montagne
   ne rencontre jamais une autre montagne"
Dit un proverbe hébreu
Les précipices se croisent
J'étais à Naples
1896
Quand j'ai reçu le "Petit Journal Illustré"
Le capitaine Dreyfus dégradé devant l'armée
Mon cinquième oncle:
Je suis chef au Club-Hôtel de Chicago
J'ai 400 gâte-sauces sous mes ordres
Mais je n'aime pas la cuisine des Yankees
Prenez bonne note de ma nouvelle adresse
Tunis etc.
Amitiés de la tante Adèle
Prenez bonne note de ma nouvelle adresse
Biarritz etc.

His Excellency's wardrobe fell overboard that went straight to
    your heart.
You died in Switzerland at the lunaticasylum in St. Aubain,
Your wits
Your funeral.
That's where I saw you for the third time
It was snowing
Me, walking behind the coffin I was arguing with the under-
    taker's men about the amount of the tip.
There were only two things in the world you loved,
A cockatoo,
And the pink fingernails of His Excellency.

There's no such thing as hope
You've got to work
Hemmed-in lives grow densest
Plants in a hotbed
Remy de Gourmont lives at 71 rue des Saints-Pères,
Timefuse or packingthread?
"A man meets a man he's been separated from but a mountain
    never meets another mountain"
Says a Hebrew proverb.
Cliffs interlock.
I was in Naples in 1896
When I got in the mail the illustrated edition of the *Petit
    Journal*
Captain Dreyfus reduced to the ranks before the army.
My fifth uncle:
I'm chef at the Club-Hotel in Chicago
400 assistant cooks under me
But I don't like the Yankees' cookery
Note my new address,
Tunis, etc.
Best wishes from Aunt Adele
Be sure to note my new address,
Biarritz etc.

Oh mon oncle, toi seul tu n'as jamais eu le mal du pays

Nice Londres Buda-Pest Bermudes Saint-Pétersbourg Tokio
    Memphis

Tous les grands hôtels se disputent tes services

Tu es le maître

Tu as inventé nombre de plats doux qui portent ton nom

Ton art

Tu te donnes tu te vends on te mange

On ne sait jamais où tu es

Tu n'aimes pas rester en place

Il paraît que tu possèdes une "Histoire de la Cuisine à travers
    tous les âges et chez tous les peuples"

En 12 vol. in-8°

Avec les portraits des plus fameux cuisiniers de l'histoire

Tu connais tous les événements

Tu as toujours été partout où il se passait quelque chose

Tu es peut-être à Paris.

Tes menus

Sont la poésie nouvelle

J'ai quitté tout cela

J'attends

La guillotine est le chef-d'œuvre de l'art plastique

Son déclic

Mouvement perpétuel

Le sang des bandits

Les chants de la lumière ébranlent les tours

Les couleurs croulent sur la ville

Affiche plus grande que toi et moi

Bouche ouverte et qui crie

Dans laquelle nous brûlons

Les trois jeunes gens ardents

Hananie Mizaël Azarie

Adam's Express C°

Derrière l'Opéra

Il faut jouer à saute-mouton

Oh my uncle, you were the only one who was never homesick
Nice London Budapest Bermuda St. Petersburg Memphis
All the big hotels fought to have you
You are a master
You have invented a number of desserts that go under your
   name
You give yourself sell yourself people eat you
Nobody ever knows where you are
You don't like to stay too long in one place
It seems that you own a *History of Cookery in All Times and
   Among All Peoples*
In 12 volumes in–8°
With the portraits of the most famous cooks of history
You're on the inside of everything that happens
You're always there when anything goes on
Perhaps you're in Paris at this minute.
Your menucards
Are the new prosody.

I'm through with all that,
I'm waiting
The guillotine is the masterpiece of plastic art
Its trigger
Perpetual motion,
Blood of gunmen
Singing light shaking all towers
Colors crumbled over the city.
A signboard bigger than you and me
Yelling with its mouth open
In which we burn
Hananiah Mishael Azariah
The three flaming youngsters
Adam's Express Co
Behind the opera
You have to play leapfrog

A la brebis qui broute
Femme-tremplin
Le beau joujou de la réclame
En route!
"Siméon, Siméon"
Paris-adieux

C'est rigolo
Il y a des heures qui sonnent
Quai-d'Orsay-Saint-Nazaire!
On passe sous la Tour Eiffel — boucler la boucle — pour
  retomber de l'autre côté du monde

Puis on continue
Les catapultes du soleil assiègent les tropiques irascibles
Riche Péruvien propriétaire de l'exploitation du guano d'An-
  gamos
On lance l'Acaraguan Bananan
A l'ombre
Les mulâtres hospitaliers
J'ai passé plus d'un hiver dans ces îles fortunées
L'oiseau-secrétaire est un éblouissement
Belles dames plantureuses
On boit des boissons glacées sur la terrasse
Un torpilleur brûle comme un cigare
Une partie de polo dans le champ d'ananas
Et les palétuviers éventent les jeunes filles studieuses
My gun
Coup de feu
Un observatoire au flanc du volcan
De gros serpents dans la rivière desséchée
Haie de cactus
Un âne claironne la queue en l'air
La petite Indienne qui louche veut se rendre à Buenos-Ayres
Le musicien allemand m'emprunte ma cravache à pommeau
  d'argent et une paire de gants de Suède

At the sign of the grazing sheep
The gadgetlady, human springboard,
The pretty toy of advertising
Allaboard
Simeon Simeon
Paris Solong.

Funny
Clocks striking the hour
Quai d'Orsay St. Nazaire
We're passing under the Eiffel Tower loop the loop to fall on
    our feet on the other side of the world

And the show goes on:
The sun's catapults pelt the sourbelly tropics
And the rich Peruvian proprietor of the guano deposits at
    Angamos who sits organizing the Acaraguan Banana
In the shade.
With hospitable mulattos
I spent more than one winter in these Fortunate Isles.
The secretarybird is a knockout
And the lovely ladies of the planters' families
Drinking iced drinks on the terrace,
The torpedoboat smokes like a cigar,
A polo game in a field of pineapples
And the mangroves carefully fanning the studious flappers
My gun
Rifleshot
An observatory on the slope of the volcano
Big snakes in the dry riverbed
A cactus hedge
A jackass braying with his tail in the air
The little Indian girl who squints wants to sell herself at
    Buenos Aires,
The German musician borrowed my silverheaded ridingcrop
    and a pair of suede gloves,

Denver, the Residence City and Commercial Center

DENVER is the capital of Colorado and the commercial metropolis of the Rocky Mountain Region. The city is in its fifty-fifth year and has a population of approximately 225,000 as indicated by the U. S. Census of 1910. Many people who have not visited Colorado, believe Denver is situated in the mountains. This city is located 12 miles east of the foothills of the Rocky Mountains, near the north central part of the state, at the junction of the Platte River and Cherry Creek. The land is rolling, giving the city perfect drainage. Altitude one mile above sea level. Area 60 square miles.

Ideal Climate, Superior Educational Advantages Unequalled Park System

DENVER has the lowest death rate of the cities of the United States.

DENVER has 29 parks; total area 1,238 acres.

DENVER has 61 grade schools, 4 high schools, 1 manual training school, 1 trade and 1 technical school.

DENVER has 11 playgrounds — 8 in parks, 3 in individual tracts.

DENVER has 209 churches of every denomination.

DENVER has 56 miles of drives in its parks.

Commercial and Manufacturing City

Annual Bank Clearings, $ 487,848,305.95.

Per capita clearings, $ 180.00.

Annual manufacturing output, $ 57,711,000 (1912).

Eighteen trunk lines entering Denver, tapping the richest agricultural sections of the United States.

DENVER has 810 factories, in which 16,251 wage earners were employed during 1911. The output of factories in DENVER in 1911 was valued at $ 52,000,000. The payroll for the year was $ 12,066,000 — OVER A MILLION DOLLARS A MONTH !

DENVER, COLORADO, BERLIN, GERMANY and MANCHESTER, ENGLAND, are cited by Economists as examples of inland cities which have become great because they are located at a sort of natural cross-roads.

For detailed information, apply to the *Denver Chamber of Commerce.* *Prospectus free.*

Ce gros Hollandais est géographe
On joue aux cartes en attendant le train
C'est l'anniversaire de la Malaise
Je reçois un paquet à mon nom, 200.000 pésétas et une lettre
     de mon sixième oncle:
Attends-moi à la factorerie jusqu'au printemps prochain
Amuse-toi bien bois sec et n'épargne pas les femmes
Le meilleur électuaire
Mon neveu . . .
Et il y avait encore quelque chose
La tristesse
Et le mal du pays.

Oh mon oncle, je t'ai attendu un an et tu n'es pas venu
Tu étais parti avec une compagnie d'astronomes qui allait
     inspecter le ciel sur la côte occidentale de la Patagonie
Tu leur servais d'interprète et de guide
Tes conseils
Ton expérience
Il n'y en avait pas deux comme toi pour viser l'horizon au
     sextant
Les instruments en équilibre
Électro-magnétiques
Dans les fjords de la Terre de Feu
Aux confins du monde
Vous pêchiez des mousses protozoaires en dérive entre deux
     eaux à la lueur des poissons électriques
Vous collectionniez des aérolithes de peroxyde de fer
Un dimanche matin:
Tu vis un évêque mitré sortir des eaux
Il avait une queue de poisson et t'aspergeait de signes de croix
Tu t'es enfui dans la montagne en hurlant comme un vrai
     blessé
La nuit même
Un ouragan détruisit le campement

The fat Hollander is a geographer;
People play cards waiting for the train,
It's the anniversary of unrest,
I receive a package addressed to me, 200,000 pesetas and a
    letter from my sixth uncle:
Wait for me at the tradingpost until next spring
Have a good time drink up strong and don't spare the women
The best electuary
My nephew . . .
And there was something else too
Gloom
Homesickness.

Oh my uncle, I waited a year for you and you never came
You had gone off with an astronomical expedition that was
    going to examine the sky from the west coast of Patagonia
You went as interpreter and guide
Your advice
Your experience
There wasn't a man could equal you getting a bead on the
    horizon with the sextant
Electromagnetic
Levels
In the fjords of the Land of Fire
On the fringes of the world
You fished out protozoic mosses drifting between two tides in
    the glimmer of electric fish
You collected aeroliths of peroxide of iron.
One Sunday morning
You saw a mitered bishop rise up out of the waters
He had a tail like a fish and sprinkled you with signs of the
    cross
You ran off into the hills howling like a wounded lemur.
That same night
A hurricane destroyed the camp

Tes compagnons durent renoncer à l'espoir de te retrouver
    vivant
Ils emportèrent soigneusement les documents scientifiques
Et au bout de trois mois,
Les pauvres intellectuels,
Ils arrivèrent un soir à un feu de gauchos où l'on causait juste-
    ment de toi
J'étais venu à ta rencontre
Tupa
La belle nature
Les étalons s'enculent
200 taureaux noirs mugissent
Tango-argentin

Bien quoi
Il n'y a donc plus de belles histoires
"La Vie des Saints"
"Das Nachtbuechlein von Schuman"
"Cymballum mundi"
"La Tariffa delle Puttane di Venegia"
"Navigation de Jean Struys, Amsterdam", 1528
"Shalom Aleïchem"
"Le crocodile de Saint-Martin"
Strindberg a démontré que la terre n'est pas ronde
Déjà Gavarni avait aboli la géométrie
Pampas
Disque
Les iroquoises du vent
Saupiquets
L'hélice des gemmes
Maggi
Byrrh
Daily Chronicle
La vague est une carrière où l'orage en sculpteur abat des
    blocs de taille
Quadriges d'écume qui prennent le mors aux dents

130

Your companions gave up the hope of finding you alive
They carefully brought back the scientific documents
And at the end of three months
The unfortunate intellectuals
Reached a gauchos' bivouac one night where the talk happened
    to be about you.
I'd come out to meet you:
Tupa,
Beauties of nature,
Stallions mounting stallions
200 black bulls bellowing
Argentine tango.

What the hell
Aren't there any more good yarns?
The Lives of the Saints
Das Nachtbuechlein von Schuman
Cymballum mundi
La Tariffa delle Puttane di Venegia
Navigation de Jean Struys, Amsterdam, 1528
Shalom Aleichem
Le Crocodile de Saint-Martin
Strindberg proved that the earth isn't round,
Already Gavarni had abolished geometry,
Pampas
Phonograph record
Iroquois, squaws of the blizzard
Salamagundi
The incidence of crystals
Maggi
Byrrh
Daily Chronicle
The wave is a quarry where the sculptor stormwind hews out
    buildingstone
Fourhorse chariots of foam with the bits in their teeth

Éternellement
Depuis le commencement du monde
Je siffle
Un frissoulis de bris

Mon septième oncle
On n'a jamais su ce qu'il est devenu
On dit que je te ressemble

Je vous dédie ce poème
Monsieur Bertrand
Vous m'avez offert des liqueurs fortes pour me prémunir
    contre les fièvres du canal
Vous vous êtes abonné à l'Argus de la Presse pour recevoir
    toutes les coupures qui me concernent.
Dernier Français de Panama (il n'y en a pas 20)
Je vous dédie ce poème
Barman du Matachine
Des milliers de Chinois sont morts où se dresse maintenant le
    Bar flamboyant
Vous distillez
Vous vous êtes enrichi en enterrant les cholériques
Envoyez-moi la photographie de la forêt de chênes-lièges qui
    pousse sur les 400 locomotives abandonnées par l'entre-
    prise française
Cadavres-vivants
Le palmier greffé dans la banne d'une grue chargée d'orchidées
Les canons d'Aspinwall rongés par les toucans
La drague aux tortues
Les pumas qui nichent dans le gazomètre défoncé
Les écluses perforées par les poissons-scie
La tuyauterie des pompes bouchée par une colonie d'iguanes
Les trains arrêtés par l'invasion des chenilles
Et l'ancre gigantesque aux armoiries de Louis XV dont vous
    n'avez su m'expliquer la présence dans la forêt

Eternally
Since the beginning of the world.
I'm whistling.
Somebody's walking over my grave!

My seventh uncle
We never knew what became of him
They say I look like him.

I'm dedicating this poem to you
Monsieur Bertrand,
You set me up to strong liquors as a preventative against the
    fevers of the Canal Zone
You subscribed to the Argus of the Press to get clippings about
    me,
Last Frenchman of Panama (there aren't 20 left),
I dedicate this poem to you
Barman of Matachinos;
Tens of thousands of Chinamen died where your burnished
    bar now stands.
You're a distiller.
You got rich burying cholera victims.
Send me the photograph of the forest of corkoaks that grows
    over the 400 locomotives abandoned by the French con-
    cession
Livingcorpses
The palmtree grafted into the arm of a crane laden with
    orchids
The pumping machinery gnawed by the toucans
The turtleinfested dredge
The puma's lairs in the cavedin gasometers
The locks perforated by sawfish
The pipeline bunged by a colony of iguanas
The trains stopped by caterpillars on the march
And the gigantic anchor with the arms of Louis XV the
    presence of which in the forest you couldn't explain to me

Tous les ans vous changez les portes de votre établissement
    incrustées de signatures
Tous ceux qui passèrent chez vous
Ces 32 portes quel témoignage
Langues vivantes de ce sacré canal que vous chérissez tant

Ce matin est le premier jour du monde
Isthme
D'où l'on voit simultanément tous les astres du ciel et toutes
    les formes de la végétation
Préexcellence des montagnes équatoriales
Zone unique
Il y a encore le vapeur de l'Amidon Paterson
Les initiales en couleurs de l'Atlantic-Pacific Tea-Trust
Le Los Angeles limited qui part à 10 h. 02 pour arriver le
    troisième jour et qui est le seul train au monde avec
    wagon-coiffeur
Le Trunk les éclipses et les petites voitures d'enfants
Pour vous apprendre à épeler l'A B C de la vie sous la férule
    des sirènes en partance
Toyo Kisen Kaïsha
J'ai du pain et du fromage
Un col propre
La poésie date d'aujourd'hui

La voie lactée autour du cou
Les deux hémisphères sur les yeux
A toute vitesse
Il n'y a plus de pannes
Si j'avais le temps de faire quelques économies je prendrais
    part au rallye aérien
J'ai réservé ma place dans le premier train qui passera le
    tunnel sous la Manche
Je suis le premier aviateur qui traverse l'Atlantique en mono-
    coque
900 millions

134

Every year you take out the doors of your place encrusted with
     signatures
All those who pass your way
The 32 doors bear witness
Living tongues of this cursed canal you're so fond of.

This morning is the first day on earth,
Isthmus
From which you can see all the stars in the sky at one time and
     all forms of vegetation
Marvel of the equatorial mountains,
Only and unique Zone.
There's still the steamboat of the Patterson *Starch*
The colored initials of the Atlantic and Pacific Tea Company
The Los Angeles Limited that leaves at 10:02 to arrive the
     third day and that is the only train in the world to carry a
     barbershop
The Grand Trunk eclipses and the little cars for children
That teach you the ABC of life under the switch of the sirens
     of departure.
Toyo Kisen Kaisha
I have bread and cheese
A clean collar
And poetry dates from today.

With the Milky Way around my neck
And the two hemispheres for goggles,
Full speed ahead.
Never stall again.
If I had time to save up a little jack I'd take part in the Air
     Circus
I've reserved my seat in the first train to go through the Chan-
     nel Tunnel
The first aviator to cross the Atlantic in a monocoupé.
900 million.

Terre Terre Eaux Océans Ciels
J'ai le mal du pays
Je suis tous les visages et j'ai peur des boîtes aux lettres
Les villes sont des ventres
Je ne suis plus les voies
Lignes
Câbles
Canaux
Ni les ponts suspendus!

Soleils lunes étoiles
Mondes apocalyptiques
Vous avez encore tous un beau rôle à jouer
Un siphon éternue
Les cancans littéraires vont leur train
Tout bas
A la Rotonde
Comme tout au fond d'un verre
J'attends

Je voudrais être la cinquième roue du char
Orage
Midi à quatorze heures
Rien et partout

Paris et Sa Banlieue.
Saint-Cloud, Sèvres, Montmorency,
Courbevoie, Bougival, Rueil, Montrouge,
Saint-Denis, Vincennes, Étampes, Melun,
Saint-Martin, Méréville, Barbizon, Forges-en-
Bière.

Juin 1913–juin 1914

Earth earth seas ocean skies
I'm homesick
I'm all these faces and I'm afraid of mailboxes
Cities are devouring maws
I can't follow the tracks any more
Lines
Cables
Canals
Nor the suspensionbridges.

Suns moons stars
Apocalyptic worlds
All of you have still your parts to play.
A siphon sneezes;
They still dance the old literary cancans
Very low
At the Rotonde
Like at the bottom of a glass.

I'm waiting.

I want to be the fifth wheel of the juggernaut
Thunderstorm
Noon at fourteen o'clock
Nothing and everywhere.

Paris and Suburbs.
Saint-Cloud, Sèvres, Montmorency,
Courbevoie, Bougival, Rueil, Montrouge,
Saint-Denis, Vincennes, Étampes, Melun,
Saint-Martin, Méréville, Barbizon, Forges-en
Bière.
June 1913–June 1914.

Translated by John Dos Passos

1. JOURNAL

Christ
Voici plus d'un an que je n'ai plus pensé à Vous
Depuis que j'ai écrit mon avant-dernier poème Pâques
Ma vie a bien changé depuis
Mais je suis toujours le même
J'ai même voulu devenir peintre
Voici les tableaux que j'ai faits et qui ce soir pendent aux
    murs
Ils m'ouvrent d'étranges vues sur moi-même qui me font
    penser à Vous.

Christ
La vie
Voilà ce que j'ai fouillé

Mes peintures me font mal
Je suis trop passionné
Tout est orangé.

J'ai passé une triste journée à penser à mes amis
Et à lire le journal

1. DIARY

Christ
It's been more than a year since I've thought of You
Since I wrote Easter my poem before last
My life has greatly changed since
But I am still the same
I even wanted to become a painter
Here are the paintings I've done and which this evening hang
    on my walls
They open strange vistas in me and make me think of You.

Christ
Life
That's what I've ransacked

My paintings hurt me
I am too intense
Everything is bright orange.

I've spent a sad day thinking of my friends
And reading the newspaper

Christ
Vie crucifiée dans le journal grand ouvert que je tiens les bras
    tendus
Envergures
Fusées
Ébullition
Cris.
On dirait un aéroplane qui tombe.
C'est moi.

Passion
Feu
Roman-feuilleton
Journal
On a beau ne pas vouloir parler de soi-même
Il faut parfois crier

Je suis l'autre
Trop sensible

Août 1913.

2. TOUR

1910
Castellamare
Je dînais d'une orange à l'ombre d'un oranger
Quand, tout à coup . . .
Ce n'était pas l'éruption du Vésuve
Ce n'était pas le nuage de sauterelles, une des dix plaies
    d'Égypte

Christ
Life crucified in the opened newspaper I'm holding my arms
       outstretched
Wingspread
Rockets
Effervescence
Cries.
You would say it's an airplane falling.
It's me.

Passion
Fire
Continued story
Newspaper
It's useless not to want to speak of oneself
You must cry out sometimes

I am the other
Too sensitive

August 1913.

2. TOWER

1910
Castelmare
I was dining on an orange in the shade of an orange tree
When, suddenly ...
It was not Vesuvius erupting
It was not the cloud of grasshoppers, one of the ten plagues
       of Egypt

Ni Pompéi
Ce n'était pas les cris ressuscités des mastodontes géants
Ce n'était pas la Trompette annoncée
Ni la grenouille de Pierre Brisset
Quand, tout à coup,
Feux
Chocs
Rebondissements
Étincelle des horizons simultanés
Mon sexe

      O Tour Eiffel!
Je ne t'ai pas chaussée d'or
Je ne t'ai pas fait danser sur les dalles de cristal
Je ne t'ai pas vouée au Python comme une vierge de Carthage
Je ne t'ai pas revêtue du péplum de la Grèce
Je ne t'ai jamais fait divaguer dans l'enceinte des menhirs
Je ne t'ai pas nommée Tige de David ni Bois de la Croix
Lignum Crucis
      O Tour Eiffel
Feu d'artifice géant de l'Exposition Universelle!
Sur le Gange
A Bénarès
Parmi les toupies onanistes des temples hindous
Et les cris colorés des multitudes de l'Orient
Tu te penches, gracieux Palmier!
C'est toi qui à l'époque légendaire du peuple hébreu
Confondis la langue des hommes
O Babel!
Et quelque mille ans plus tard, c'est toi qui retombais en
    langues de feu sur les Apôtres rassemblés dans ton église
En pleine mer tu es un mât
Et au Pôle-Nord
Tu resplendis avec toute la magnificence de l'aurore boréale de
    ta télégraphie sans fil

Nor Pompeii
It was not the reviving cries of giant mastodons
It was not the Last Trumpet
Nor Pierre Brisset's toad
When, suddenly,
Flames
Shocks
Reverberations
Igniting of simultaneous horizons
My sex

      O Eiffel Tower!
I have not shod you in gold
I have not made you dance on crystal flagstones
I have not pledged you to the Python like a Carthaginian virgin
I have not clothed you in the Grecian peplos
I have never had you raving within the circle of sacred
      menhirs
I have not named you Staff of David nor Wood of the Cross
Lignum Crucis
      O Eiffel Tower
Giant fireworks of the Universal Fair!
On the Ganges
At Benares
Among the onanistic dervishes of Hindu temples
And the brilliant cries of Oriental multitudes
You bow, gracious Palmtree!
It was you who in the legendary era of the people of Israel
Mingled the tongues of men
O Babel!
And several thousand years later, it was you who fell in
      tongues of fire upon the Apostles gathered in your church
On the open sea you are a mast
And at the North Pole
You shine with all the splendor of the aurora borealis of your
      wireless telegraph

143

Les lianes s'enchevêtrent aux eucalyptus
Et tu flottes, vieux tronc, sur le Mississipi
Quand
Ta gueule s'ouvre
Et un caïman saisit la cuisse d'un nègre
En Europe tu es comme un gibet
(Je voudrais être la tour, pendre à la Tour Eiffel!)
Et quand le soleil se couche derrière toi
La tête de Bonnot roule sous la guillotine
Au cœur de l'Afrique c'est toi qui cours
Girafe
Autruche
Boa
Équateur
Moussons
En Australie tu as toujours été tabou
Tu es la gaffe que le capitaine Cook employait pour diriger
    son bateau d'aventuriers
O sonde céleste!
Pour le Simultané Delaunay, à qui je dédie ce poème,
Tu es le pinceau qu'il trempe dans la lumière

Gong tam-tam zanzibar bête de la jungle rayons-X express
    bistouri symphonie
Tu es tout
Tour
Dieu antique
Bête moderne
Spectre solaire
Sujet de mon poème
Tour
Tour du monde
Tour en mouvement

Août 1913.

144

Vines entwine about the eucalyptus
And you float, ancient log, on the Mississippi
Your maw opens
And a cayman grabs a Negro's leg
In Europe you're like a gallows
(I would like to be the tower, to hang on the Eiffel Tower!)
And when the sun goes down behind you
Bonnot's head rolls under the guillotine
In the heart of Africa it's you who run
Giraffe
Ostrich
Serpent
Equator
Monsoons
In Australia you've always been taboo
You are the boathook that Captain Cook used to control his
     ship of adventurers
O divine soundingline!
For the Simultaneous painter Delaunay, to whom I dedicate
     this poem,
You are the brush he dips in light

Gong tam-tam zanzibar jungle beast X-rays express scalpel
     symphony
You are everything
Tower
Ancient god
Modern beast
Solar spectrum
Subject of my poem
Tower
Globe-circling tower
Tower in motion

                                        August 1913.

3. CONTRASTES

Les fenêtres de ma poésie sont grand'ouvertes sur les boule-
　　vards et dans ses vitrines
Brillent
Les pierreries de la lumière
Écoute les violons des limousines et les xylophones des linotypes
Le pocheur se lave dans l'essuie-main du ciel
Tout est taches de couleur
Et les chapeaux des femmes qui passent sont des comètes dans
　　l'incendie du soir

L'unité
Il n'y a plus d'unité
Toutes les horloges marquent maintenant 24 heures après
　　avoir été retardées de dix minutes
Il n'y a plus de temps.
Il n'y a plus d'argent.
A la Chambre
On gâche les éléments merveilleux de la matière première

Chez le bistro
Les ouvriers en blouse bleue boivent du vin rouge
Tous les samedis poule au gibier
On joue
On parie
De temps en temps un bandit passe en automobile
Ou un enfant joue avec l'Arc de Triomphe . . .
Je conseille à M. Cochon de loger ses protégés à la Tour Eiffel.

Aujourd'hui
Changement de propriétaire

3. CONTRASTS

The windows of my poetry are wide open to the boulevards
     and in its showcases
Shine
Jewels of light
Listen to the limousines' violins and the linotypists' xylophones
The inept painter washes with the sky's wash cloth
Everything is splashes of color
And the hats of the women passersby are comets in the
     evening bonfire

Unity
There is no more unity
All the clocks are now showing midnight after having been
     set back ten minutes
There is no more time.
There's no more money.
In the legislature
They're spoiling the marvelous elements of elemental matter

In the corner bar
The workmen in blue shirts are drinking red wine
Every Saturday chicken in the pot
They play
They bet
From time to time a bandit passes in a car
Or a child plays with the Arch of Triumph . . .
I advise Mr. Big to quarter his protegés at the Eiffel Tower

Today
Change of owner

Le Saint-Esprit se détaille chez les plus petits boutiquiers
Je lis avec ravissement les bandes de calicot
De coquelicot
Il n'y a que les pierres ponces de la Sorbonne qui ne sont
    jamais fleuries
L'enseigne de la Samaritaine laboure par contre la Seine
Et du côté de Saint-Séverin
J'entends
Les sonnettes acharnées des tramways

Il pleut les globes électriques
Montrouge Gare de l'Est Métro Nord-Sud bateaux-mouches
    monde
Tout est halo
Profondeur
Rue de Buci on crie "L'Intransigeant" et "Paris-Sports"
L'aérodrome du ciel est maintenant, embrasé, un tableau de
    Cimabue
Quand par devant
Les hommes sont
Longs
Noirs
Tristes
Et fument, cheminées d'usine

Octobre 1913.

4.

I. PORTRAIT

Il dort
Il est éveillé

The Holy Ghost is on sale in the smallest shops
With increasing delight I read the strips of calico
Of marigold
Only the Sorbonne pumice stones are never in bloom
The "Samaritan's" signboard ploughs the Seine
And over by Saint Severin
I can hear
The trolley's excited clanging

It's raining electric light bulbs
Montrouge Gare de l'Est Metro North–South tourist-boats
    world
All is shrouded in halos
Impenetrable
On the Rue de Buci they're hawking *L'Intransigeant* and
    Paris-Sports
The celestial airport is now, in flames, a painting by Cimabue
While in the foreground
Men are
Long
Dark
Sad
And smoking, factory chimneys

October 1913.

4.

I. PORTRAIT

He is sleeping
He is awake

Tout à coup, il peint
Il prend une église et peint avec une église
Il prend une vache et peint avec une vache
Avec une sardine
Avec des têtes, des mains, des couteaux
Il peint avec un nerf de bœuf
Il peint avec toutes les sales passions d'une petite ville juive
Avec toute la sexualité exacerbée de la province russe
Pour la France
Sans sensualité
Il peint avec ses cuisses
Il a les yeux au cul
Et c'est tout à coup votre portrait
C'est toi lecteur
C'est moi
C'est lui
C'est sa fiancée
C'est l'épicier du coin
La vachère
La sage-femme
Il y a des baquets de sang
On y lave les nouveau-nés
Des ciels de folie
Bouches de modernité
La Tour en tire-bouchon
Des mains
Le Christ
Le Christ c'est lui
Il a passé son enfance sur la Croix
Il se suicide tous les jours
Tout à coup, il ne peint plus
Il était éveillé
Il dort maintenant
Il s'étrangle avec sa cravate
Chagall est étonné de vivre encore

Suddenly, he paints
He takes a church and paints with a church
He takes a cow and paints with a cow
With a sardine
With heads, hands, knives
He paints with a bull's pizzle
He paints with all the foul passions of a little Jewish city
With all the heightened sexuality of provincial Russia
For France
Without sensuality
He paints with his thighs
He has eyes in his ass
And all of a sudden it's your portrait
It's you reader
It's me
It's him
It's his fiancée
It's the corner grocer
The milkmaid
The midwife
There are buckets of blood
The newly born are washed in them
Skies in torment
Modernistic mouths
The Tower spiraling
Hands
Christ
He's Christ
He spent his childhood on the Cross
He commits suicide every day
Suddenly, he's no longer painting
He was awake
He's asleep now
He is choking himself with his tie
Chagall is surprised he's still alive

La Ruche
Escaliers, portes, escaliers
Et sa porte s'ouvre comme un journal
Couverte de cartes de visite
Puis elle se ferme.
Désordre, on est en plein désordre
Des photographies de Léger, des photographies de Tobeen,
    qu'on ne voit pas
Et au dos
Au dos
Des œuvres frénétiques
Esquisses, dessins, des œuvres frénétiques
Et des tableaux . . .
Bouteilles vides
"Nous garantissons la pureté absolue de notre sauce tomate"
Dit une étiquette
La fenêtre est un almanach
Quand les grues gigantesques des éclairs vident les péniches du
    ciel à grand fracas et déversent des bannes de tonnerre
Il en tombe

Pêle-mêle

Des cosaques le Christ un soleil en décomposition
Des toits
Des somnambules des chèvres
Un lycanthrope
Pétrus Borel
La folie l'hiver
Un génie fendu comme une pêche
Lautréamont
Chagall
Pauvre gosse auprès de ma femme
Délectation morose

The "Ruche"
Stairs, doors, stairs
And his door opens like a newspaper
Covered with visiting cards
Then it closes.
Disorder, wild disorder
Photographs of Léger, photographs of Tobeen, which you
    can't see
And on the back
On the back
Frenzied drawings
Sketches, designs, frenzied drawings
And paintings . . .
Empty bottles
"We guarantee the absolute purity of our tomato sauce"
Says one label
The window is an almanac
When the lightning like gigantic storks brawling empties the
    sky barges and tumbles out hampers of thunder
Out fall

Pell-mell

Cossacks Christ a sun decomposing
Roofs
Sleepwalkers goats
A werewolf
Petrus Borel
Madness winter
A genie split open like a peach
Lautréamont
Chagall
Poor kid beside my wife
Morose delight

Les souliers sont éculés
Une vieille marmite pleine de chocolat
Une lampe qui se dédouble
Et mon ivresse quand je lui rends visite
Des bouteilles vides
Des bouteilles
Zina
(Nous avons beaucoup parlé d'elle)
Chagall
Chagall
Dans les échelles de la lumière

Octobre 1913.

5. MA DANSE

Platon n'accorde pas droit de cité au poète
Juif errant
Don Juan métaphysique
Les amis, les proches
Tu n'as plus de coutumes et pas encore d'habitudes
Il faut échapper à la tyrannie des revues
Littérature
Vie pauvre
Orgueil déplacé
Masque
La femme, la danse que Nietzsche a voulu nous apprendre à
     danser
La femme
Mais l'ironie?

His shoes are rent
An old pot filled with chocolate
A lamp casting its own shadow
And my drunkenness when I visit him
Empty bottles
Bottles
Zina
(We've talked a great deal about her)
Chagall
Chagall
In rungs of light

October 1913.

5. MY DANCE

Plato refuses the poet citizenship
Wandering Jew
Metaphysical Don Juan
Friends, relations
You've forgotten your customs and acquired no habits
You must escape the tyranny of the magazines
Literature
Impoverished life
Misplaced pride
Mask
Woman, the dance Nietzsche wanted to teach us to dance
Woman
But the irony?

Va-et-vient continuel
Vagabondage spécial
Tous les hommes, tous les pays
C'est ainsi que tu n'es plus à charge
Tu ne te fais plus sentir . . .

Je suis un monsieur qui en des express fabuleux traverse les
        toujours mêmes Europes et regarde découragé par la
        portière
Le paysage ne m'intéresse plus
Mais la danse du paysage
La danse du paysage
Danse-paysage
Paritatitata
Je tout-tourne

Février 1914.

6. SUR LA ROBE ELLE A UN CORPS

Le corps de la femme est aussi bosselé que mon crâne
Glorieuse
Si tu t'incarnes avec esprit
Les couturiers font un sot métier
Autant que la phrénologie
Mes yeux sont des kilos qui pèsent la sensualité des femmes

Tout ce qui fuit, saille avance dans la profondeur
Les étoiles creusent le ciel
Les couleurs déshabillent
"Sur la robe elle a un corps"

156

Always coming and going
A special kind of bumming
All men, all countries
That's how you are no longer a burden
You are weightless

I'm a gentleman who is crossing always the same Europes in
    fabulous express trains and in despair looks out the
    window
The landscape doesn't interest me any more
But the dance of the landscape
Dance-landscape
Ladeedadeeda
I'm turning in all directions

                                        February 1914.

6. ON HER DRESS SHE HAS A BODY

A woman's body is as hilly as my skull
All-glorious
Matter become flesh wittily
Dressmaking is a silly business
Like phrenology
My eyes are pounds that weigh the sensuality of women

Everything that flees, overflows moves into depths
Stars hollow out the sky
Colors undress
"On her dress she has a body"

Sous les bras des bruyères mains lunules et pistils quand les
     eaux se déversent dans le dos avec les omoplates glauques
Le ventre un disque qui bouge
La double coque des seins passe sous le pont des arcs-en-ciel
Ventre
Disque
Soleil
Les cris perpendiculaires des couleurs tombent sur les cuisses
"Épée de Saint Michel"

Il y a des mains qui se tendent
Il y a dans la traîne la bête tous les yeux toutes les fanfares
     tous les habitués du bal Bullier
Et sur la hanche
La signature du poète

Février 1914.

7. HAMAC

Onoto-visage
Cadran compliqué de la Gare Saint-Lazare
Apollinaire
Avance, retarde, s'arrête parfois.
Européen
Voyageur occidental
Pourquoi ne m'accompagnes-tu pas en Amérique?
J'ai pleuré au débarcadère
New York

Under her arms heather hands crescents and pistils while
　　waters empty in her back with its glaucous shoulder
　　blades
Her stomach a restless disk
The double hull of her breasts passes under the rainbow bridge
Stomach
Disk
Sun
The perpendicular cries of colors fall on her thighs
"Saint Michael's sword"

There are hands which reach out
There is in her train that beast all the eyes all the bands all
　　the regulars of the Bullier Dance Hall
And on her hip
The poet has signed his name

　　　　　　　　　　　　　　　　　　February 1914.

7. HAMMOCK

Onoto-visage
Complicated watch face of the Gare Saint-Lazare
Apollinaire
Runs, slows down, stops sometimes.
European
Western traveler
Why won't you come with me to America?
I wept at the sailing
New York

Les vaisseaux secouent la vaisselle
Rome Prague Londres Nice Paris
Oxo-Liebig fait frise dans ta chambre
Les livres en estacade

Les tromblons tirent à noix de coco
"Julie ou j'ai perdu ma rose"

Futuriste

Tu as longtemps écrit à l'ombre d'un tableau
A l'Arabesque tu songeais
O toi le plus heureux de nous tous
Car Rousseau a fait ton portrait
Aux étoiles
Les œillets du poète "Sweet Williams"

Apollinaire
1900–1911
Durant 12 ans seul poète de France

Décembre 1913.

8. MARDI-GRAS

Les gratte-ciel s'écartèlent
J'ai trouvé tout au fond Canudo non rogné
Pour cinq sous
Chez un bouquiniste de la 14e rue
Religieusement

Ships shake the dishes
Rome Prague London Nice Paris
In your room Oxo-Liebig makes a frieze
Books as piers

Blunderbusses shoot coconuts
"Julia or I've lost my rose"

Futurist

For a long time you have been writing in the shelter of a
    painting
You used to dream about the perfect arabesque
O you the happiest of us all
For Rousseau painted your portrait
In the stars
The poet's Sweet Williams "Oeillets"

Apollinaire
1900–1911
For 12 years the only poet in France

December 1913.

8. MARDI GRAS

The skyscrapers break asunder
At the very bottom I found Canudo the pages uncut
For twenty-five cents
In a shop on 14th Street
Religiously

Ton improvisation sur la IXe Symphonie de Beethoven
On voit New York comme la Venise mercantile de l'océan
    occidental

La Croix s'ouvre
Danse
Il n'y a pas de commune
Il n'y a pas d'aéropage
Il n'y a pas de pyramide spirituelle
Je ne comprends pas très bien le mot "Impérialisme"
Mais dans ton grenier
Parmi les ouistitis les Indiens les belles dames
Le poète est venu
Verbe coloré

Il y a des heures qui sonnent
Montjoie!
L'olifant de Roland
Mon taudis de New York
Les livres
Les messages télégraphiques
Et le soleil t'apporte le beau corps d'aujourd'hui dans les
    coupures des journaux
Ces langes

Février 1914.

9. CRÉPITEMENTS

Les arcencielesques dissonances de la Tour dans sa télégraphie
    sans fil
Midi
Minuit
On se dit merde de tous les coins de l'univers

Your improvisation on Beethoven's 9th Symphony
New York is considered the mercantile Venice of the Western
    Ocean

The Cross opens
Dances
There's no parish hall
There's no airport
There's no holy pyramid
I'm not clear about the meaning of the word "Imperialism"
But in your garret
Among the South American monkeys the Indians the beauti-
    ful women
The poet has come
The Word in color

There are hours which ring
Montjoie!
Roland's olifant
My New York hovel
Books
Telegraph messages
And the sun brings you today's handsome body in newspaper
    clippings
Those swaddling clothes

February 1914.

9. CRACKLINGS

The rainbowed dissonances of the Tower in its wireless
    telegraph
Noon
Midnight
One hears "shit" from every corner of the universe

Étincelles
Jaune de chrome
On est en contact
De tous les côtés les transatlantiques s'approchent
S'éloignent
Toutes les montres sont mises à l'heure
Et les cloches sonnent
"Paris-Midi" annonce qu'un professeur allemand a été mangé
      par les cannibales au Congo
C'est bien fait
"L'Intransigeant" ce soir publie des vers pour cartes postales
C'est idiot quand tous les astrologues cambriolent les étoiles
On n'y voit plus
J'interroge le ciel
L'Institut Météorologique annonce du mauvais temps
Il n'y a pas de futurisme
Il n'y a pas de simultanéité
Bodin a brûlé toutes les sorcières
Il n'y a rien
Il n'y a plus d'horoscopes et il faut travailler
Je suis inquiet
L'Esprit
Je vais partir en voyage
Et j'envoie ce poème dépouillé à mon ami R . . .

Septembre 1913.

10. DERNIÈRE HEURE

"Oklahoma, 20 janvier 1914"
Trois forçats se procurent des revolvers
Ils tuent leur geôlier et s'emparent des clefs de la prison

Sparks
Chrome yellow
We are in contact
From every side ocean liners are approaching
Moving away
All the watches are set
And the clocks are ringing
Paris-Midi announces that a German professor has been eaten
    by cannibals in the Congo
Good work
L'Intransigeant this evening is publishing verses for postcards
It's idiotic when all the astrologers are robbing the stars
Our view is cut off
I question the sky
The Weather Bureau announces bad weather
There is no futurism
There is no simultaneity
Bodin has burned all the witches
There is nothing
There are no more horoscopes and we must work
I am restless
The Holy Ghost
I'm going to leave on a trip
And I send this naked poem to my friend R . . .

September 1913.

10. LATEST REPORT

"Oklahoma, January 20, 1914"
Three convicts get hold of pistols
They kill their jailer and take the jail keys

Ils se précipitent hors de leurs cellules et tuent quatre gardiens
   dans la cour
Puis ils s'emparent de la jeune sténo-dactylographe de la prison
Et montent dans une voiture qui les attendait à la porte
Ils partent à toute vitesse
Pendant que les gardiens déchargent leurs revolvers dans la
   direction des fugitifs

Quelques gardiens sautent à cheval et se lancent à la poursuite
   des forçats
Des deux côtés des coups de feu sont échangés
La jeune fille est blessée d'un coup de feu tiré par un des
   gardiens

Une balle frappe à mort le cheval qui emportait la voiture
Les gardiens peuvent approcher
Ils trouvent les forçats morts le corps criblé de balles
Mr. Thomas, ancien membre du Congrès qui visitait la prison
Félicite la jeune fille

Télégramme-poème copié dans "Paris-Midi"

Janvier 1914.

11. BOMBAY-EXPRESS

La vie que j'ai menée
M'empêche de me suicider
Tout bondit
Les femmes roulent sous les roues
Avec de grands cris
Les tape-cul en éventail sont à la porte des gares.
J'ai de la musique sous les ongles.

They rush out of their cells and kill four guards in the
    courtyard
Then they kidnap the young prison stenographer
And get into a carriage which was waiting for them at the
    gate
They leave at top speed
While the guards empty their revolvers after the fugitives

Some of the guards jump on horses and rush in pursuit of the
    convicts
Shots are fired from both sides
The girl is wounded by a shot fired by one of the guards

A bullet kills the horse which was pulling the carriage
The guards can approach
They find the convicts dead their bodies riddled with bullets
Mr. Thomas, former member of Congress who was visiting the
    prison,
Congratulates the young girl

Telegram-poem copied from *Paris-Midi*

January 1914.

11. BOMBAY EXPRESS

The life I've led
Keeps me from committing suicide
Everything's leaping
Women are wallowing under wheels
With loud cries
The fan-shaped gigs are waiting at the station gates.
I have music under my fingernails.

Je n'ai jamais aimé Mascagni
Ni l'art ni les Artistes
Ni les barrières ni les ponts
Ni les trombones ni les pistons
Je ne sais plus rien
Je ne comprends plus . . .
Cette caresse
Que la carte géographique en frissonne

Cette année ou l'année prochaine
La critique d'art est aussi imbécile que l'espéranto
Brindisi
Au revoir au revoir

Je suis né dans cette ville
Et mon fils également
Lui dont le front est comme le vagin de sa mère
Il y a des pensées qui font sursauter les autobus
Je ne lis plus les livres qui ne se trouvent que dans les
    bibliothèques
Bel A B C du monde

Bon voyage!

Que je t'emporte
Toi qui ris du vermillon

Avril 1914.

12. F.I.A.T.

J'ai l'ouïe déchirée

J'envie ton repos
Grand paquebot des usines
A l'ancre
Dans la banlieue des villes

I've never liked Mascagni
Nor art nor Artists
Nor gates nor bridges
Nor trombones nor trumpets
I don't know anything anymore
I no longer understand . . .
This caress
From which the map trembles

This year or next year
Art criticism is as imbecilic as Esperanto
Brindisi
Goodbye goodbye

I was born in this city
And my son too
The one whose forehead is like his mother's vagina
There are thoughts that make the buses start up
I no longer read books that are found only in libraries
Handsome alphabetbook of the world

Bon voyage!

Let me carry you off
You who laugh at red

April 1914.

12. F.I.A.T.

My hearing is torn

I envy your ease
Ocean liner of factories
At anchor
In the suburbs of cities

Je voudrais m'être vidé
Comme toi
Après ton accouchement
Les pneumatiques vessent dans mon dos
J'ai des pommettes électriques au bout des nerfs

Ta chambre blanche moderne nickelée
Le berceau
Les rares bruits de l'hôpital
Sainte Clothilde
Je suis toujours en fièvre
Paris-Adresses

Être à ta place
Tournant brusque!
C'est la première fois que j'envie une femme
Que je voudrais être femme
Être femme
Dans l'univers
Dans la vie
Être
Et s'ouvrir à l'avenir enfantin
Moi qui suis ébloui

Phares Blériot
Mise en marche automatique
Vois

Mon stylo caracole

Caltez!

Avril 1914.

I would like to have emptied myself
Like you
After your confinement
The air pumps fart in my back
I have electric knobs at my nerves' ends

Your white room modern nickel-plated
The cradle
The sparse noises of the hospital
Saint Clothilde
I am always feverish
Paris Addresses

To be in your place
Sudden shift!
It's the first time I've envied a woman
That I've wanted to be a woman
To be a woman
In the universe
In life
To be
And to expose oneself to the childbearing future
The prospect dazzles me

Blériot headlights
Automatic operation
See

My pen maneuvers

Move on!

April 1914.

13. AUX 5 COINS

Oser et faire du bruit
Tout est couleur mouvement explosion lumière
La vie fleurit aux fenêtres du soleil
Qui se fond dans ma bouche
Je suis mûr
Et je tombe translucide dans la rue

Tu parles, mon vieux

Je ne sais pas ouvrir les yeux?
Bouche d'or
La poésie est en jeu

Février 1914.

14. NATURES MORTES

Pour Roger de la Fresnaye

"Vert"
Le gros trot des artilleurs passe sur la géométrie
Je me dépouille
Je ne serais bientôt qu'en acier
Sans l'équerre de la lumière
"Jaune"
Clairon de modernité
Le classeur américain
Est aussi sec et

13. AT THE 5 CORNERS

To dare and to make a commotion
Everything is color movement explosion light
Life is blooming in the windows of the sun
Which is melting in my mouth
I am ripe
And I fall translucent into the street

You're kidding, man

Don't I know how to open my eyes?
Mouth of gold
Poetry is at stake

February 1914.

14. STILL LIFES

For Roger de la Fresnaye

"Green"
The heavy tread of the artillerymen passes over geometry
I strip myself
I should soon be only steel
Without light's square rule
"Yellow"
Trumpet of modernity
The American portfolio
Is as dry and

Frais
Que vertes les campagnes premières
Normandie
Et la table de l'architecte
Est ainsi strictement belle
"Noir"
Avec une bouteille d'encre de Chine
Et des chemises bleues
"Bleu"
"Rouge"
Puis il y a aussi un litre, un litre de sensualité
Et cette haute nouveauté
"Blanc"
Des feuilles de papier blanc

Avril 1914.

15. FANTÔMAS

Tu as étudié le grand-siècle dans l'"Histoire de la Marine
    française" par Eugène
Sue
"Paris, au Dépôt de la Librairie", 1835,
"4 vol. in-16 jésus"
Fine fleur des pois du catholicisme pur
Moraliste
Plutarque
Le simultanéisme est passéiste

Cool
As green the original countrysides
Normandy
And the architect's drawing board
Is just as firmly beautiful
"Black"
With a bottle of Chinese ink
And blue shirts
"Blue"
"Red"
There is also a liter, a liter of sensuality
And that newest of the new
"White"
Sheets of white paper

April 1914.

15. FANTOMAS

You studied the great century in the *History of the French
    Navy* by Eugène
Sue
"Paris, au Dépôt de la Librairie," 1835,
"4 vol. in–16 jésus"
Delicate pea flower of pure Catholicism
Moralist
Plutarch
Simultanism is passé

Tu m'as mené au Cap chez le père Moche au Mexique
Et tu m'as ramené à Saint-Pétersbourg où j'avais déjà été
C'est bien par là
On tourne à droite pour aller prendre le tramway
Ton argot est vivant ainsi que la niaiserie sentimentale de ton
    cœur qui beugle
Alma mater Humanité Vache
Mais tout ce qui est machinerie mise en scène changement de
    décors etc. etc.
Est directement plagié de Homère, ce châtelet

Il y a aussi une jolie page
    ". . . vous vous imaginiez monsieur Barzum, que j'al-
    lais tranquillement vous permettre de ruiner mes projets,
    de livrer ma fille à la justice, vous aviez pensé cela? . . .
    allons! sous votre apparence d'homme intelligent, vous
    n'étiez qu'un imbécile . . ."
Et ce n'est pas mon moindre mérite que de citer le roi des
    voleurs
"Vol. 21, le Train perdu, p. 367."

Nous avons encore beaucoup de traits communs
J'ai été en prison
J'ai dépensé des fortunes mal acquises
Je connais plus de 120.000 timbres-poste tous différents et
    plus joyeux que les Nᵒ Nᵒ du Louvre
Et
Comme toi
Héraldiste industriel
J'ai étudié les marques de fabrique enregistrées à l'Office
    international des Patentes internationales

Il y a encore de jolis coups à faire
Tous les matins de 9 à 11

Mars 1914.

176

You led me to the Cape to Father Moche in Mexico
And you brought me back to St. Petersburg where I had
    already been
It's right over there
You turn to the right to take the streetcar
Your slang is as authentic as the sentimental bumbling of your
    bellowing heart
Alma mater Humanity Cow
But all that is machinery theatrics scene changing etc., etc.,
Is directly plagiarized from Homer, that theatre

There is also a fine page
    ". . . did you think monsieur Barzum, that I would calmly
    allow you to ruin my plans, allow you to hand over my
    daughter to the police, had you really thought that? . . .
    come on! all the while masquerading as an intelligent
    man, you were nothing more than an imbecile . . ."
And it is not my least merit to cite the king of the thieves
"Vol. 21, The Disappearing Train, p. 367."

We still have much in common
I have been in jail
I've spent my ill-gotten gains
I am familiar with more than 120,000 postage stamps, each
    different and more joyful than the Louvre's numbered
    numbers
And
Like you
Industrial genealogist
I have studied the trademarks registered at the International
    Office of International Patents

There are still lovely little thefts to bring off
Every morning from 9 to 11

March 1914.

16. TITRES

Formes sueurs chevelures
Le bond d'être
Dépouillé
Premier poème sans métaphores
Sans images
Nouvelles
L'esprit nouveau
Les accidents des féeries
400 fenêtres ouvertes
L'hélice des gemmes des foires des menstrues
Le cône rabougri
Les déménagements à genoux
Dans les dragues
A travers l'accordéon du ciel et des voix télescopées
Quand le journal fermente comme un éclair claquemuré

Manchette

Juillet 1914.

17. MEE TOO BUGGI

Comme chez les Grecs on croit que tout homme bien élevé
      doit savoir pincer la lyre
Donne-moi le fango-fango
Que je l'applique à mon nez
Un son doux et grave
De la narine droite
Il y a la description des paysages

16. HEADLINES

Shapes sweat tresses
The leap of being
Stripped
First poem without metaphors
Without images
New
The new spirit
The unexpected in fairytale extravaganzas
400 open windows
The facets of gems   the runs   menses
The stunted cone
Moving on your knees
In dredgers
Across the accordion of the sky and telescoped voices
When the newspaper ferments like a cooped-up lightning bolt

Headline

July 1914.

17. ME TOO BOOGIE

Like the Greeks we think every properly educated man should
      know how to pluck the lyre
Give me the fango-fango
Let me press it to my nose
A sweet, sonorous sound
From the right nostril
There is the description of landscapes

Le récit des événements passés
Une relation des contrées lointaines
Bolotoo
Papalangi
Le poète entre autres choses fait la description des animaux
Les maisons sont renversées par d'énormes oiseaux
Les femmes sont trop habillées
Rimes et mesures dépourvues
Si l'on fait grâce à un peu d'exagération
L'homme qui se coupa lui-même la jambe réussissait dans le
    genre simple et gai
Mee low folla
Mariwagi bat le tambour à l'entrée da sa maison

Juillet 1914.

18. LA TÊTE

La guillotine est le chef-d'œuvre de l'art plastique
Son déclic
Crée le mouvement perpétuel
Tout le monde connaît l'œuf de Christophe Colomb
Qui était un œuf plat, un œuf fixe, l'œuf d'un inventeur
La sculpture d'Archipenko est le premier œuf ovoïdal
Maintenu en équilibre intense
Comme une toupie immobile
Sur sa pointe animée
Vitesse
Il se dépouille
Des ondes multicolores
Des zones de couleur
Et tourne dans la profondeur

The recital of past events
A narrative of distant countries
Bolotoo
Papalangi
The poet among other things describes animals
Houses are toppled over by enormous birds
Women wear too many clothes
Scanty rhymes and measures
If you allow for a little exaggeration
The man who cut off his own leg succeeded in the light,
    simple genre
Me low fellah
Mariwagi is beating the drum in the doorway of his house

July 1914.

18. THE HEAD

The guillotine is the masterpiece of plastic art
Its click
Creates perpetual motion
Everybody is familiar with Christopher Columbus' egg
Which was a flat egg, a solid egg, the egg of an inventor
The sculpture of Archipenko is the first ovoid egg
Held in tense balance
Like a motionless top
On its spinning point
Speed
It strips itself
Many-colored bands
Colored zones
And turns in depth

Nu.
Neuf.
Total.

Juillet 1914.

19. CONSTRUCTION

De la couleur, de la couleur et des couleurs . . .
Voici Léger qui grandit comme le soleil de l'époque tertiaire
Et qui durcit
Et qui fixe
La nature morte
La croûte terrestre
Le liquide
Le brumeux
Tout ce qui se ternit
La géométrie nuageuse
Le fil à plomb qui se résorbe
Ossification.
Locomotion.
Tout grouille
L'esprit s'anime soudain et s'habille à son tour comme les
    animaux et les plantes
Prodigieusement
Et voici
La peinture devient cette chose énorme qui bouge
La roue
La vie
La machine
L'âme humaine
Une culasse de 75
Mon portrait

Février 1919.

Naked.
New.
Total.

19. CONSTRUCTION

Color, color, and more color . . .
See Léger expanding like the sun of the tertiary epoch
And hardening
And settling
Still life
Earthy crust
Liquid
Milky
All that tarnishes
Cloudy geometry
The plumb-line that retracts
Ossification.
Locomotion.
Everything swarms
The spirit suddenly comes to life and in its turn clothes itself
    like animals and plants
Prodigiously
And now
The painting becomes that enormous, restless thing
The wheel
Life
The machine
The human soul
A 75mm. breech
My portrait

February 1919.

LA GUERRE AU LUXEMBOURG

*Ces ENFANTINES sont dédiées à mes
camarades de la Légion Étrangère
Mieczyslaw KOHN, Polonais tué à Frise;
Victor* Chapman, *Américain tué à Verdun;
Xavier de CARVALHO, Portugais tué à
la ferme de Navarin; Engagés Volontaires
morts pour la France*
**Blaise Cendrars
MCMXVI**

"Une deux une deux
Et tout ira bien . . ."
Ils chantaient
Un blessé battait la mesure avec sa béquille
Sous le bandeau son œil
Le sourire du Luxembourg
Et les fumées des usines de munitions
Au-dessus des frondaisons d'or
Pâle automne fin d'été
On ne peut rien oublier
Il n'y a que les petits enfants qui jouent à la guerre
La Somme Verdun
Mon grand frère est aux Dardanelles
Comme c'est beau
Un fusil   MOI!
Cris voix flûtées
Cris   MOI!

THE WAR IN THE LUXEMBOURG GARDENS

*These ENFANTINES are dedicated
to my comrades in the Foreign Legion
Mieczyslaw Kohn, Pole killed at Frise;
Victor Chapman, American killed at
Verdun; Xavier de Carvalho, Portu-
guese killed at the Navarin farm;
volunteers who died for France*
    Blaise Cendrars
    MCMXVI

"One two one two
And everything will be just fine . . ."
They were singing
A wounded man was beating time with his crutch
Under the bandage his eye
The smile of the Luxembourg
And smoke from the munitions factories
Above gold foliage
Pale autumn summer's end
We can't forget anything
Only children play at war
The Somme Verdun
My big brother is in the Dardanelles
How fine it is
A gun   ME!
Cries flutelike voices
Cries   ME!

Les mains se tendent
Je ressemble à papa
On a aussi des canons
Une fillette fait le cycliste   MOI!
Un dada caracole
Dans le bassin les flottilles s'entre-croisent
Le méridien de Paris est dans le jet d'eau
On part à l'assaut du garde qui seul a un sabre authentique
Et on le tue à force de rire
Sur les palmiers encaissés le soleil pend
Médaille Militaire
On applaudit le dirigeable qui passe du côté de la Tour Eiffel
Puis on relève les morts
Tout le monde veut en être
Ou tout au moins blessé   ROUGE
Coupe coupe
Coupe le bras coupe la tête   BLANC
On donne tout
Croix-Rouge   BLEU
Les infirmières ont 6 ans
Leur cœur est plein d'émotion
On enlève les yeux aux poupées pour réparer les aveugles
J'y vois! j'y vois!
Ceux qui faisaient les Turcs sont maintenant brancardiers
Et ceux qui faisaient les morts ressuscitent pour assister à la
        merveilleuse opération
A présent on consulte les journaux illustrés
Les photographies
On se souvient de ce que l'on a vu au cinéma
Ça devient plus sérieux
On crie et l'on cogne mieux que Guignol
Et au plus fort de la mêlée
Chaud chaudes
Tout le monde se sauve pour aller manger les gaufres

Hands reach out
I look like papa
We also have cannons
A little girl mimics the cyclist   ME!
A hobbyhorse caracols
In the fountain fleets crisscross
The Paris meridian is in the water spray
We're off to waylay the guard who's the only one with an
        authentic saber
And we kill him with laughter
The sun hangs from potted palms
Military Medal
We applaud the dirigible passing in the direction of the Eiffel
        Tower
Then we gather up the dead
Everybody wants to be one
Or at least wounded   RED
Cut cut
Cut off the arm cut off the head   WHITE
We give our all
Red Cross   BLUE
The nurses are six years old
Their hearts are filled with emotion
We take out the dolls' eyes to heal the blind
I can see! I can see!
The ones who were playing Turks are now stretcher-bearers
And those who were playing the dead are reviving to watch
        the wonderful operation
Now we're consulting Sunday rotogravures
Photographs
We remember what we saw in the movies
It's becoming more serious
We shout and thump better than Punch and Judy
And at the height of the fray
Sweating hot
Everybody runs away to eat honeywafers

Elles sont prêtes.   R
Il est cinq heures.   Ê
Les grilles se ferment.   V
On rentre.   E
Il fait soir.   U
On attend le zeppelin qui ne vient pas   R
Las   S
Les yeux aux fusées des étoiles
Tandis que les bonnes vous tirent par la main
Et que les mamans trébuchent sur les grandes automobiles
    d'ombre
Le lendemain ou un autre jour
Il y a une tranchée dans le tas de sable
Il y a un petit bois dans le tas de sable
Des villes
Une maison
Tout le pays   La Mer
Et peut-être bien la mer
L'artillerie improvisée tourne autour des barbelés imaginaires
Un cerf-volant rapide comme un avion de chasse
Les arbres se dégonflent et les feuilles tombent pardessus bord
    et tournent en parachute
Les 3 veines du drapeau se gonflent à chaque coup de l'obusier
    du vent
Tu ne seras pas emportée petite arche de sable
Enfants prodiges, plus que les ingénieurs
On joue en riant au tank aux gaz-asphyxiants au sous-marin-
    devant-new-york-qui-ne-peut-pas-passer
Je suis Australien, tu es nègre, il se lave pour faire la-vie-des-
    soldats-anglais-en-belgique
Casquette russe
1 Légion d'honneur en chocolat vaut 3 boutons d'uniforme
Voilà le général qui passe
Une petite fille dit:

They are ready.   D
It is five o'clock.   R
The gates are locked.   E
We return home.   A
It's getting dark.   M
We wait for the zeppelin which does not come   E
Tired   R
Eyes fixed on shooting stars   S
While maids pull you along by the hand
And the mothers stumble over great shadowy cars
Tomorrow or some other day
There will be a trench in the sandbox
There will be a little grove in the sandbox
Cities
A house
The whole country   The Sea
And perhaps even the sea
Improvised artillery turns around imaginary barbed wire
A kite as swift as a fighter plane
The trees collapse and the leaves fall overboard and turn
    into parachutes
The 3 veins of the flag swell at each direct hit by the wind's
    shelling
You'll not be blown away little sand Ark
Prodigious children, more than engineers
Laughing we play asphyxiating-gas-throwing tanks we play
    submarines-outside-New-York-which may-not-pass
I am Australian, you are Negro, he's washing himself "to
    bring to life British soldiers in Belgium"
Russian helmet
1 chocolate Legion of Honor is worth 3 uniform buttons
There's the general passing
A little girl says:

J'aime beaucoup ma nouvelle maman américaine
Et un petit garçon : — Non pas Jules Verne mais achète-moi
    encore le beau communiqué du dimanche

A PARIS
Le jour de la Victoire quand les soldats reviendront . . .
Tout le monde voudra LES voir
Le soleil ouvrira de bonne heure comme un marchand de
    nougat un jour de fête
Il fera printemps au Bois de Boulogne ou du côté de Meudon
Toutes les automobiles seront parfumées et les pauvres che-
    vaux mangeront des fleurs
Aux fenêtres les petites orphelines de la guerre auront toutes
    une belle robe patriotique
Sur les marronniers des boulevards les photographes à cali-
    fourchon braqueront leur œil à déclic
On fera cercle autour de l'opérateur du cinéma qui mieux
    qu'un mangeur de serpents engloutira le cortège histori-
    que
Dans l'après-midi
Les blessés accrocheront leurs Médailles à l'Arc-de-Triomphe
    et rentreront à la maison sans boiter
Puis
Le soir
La place de l'Étoile montera au ciel
Le Dôme des Invalides chantera sur Paris comme une
    immense cloche d'or
Et les mille voix des journaux acclameront la Marseillaise
Femme de France

Paris, octobre 1916.

"I'm very fond of my new American mama"
And a little boy: "No! not Jules Verne buy me instead another
  nice Sunday Dispatch"

IN PARIS
On Victory Day when the soldiers return . . .
Everyone will want to see THEM
The sun will open up early like a candy store on a holiday
It will be spring in the Bois de Boulogne or near Meudon
All the automobiles will be perfumed and the poor horses will
  eat flowers
At the windows little war orphans will all be wearing pretty
  patriotic dresses
From the chestnut trees along the boulevard the photographers
  will aim their clicking eye
We will form a circle around the movie cameraman who more
  efficiently than a snake-eater will engulf the historic pro-
  cession
In the afternoon
The wounded will affix their medals at the Arch of Triumph
  and will return home without limping
Then
That evening
The Place de l'Étoile will rise into the sky
The dome of the Invalides will sing over Paris like an
  immense golden bell
And the newspapers' thousand voices will acclaim the Mar-
  seillaise
First Lady of France

                                        Paris, October 1916.

191

HOMMAGE À GUILLAUME APOLLINAIRE

Le pain lève
La France
Paris
Toute une génération
Je m'adresse aux poètes qui étaient présents
Amis
Apollinaire n'est pas mort
Vous avez suivi un corbillard vide
Apollinaire est un mage
C'est lui qui souriait dans la soie des drapeaux aux fenêtres
Il s'amusait à vous jeter des fleurs et des couronnes
Tandis que vous passiez derrière son corbillard
Puis il a acheté une petite cocarde tricolore
Je l'ai vu le soir même manifester sur les boulevards
Il était à cheval sur le moteur d'un camion américain et
    brandissait un énorme drapeau international déployé
    comme un avion
VIVE LA FRANCE

IN HONOR OF GUILLAUME APOLLINAIRE

The bread is rising
France
Paris
A whole generation
I am speaking to the poets who were present
Friends
Apollinaire is not dead
You followed an empty hearse
Apollinaire is a sorcerer
It was he smiling in the silk folds of flags at the windows
He was amusing himself throwing flowers and wreaths at you
While you were following his hearse
Then he bought a little tricolor rosette
I saw him that same evening demonstrating along the boule-
    vards
He was straddling the hood of an American truck and brand-
    ishing an enormous international flag flying like an air-
    plane
LONG LIVE FRANCE

Les temps passent
Les années s'écoulent comme des nuages
Les soldats sont rentrés chez eux
A la maison
Dans leur pays
Et voilà que se lève une nouvelle génération
Le rêve des MAMELLES se réalise!
Des petits Français, moitié anglais, moitié nègre, moitié
    russe, un peu belge, italien, annamite, tchèque
L'un à l'accent canadien, l'autre les yeux hindous
Dents face os jointures galbe démarche sourire
Ils ont tous quelque chose d'étranger et sont pourtant bien de
    chez nous
Au milieu d'eux, Apollinaire, comme cette statue du Nil, le
    père des eaux, étendu avec des gosses qui lui coulent de
    partout
Entre les pieds, sous les aisselles, dans la barbe
Ils ressemblent à leur père et se départent de lui
Et ils parlent tous la langue d'Apollinaire

Paris, novembre 1918.

Time passes
The years slip away like clouds
The soldiers are back again
In their home
In their country
And there's a new generation rising
The dream of TIRESIAS' BREASTS is realized!
Little Frenchmen, half English, half Negro, half Russian,
   some Belgian, Italian, Annamite, Czech,
One with a Canadian accent, another with Hindu eyes
Teeth face bones joints curve gait smile
They all have something foreign about them and yet are
   really from among us
In their midst, Apollinaire, like that statue of the Nile, the
   father of waters, stretched out with children everywhere
   flowing from him
From between his feet, under his armpits, in his beard,
They look like their father and are different
And they all speak the language of Apollinaire

Paris, November 1918.

from **Sonnets dénaturés**

ACADÉMIE MÉDRANO

A Conrad Moricand

Danse avec ta langue, Poète, fais un entrechat
Un tour de piste
                sur un tout petit basset
                          noir ou haquenée
Mesure les beaux vers mesurés et fixe les formes fixes
Que sont LES BELLES LETTRES apprises
Regarde:
                  Les Affiches se fichent de toi te
                        mordent avec leurs dents
                        en couleur entre les doigts
                        de pied
La fille du directeur a des lumières électriques
Les jongleurs sont aussi les trapézistes
                    xuellirép tuaS
          teuof ed puoC
aç-emirpxE
Le clown est dans le tonneau malaxé

196

MEDRANO ACADEMY

To Conrad Moricand

Dance with your tongue, Poet, perform an entrechat
Once around the circus ring
                              on a very small black basset-
                                                        hound or nag
Time the beautifully cadenced lines and fix the fixed forms
That signify BELLES-LETTRES mastered
Look:

Signboards mock you bite you with
                                    their multicolored teeth
                                    between your toes
The director's daughter has electric lights
The jugglers are also trapeze artists
                          suolirep paeL
            gnikcarc pihW
ti-sserpxE
The clown is in the mixing bowl

Il faut que ta langue $\begin{cases} \text{passe à la caisse} \\ \text{fasse l'orchestre} \end{cases}$ les soirs où

Les **Billets de faveur** sont supprimés.

Novembre 1916.

Your tongue must ⎧ take over the box office
⎨   on evenings
⎩ replace the orchestra

All **passes** are suspended.

November 1916.

LE MUSICKISSME

A Erik Satie

Que nous chaut Venizelos

Seul Raymond ■ mettons Duncan trousse
encore la défroque grecque

Musique aux oreilles végétales

Autant qu'éléphantiaques

Les poissons crient dans le gulf-stream

Bidon juteux plus que figue

Et la voix basque du microphone marin

Duo de music-hall

Sur accompagnement d'auto

Gong

Le phoque musicien

50 mesures de do-ré do-ré do-ré do-ré do-ré
do-ré do-ré do-ré do-ré do-ré do-ré do-ré

Ça y est!

Et un accord diminué en la bémol mineur
                                        ETC.!

Quand c'est beau un beau joujou bruiteur
danse la sonnette

Entr'acte

A la rentrée

"Thème": CHARLOT chef d'orchestre bat la mesure

Devant

L'européen chapeauté et sa femme en corset

"Contrepoint": Danse

Devant l'européen ahuri et sa femme

Aussi

"Coda": Chante

Ce qu'il fallait démontrer

Novembre 1916.

MUSICKING

To Erik Satie

What does Venizelos mean to us
Only Raymond ■ let's say Duncan
    still hikes up a Greek robe
Music with vegetable ears
Almost elephantearish
Fish cry out in the gulf stream
Oozing canteen more than fig
The Basque voice of the marine microphone
Music hall duet
With automobile accompaniment
Gong
Musician seal
50 measures of do-re do-re do-re do-re do-re
    do-re do-re do-re do-re do-re do-re do-re
That's it!
And a diminished chord in B flat minor
                    ETC.!
When it's nice out a pretty toy cricket dances
    the bell dance
Intermission
Curtain time
"Theme": CHARLIE the orchestra leader beats time
In front of
The hatted European and his corseted wife
"Counterpoint": Dances
In front of the bewildered European
    and his wife
Also
"Coda": Sings
Quod erat demonstrandum

November 1916.

ÎLES

VII. LÉGER ET SUBTIL

L'air est embaumé
Musc ambre et fleur de citronnier
Le seul fait d'exister est un véritable bonheur

1924.

XI. AMOLLI

Jardin touffu comme une clairière
Sur le rivage paresse l'éternelle chanson bruissante du vent
    dans les feuillages des filaos
Coiffé d'un léger chapeau de rotin armé d'un grand parasol
    de papier
Je contemple les jeux des mouettes et des cormorans
Ou j'examine une fleur
Ou quelque pierre
A chaque geste j'épouvante les écureuils et les rats palmistes

from **Documentaries**

ISLANDS

VII. LIGHT AND SUBTLE

The air is perfumed
Amber musk and citron bud
The very fact of existing is real happiness

1924.

XI. ENERVATED

Garden hedged like a forest clearing
On the bank the eternal song of the roaring wind idles in the
     branches of the *filaos*
Wearing a light rattan hat armed with a large paper parasol
I contemplate the games of gulls and cormorants
Or I examine a flower
Or a stone
With each gesture I frighten the squirrels and the palm rats

Par la fenêtre ouverte je vois la coque allongée d'un steamer
    de moyen tonnage
Ancré à environ deux kilomètres de la côte et qu'entourent
    déjà les jonques les sampans et les barques chargés de
    fruits et de marchandises locales
Enfin le soleil se couche

L'air est d'une pureté cristalline
Les mêmes rossignols s'égosillent
Et les grandes chauves-souris vampires passent silencieusement
    devant la lune sur leurs ailes de velours

Passe une jeune fille complètement nue
La tête couverte d'un de ces anciens casques qui font au-
    jourd'hui la joie des collectionneurs
Elle tient à la main un gros bouquet de fleurs pâles et d'une
    pénétrante odeur qui rappelle à la fois la tubéreuse et le
    narcisse
Elle s'arrête court devant la porte du jardin
Des mouches phosphorescentes sont venues se poser sur la
    corne qui somme son casque et ajoutent encore au fan-
    tastique de l'apparition

Rumeurs nocturnes
Branches mortes qui se cassent
Soupirs de bêtes en rut
Rampements
Bruissements d'insectes
Oiseaux au nid
Voix chuchotées

Les platanes géants sont gris pâle sous la lune
Du sommet de leur voûte retombent des lianes légères qu'une
    bouche invisible balance dans la brise

Les étoiles fondent comme du sucre

1924.

Through the open window I can see the elongated shell of a
    medium tonnage steamer
Anchored about two kilometers from the coast and already
    surrounded by junks sampans and canoes loaded with
    fruits and local products
Finally the sun sets

The air has a crystalline purity
The same nightingales are singing themselves hoarse
And the great vampire bats pass silently before the moon on
    velvet wings

There passes a completely nude girl
Her head covered with one of those old helmets that today
    delight collectors
She is holding a thick bouquet of pale flowers with a heady
    odor that recalls both the tuberose and the narcissus
She stops short in front of the garden gate
Phosphorescent flies have come to rest on the horn that crowns
    her cap and add even more to the strangeness of her
    appearance

Night rumblings
Dead branches breaking
Sighs of rutting animals
Creepings
Soughing insects
Nesting birds
Whispering voices

The giant plane trees are pale grey under the moon
From the top of their vault fall slender vines that an invisible
    mouth swings in the breeze

The stars melt like sugar

                                                    1924.

1. LE FORMOSE

DANS LE RAPIDE DE 19 H. 40

Voici des années que je n'ai plus pris le train
J'ai fait des randonnées en auto
En avion
Un voyage en mer et j'en refais un autre un plus long

Ce soir me voici tout à coup dans ce bruit de chemin de fer
      qui m'était si familier autrefois
Et il me semble que je le comprends mieux qu'alors

Wagon-restaurant
On ne distingue rien dehors
Il fait nuit noire
Le quart de lune ne bouge pas quand on le regarde
Mais il est tantôt à gauche, tantôt à droite du train

Le rapide fait du 110 à l'heure
Je ne vois rien

1. THE FORMOSA

THE 7:40 EXPRESS

It's been years since I've taken the train
I've traveled by car
By plane
An ocean voyage and I'm making an even longer one

All of a sudden here I am this evening in this train racket that
      was once so familiar to me
And it seems that I understand it better than I did then

Dining car
You can't see anything outside
It's pitch black
The quarter moon doesn't budge when I look at it
But it's now to the left, now to the right of the train

The express is traveling 110 kilometers an hour
I can't see anything

Cette sourde stridence qui me fait bourdonner les tympans—
    le gauche en est endolori—c'est le passage d'une tranchée
    maçonnée
Puis c'est la cataracte d'un pont métallique
La harpe martelée des aiguilles la gifle d'une gare le double
    crochet à la mâchoire d'un tunnel furibond
Quand le train ralentit à cause des inondations on entend un
    bruit de water-chute et les pistons échauffés de la cent
    tonnes au milieu des bruits de vaisselle et de frein
Le Havre autobus ascenseur
J'ouvre les persiennes de la chambre d'hôtel
Je me penche sur les bassins du port et la grande lueur froide
    d'une nuit étoilée
Une femme chatouillée glousse sur le quai
Une chaîne sans fin tousse geint travaille

Je m'endors la fenêtre ouverte sur ce bruit de bassecour
Comme à la campagne

TU ES PLUS BELLE QUE LE CIEL ET LA MER

Quand tu aimes il faut partir
Quitte ta femme quitte ton enfant
Quitte ton ami quitte ton amie
Quitte ton amante quitte ton amant
Quand tu aimes il faut partir

Le monde est plein de nègres et de négresses
Des femmes des hommes des hommes des femmes
Regarde les beaux magasins
Ce fiacre cet homme cette femme ce fiacre
Et toutes les belles marchandises

Il y a l'air il y a le vent
Les montagnes l'eau le ciel la terre
Les enfants les animaux
Les plantes et le charbon de terre

This dull keening that makes my eardrums hum — the left
one is aching from it — marks our passing through an
open tunnel
Then it's the sound cascading from a metal bridge
The precisely plucked harp of switches the slap of a station the
double detour in the jaw of a raging tunnel
When the train slows down because of floodwaters you can
hear the sound of water churning and of pistons steaming
under pressure in the midst of the din of dishes and
brakes
Le Havre bus elevator
I open the blinds of my hotel room
I lean out on the wet docks and the great cold light of a
starry night
An excited woman clucks on the quay
An endless chain coughs strains labors

I go to sleep my window open to this backyard clamor
As in the country

YOU ARE LOVELIER THAN THE SKY AND SEA

When you're in love you must leave
Leave your wife leave your child
Leave your friend leave your sweetheart
Leave your lover
When you're in love you must leave

The world is full of Negroes and Negresses
Of women men men women
Look at the fine shops
That cab that man that woman that cab
And all the fine merchandise

There is the air the wind
The mountains the water sky earth
Children animals
Plants and coal

Apprends à vendre à acheter à revendre
Donne prends donne prends
Quand tu aimes il faut savoir
Chanter courir manger boire
Siffler
Et apprendre à travailler

Quand tu aimes il faut partir
Ne larmoie pas en souriant
Ne te niche pas entre deux seins
Respire marche pars va-t-en

Je prends mon bain et je regarde
Je vois la bouche que je connais
La main la jambe Le l'œil
Je prends mon bain et je regarde

Le monde entier est toujours là
La vie pleine de choses surprenantes
Je sors de la pharmacie
Je descends juste de la bascule
Je pèse mes 80 kilos
Je t'aime

BILBAO

Nous arrivons bien avant l'aube dans la rade de Bilbao

Une crique de montagnes basses et de collines à contrejour
noir velours piqué des lumières de la ville

Ce décor simple et bien composé me rappelle et au risque de
passer pour un imbécile puisque je suis en Espagne je le
répète me rappelle un décor de Picasso

Il y a des barquettes montées par deux hommes seulement et
munies d'une toute petite voile triangulaire qui prennent
déjà le large

Deux marsouins font la roue

210

Learn to sell buy resell
Give take give take
When you're in love you must know how
To sing run eat drink
Whistle
And learn to work

When you're in love you must leave
Don't whimper through your smiles
Don't build a nest between two breasts
Breathe walk leave go away

I take my bath and look
I see the mouth I know
The hand the leg The, the eye
I take my bath and look

The whole world is always there
Life full of surprises
I leave the drugstore
I have just weighed myself
I weigh my 192 pounds
I love you

BILBAO

We reach the Bilbao basin well before dawn
A bay with low mountains and hills shaded in black velvet
    pierced by the city lights
This simple, well-balanced setting reminds me and at the risk
    of being considered an imbecile since I am in Spain I
    repeat reminds me of a Picasso setting
There are skiffs operated by only two men, outfitted with a
    tiny triangular sail and already putting out to sea
Two porpoises bend into circles

Dès que le soleil se lève de derrière les montagnes
Ce décor si simple
Est envahi
Par un déluge de couleurs
Qui vont de l'indigo au pourpre
Et qui transforment Picasso en expressionniste allemand
Les extrêmes se touchent

LETTRE-OCÉAN

La lettre-océan n'est pas un nouveau genre poétique
C'est un message pratique à tarif régressif et bien meilleur
    marché qu'un radio
On s'en sert beaucoup à bord pour liquider des affaires que
    l'on n'a pas eu le temps de régler avant son départ et pour
    donner des dernières instructions
C'est également un messager sentimental qui vient vous dire
    bonjour de ma part entre deux escales aussi éloignées que
    Leixoës et Dakar alors que me sachant en mer pour six
    jours on ne s'attend pas à recevoir de mes nouvelles
Je m'en servirai encore durant la traversé du sud-atlantique
    entre Dakar et Rio-de-Janeiro pour porter des messages en
    arrière car on ne peut s'en servir que dans ce sens-là
La lettre-océan n'a pas été inventée pour faire da la poésie
Mais quand on voyage quand on commerce quand on est à
    bord quand on envoie des lettres-océan
On fait de la poésie

BIJOU-CONCERT

Non
Jamais plus
Je ne foutrai les pieds dans un beuglant colonial
Je voudrais être ce pauvre nègre je voudrais être ce pauvre
    nègre qui reste à la porte
Car les belles négresses seraient mes sœurs

As soon as the sun rises from behind the mountains
This simple setting
Is invaded
By a flood of colors
Which range from indigo to purple
And transform Picasso into a German expressionist
The extremes meet

OCEAN LETTER

The ocean letter is not a new poetic genre
It's a practical message at decreasing rates and much cheaper
     than a radiogram
It's used a great deal on board to dispose of matters that you
     didn't have time to handle before you left and to give
     final instructions
It is also a sentimental messenger who comes to tell you hello
     for me between two ports as far apart as Leixões and
     Dakar when knowing I'm at sea for six days you're not
     expecting to hear from me
I will also make use of it during the South Atlantic crossing
     between Dakar and Rio de Janeiro to carry messages
     backwards because you can only use it in that direction
The ocean letter was not invented for composing poetry
But when you're traveling when you're businessing when
     you're on board when you send ocean letters
You're making poetry

CAMEO CONCERT

No
Never again
Will I set foot in a colonial music hall
I would like to be that poor Negro I would like to be that
     poor Negro who stays at the door
For the beautiful Negresses would be my sisters

Et non pas
Et non pas
Ces sales vaches françaises espagnoles serbes allemandes qui
    meublent les loisirs des fonctionnaires cafardeux en mal
    d'un Paris de garnison et qui ne savent comment tuer le
    temps
Je voudrais être ce pauvre nègre et perdre mon temps

1924.

And not
And not
Those dirty French Spanish Serbian German cows who fill up
    the leisure time of bored officials longing for a garrison-
    town Paris and who don't know how to kill time
I would like to be that poor Negro and waste my time

                                                    1924.

AU CŒUR DU MONDE

Fragment retrouvé

Ce ciel de Paris est plus pur qu'un ciel d'hiver lucide de froid
Jamais je ne vis de nuits plus sidérales et plus touffues que ce
    printemps
Où les arbres des boulevards sont comme les ombres du ciel,
Frondaisons dans les rivières mêlées aux oreilles d'éléphant,
Feuilles de platanes, lourds marronniers.

Un nénuphar sur la Seine, c'est la lune au fil de l'eau
La Voie Lactée dans le ciel se pâme sur Paris et l'étreint
Folle et nue et renversée, sa bouche suce Notre-Dame.
La Grande Ourse et la Petite Ourse grognent autour de Saint-
    Merry.
Ma main coupée brille au ciel dans la constellation d'Orion.

Dans cette lumière froide et crue, tremblotante, plus qu'irréelle,
Paris est comme l'image refroidie d'une plante
Qui réapparaît dans sa cendre. Triste simulacre.
Tirées au cordeau et sans âge, les maisons et les rues ne sont
Que pierre et fer en tas dans un désert invraisemblable.

AT THE HEART OF THE WORLD

Rediscovered fragment

This sky over Paris is purer than a winter sky lucid with cold
I have never seen such starry, luxuriant nights as this spring
When the trees along the boulevards are like shadows from the
    sky,
Foliage in rivers thick with elephants' ears,
Plane tree leaves, heavy chestnut trees.

A lily on the Seine is the moon at the water's level
The Milky Way swoons on Paris and embraces it
Mad, naked, sprawled out, its mouth sucks at Notre Dame.
The Great Bear and the Little Bear growl around Saint Merry.
My amputated hand shines in the sky in the Orion constel-
    lation.

In this hard, cold light, flickering, more than unreal,
Paris is like the frozen image of a plant
Reviving in its ashes. Pitiful specter.
In unswerving line and ageless, the houses and streets are only
Stone and iron heaped up in an unbelievable desert.

Babylone et la Thébaïde ne sont pas plus mortes, cette nuit,
    que la ville morte de Paris
Bleue et verte, encre et goudron, ses arêtes blanchies aux
    étoiles.
Pas un bruit. Pas un passant. C'est le lourd silence de guerre.
Mon œil va des pissotières à l'œil violet des réverbères.
C'est le seul espace éclairé où traîner mon inquiétude.

C'est ainsi que tous les soirs je traverse tout Paris à pied
Des Batignolles au Quartier Latin comme je traverserais les
    Andes
Sous les feux de nouvelles étoiles, plus grandes et plus
    consternantes,
La Croix du Sud plus prodigieuse à chaque pas que l'on fait
    vers elle émergeant de l'ancien monde
Sur son nouveau continent.

Je suis l'homme qui n'a plus de passé.— Seul mon moignon
    me fait mal.—
J'ai loué une chambre d'hôtel pour être bien seul avec moi-
    même.
J'ai un panier d'osier tout neuf qui s'emplit de mes manuscrits.
Je n'ai ni livres ni tableau, aucun bibelot esthétique.

Un journal traîne sur ma table.
Je travaille dans ma chambre nue, derrière une glace dépolie,
Pieds nus sur du carrelage rouge, et jouant avec des ballons et
    une petite trompette d'enfant:
Je travaille à la FIN DU MONDE.

Babylon and the Thebaid are no less dead tonight than the
     dead city of Paris
Blue and green, ink and pitch, its arches starwashed.
Not a sound. No passersby. It is the heavy silence of war.
My eyes travel from the urinaries to the violet eye of the
     street lamps.
It is the only lighted space to which I can drag my uneasiness.

So it is that every evening I cross Paris on foot
From the Batignolles to the Latin Quarter just as I would
     cross the Andes
In the fires of new stars, ever larger and more overwhelming,
The Southern cross more stupendous at each step one takes
     toward it, emerging from the old world
Onto its new continent.

I am the man who has no more past.— Only my stump aches.—
I rented a hotel room to be truly alone with myself.
I have a brand-new wicker basket filling up with my manu-
     scripts.
I have neither books nor paintings, no esthetic geegaws.

A newspaper is yellowing on my worktable.
I work in my bare room, behind a frosted glass,
Bare feet on red linoleum, playing with balloons and a little
     child's trumpet:
I am working on LA FIN DU MONDE.

LE VENTRE DE MA MÈRE

C'est mon premier domicile
Il était tout arrondi
Bien souvent je m'imagine
Ce que je pouvais bien être ...

Les pieds sur ton cœur maman
Les genoux tout contre ton foie
Les mains crispées au canal
Qui aboutissait à ton ventre

Le dos tordu en spirale
Les oreilles pleines les yeux vides
Tout recroquevillé tendu
La tête presque hors de ton corps

Mon crâne à ton orifice
Je jouis de ta santé
De la chaleur de ton sang
Des étreintes de papa

Bien souvent un feu hybride
Électrisait mes ténèbres
Un choc au crâne me détendait
Et je ruais sur ton cœur

Le grand muscle de ton vagin
Se resserrait alors durement
Je me laissais douloureusement faire
Et tu m'inondais de ton sang

MY MOTHER'S BELLY

It was my first residence
It was quite round
Often I imagine
What I must have been like . . .

My feet on your heart mama
My knees tight against your liver
My hands grasping the canal
That ended at your belly

My back twisted into a spiral
My ears filled my eyes empty
Tightly curled up
My head almost out of your body

My skull at your cervix
I delighted in your health
In the warmth of your blood
In papa's embraces

Often a mongrel fire
Electrified my darkness
A shock to my skull relaxed me
And I kicked against your heart

The big muscle of your vagina
Tightened fiercely
Sadly I gave in
And you flooded me with your blood

Mon front est encore bosselé
De ces bourrades de mon père
Pourquoi faut-il se laisser faire
Ainsi à moitié étranglé?

Si j'avais pu ouvrir la bouche
Je t'aurais mordu
Si j'avais pu déjà parler
J'aurais dit:

Merde, je ne veux pas vivre!

My forehead is still dented
From my father's thrusts
Why must one let himself be thus
Half-strangled

If I could have opened my mouth
I would have bitten you
If I could have spoken then
I would have said:

Shit, I don't want to live!

PROSE

from **The Detonated Man (1945)**

Writing is a fire that ignites a welter of ideas and makes chains of images flame before reducing them to spitting coals and settling ashes. But if the flame releases the alarm, the spontaneity of the fire remains a mystery. For writing is burning up alive, but it is also a rebirth from its own ashes.

PROFOUND TODAY (1917)

I'm no longer certain whether I'm looking at a starry sky with the naked eye or at a drop of water under a microscope. Since the origin of his species, the horse has been moving, supple and mathematical. Machines are already catching up with him, passing him by. Locomotives rear up and steamers whinny over the water. A typewriter may never make an etymological spelling mistake, while the scholar stammers, swallows his words, wears out his dentures on antique consonants. When I think, all my senses light up and I should like to violate everybody, and when I abandon myself to my destructive instincts, I find the triangle of a metaphysical solution. Inexhaustible coal mines! Cosmogonies revive in manufacturers' trademarks. Extravagant signboards over the multicolored city, with the ribbon of streetcars climbing the avenue, howling monkeys holding one another by the tail, and the incendiary orchid clusters of architectures that fall on top of them and kill them. In the air, the virgin cry of trolleys! Raw matter is as well trained as the Indian chieftain's stallion. It obeys the slightest signal. Pressure of a finger. Steam pressure sets the connecting rod in motion. Copper wire makes the frog's foot start. Everything is sensitized. Is within eye's reach. Almost touches. Where is man? The gesture of infusoria is more tragic than the story of a woman's heart. The life of plants more moving than a detective story. The musculature of the back in motion is a ballet. This piece of fabric should be set to music and this tincan is a poem of ingenuity. Everything changes proportion, angle, appearance. Everything moves away, comes closer, mounts up, fails, laughs, states its position, and is enraged. Products from the five parts of the world show up in the same dish, on the same dress. We are nourished by the sweating of gold at each meal, at each kiss. Everything is artificial and very real. Eyes. The hand. The immense fur of figures on which I bed down my bank. The sexual passion of factories. The turning wheel. The gliding wing. The voice retreating along a wire. Your ear in an ear trumpet. Your sense of orientation. Your rhythm. You dissolve the world in the mold of your skull. Your brain becomes hollow. Unsuspected depth in which you collect the mighty flower of explosives. Like a religion, a mysterious pill speeds up your digestion. You lose yourself in the labyrinth of stores where you give up all claims on yourself to become everybody. With Mr. Book you smoke the five-cent Havana cigar pictured in the ads. You become part of that great anonymous body: the café. I can no longer recognize myself in the mirror, liquor has erased my features. He embraces the fashion shop like a bridegroom. We are all alarm clocks. Your hooves beat tattoos in the train station corrals to tame the beast of your impatience. They leave. They scatter. Skyrocket. In all directions. European capitals are in the trajectory of their inertia. A terrible whistle blast wracks the continent. The colonies lie in the net. Here's Egypt riding a camel. Enjoy winter sports in Engadine. Read about the Golf's Hotels in the palm trees. Think about four hundred windows in bright sunlight. We unfold the horizon of time schedules and dream about South Sea islands. Romanticism. Landscape streamers ripple at the windows while from garland-like trains fall flowers that take root and name— forgotten villages! Moving on your knees in the accordion of the sky through telescoping voices. The most blasé go the farthest. Motionless. For whole days. Like Socrates. With activity inside their head. The Eiffel Tower comes and goes at the summit. The sun, a cloud, a mite is sufficient to lengthen it, to shorten it. Metallic bridges are just as mysterious and sensitive. Watches set themselves. From every side ocean liners advance toward their rendezvous. Then the semaphore signals. A blue eye opens. The red closes. Soon there's nothing but color. Joint penetration. Record. Rhythm. Dance. An orange and a violet eat up one another. The chessboard port. In each square sinks everything you won by inventing the game, Dr. Alamedes. Hydraulic cranes empty thundering wagons. Helter-skelter. East. West. South. North. Everything struts along the piers while the lion in the sky strangles the cows of dusk. There are cargoes of fruit on the ground and on roofs. Barrels of fire. Cinnamon. European women are like undersea flowers in the face of the savage labor of the stevedores and the dark red apotheosis of the machines. You get a streetcar in your back. A trap opens under your foot. You have a tunnel in your eye. You climb to the sixteenth floor drawn by your hair. Smoking your pipe and your hands at the faucets— hot water, cold water—you dream about the commandant's wife whom you're going to play footsy with in a little while. Gold bridgework her smile and her accent is charming. And you let yourself glide down to dinner. Tongues are stuffed. You have to contort your face to make yourself understood. Gesticulating and laughing very loud. Madame dries her mouth with her loincloth napkin. Zephyr beef. Eureka coffee. Pimodan or Pamodan. In my rocking chair I'm like a Negro fetish, angular in the heraldic electricity. The orchestra plays "Louise." I amuse myself by riddling with pinpricks this fat goatskin body floating at eye's level. Diver, in the smoke from my cigar, alone, I hear the senti-mental music dying that makes my helmet ring. My lead soles hold me erect and I advance, slow, grotesque, tight around the collar, and lean awkwardly over the marshy lives of women. Your eye, sea horse, trembles, makes a comma, and passes on. Between two waters the phallus, bushy, complicated, sparse. This cuttlefish envelops me in its inky cloud and I disappear like a pilot. I can hear the water's motors, the metalworking machinery of air vents. A thousand suction pores function, secrete iodine. Skin turns to jelly, transparent, sends out spokes like anemone flesh. Nerve centers polarize. Independence of all functions. The eye reaches out to touch; the back eats; the finger sees. Tufts of grassy arms undulate. Sponge of the depths, the brain breathes softly. Thighs remember and make swimming movements. The storm pulls out your tonsils. A cry passes over you like the shadow of an iceberg. It freezes and parts. The being reassembles with difficulty. Hunger draws up the limbs and groups them around the void the belly has become. The body dons again the uniform of weight. The spirit, scattered all over, concentrates intó the rosette of understanding. I am a man. You are a woman. So long. Each one goes back to his room. There are shoes in front of the door. Don't mix them up. Mine are yellow. The bellhop waits for his tip. I give him the shield from my coat of arms. I have forgotten to sleep. My glottis moves. This suicide attempt is a regicide. I am impaled on my own sensitiveness. The night hounds come to lick the blood running down my legs. They change it into light. The silence is such that you can hear the universe's mainspring tightening. A click. Suddenly everything has grown a notch. It is today. Handsome, steaming horse. Illnesses rise in the sky like stars on the horizon. And here is Betelgeuse, mistress of the seventh house. Believe me, everything is clear, orderly, simple, and natural. Mineral breathes, vegetable eats, animal feels, man crystallizes. Prodigious today. Sounding line. Antenna. Door—face—whirl-wind. You live. Off center. In complete isolation. In anonymous communion. With all that is root and crown and which throbs, enjoys, and is moved to ecstasy. Phenomena of that congenital hallucination that is life in all its manifestations and the continuous activity of awareness. The motor turns in a spiral. Rhythm speaks. Body chemistry. You are.

Cannes, February 13, 1917.

231

MARC CHAGALL (1912)

Man is alone — quite alone. At his birth he fell into a tub.

It's raining tonight. It is dark. I seem to hear in the silence heavy steps in puddles of water. It's the mammoth tread of clouds moving across the sky. But is there still a sky? I touch at all points Man's stomped-on heart, that dark heart, stomped on, ground up by the heavy tread of suffering and weeping.

It's raining blood.

The wheels of madness turn in the sky's ruts and spatter God's face with mud! Clouds jump as if in a stupor.

The moon swells forth. No, it's really God's face. A desolate, smooth face. A bald, very round head. You would think the mouth was going to cave in. Two tears cling to the cheeks.

Ah, I believe it's my own head rocking, desolate, in space.

A cloud moves.

Two bear's feet stand on my shoulders and, up there, a carnal tongue licks God's eyes. Now I can only see my face in the clouds and a dog's tongue darting, hot, from a cloud.

Something moves. A section of the night falls in ruins. Is it you, Woman?

Pity.

Paris, April 1912.

from **Modernities**

PABLO PICASSO (1919)

Picasso. I don't know of a more tormented temperament, a more restless spirit, of more rapid and subtler fingers and brushes. His fire, skill, pride, the feeling for balance, love, cruelty, elegance, line, arabesque, perversity, the unusual, the occult, his very acute sense of taste ally him to Gilles de Rais and make of his output as much of an intellectual achievement as that of a man of letters. This is so rare in painting that it is worth being taken note of. I do not say that Picasso creates literature (as did Gustave Moreau), but I do claim that he has been the first to introduce into painting certain techniques considered, until now, exclusively literary. Neither study nor copy of reality. True absorption. Contemplation. Magnetism and intuition. Here is the first liberated painter. He creates. He has that mysterious sense of metaphysical correspondences and is in possession of the secret cipher of the world. He evokes, he transposes. He strips bare enigmatically. He insists. He points with his finger. He never blinks for he has the transfigured eyes of faith. He affirms life. He adores. Dazzled. Nor is there in him any scientific analysis, any Protestant theory, any preconceived lies; but only the eternal religion of the catholic senses and that overwhelming truth of the heart. For he loves. And everything that comes from his hand is alive, always.

He is, above all else, the painter of the true. Man, animal, plant, dumb matter, the spare abstraction, all lives, grows, suffers, copulates, multiplies, disappears, moves, still grows, threatens, imposes itself, crystallizes. He is the only man in the world who knows how to paint heat, cold, hunger, thirst, perfume, odor, fatigue, desire, envy, paralysis, throbbing, twitching, obscure jolts of the "enormous, delicate" unconscious. Then his literary demon intervenes. The painter cuts, pierces, saws, stabs, quarters, rips, strangles. Suddenly matter is there. Before your eye. Perceptibly

233

larger. This gives us the key to Picasso's Cubism, which is not of a purely esthetic order, as his imitators have believed, but is rather an exorcism of a religious nature which reveals the latent spiritual reality of the world. And it is still love. An idealistic transposition.

Given Picasso's peculiarly literary temperament, I consider his investigations of matter as rapid notations, keen, picturesque, striking, of depths, of Natural Histories in the manner of Jules Renard. And if Jules Renard has been christened "the eye," I shall call Picasso "the look" — a look at once mystic, tender, direct, cruel, savage, voluptuous, sadistic.

Since the war, the master, Picasso, has magnificently isolated himself, has again grown and moved away, in his own sense, filled with logic, agility, and grace. Like his Harlequins, his painting always wears a mask on its face. Too bad for those who have let themselves be taken in by this mystery. Picasso wants no more disciples. He knows. He is jealous of the face, of the serenity of his painting.

Paris, May 29, 1919.

from **Modernities**

THE EIFFEL TOWER (1924)

For Madame Sonia Delaunay

. . . . .

. . . In the years 1910, 1911, Robert Delaunay and I were perhaps the only ones in Paris talking about machines and art and with a vague awareness of the great transformation of the modern world.

234

At that time, I was working in Chartres, with B . . . , on the perfecting of his plane with variable angles of incidence, and Robert, who had worked for a time as journeyman mechanic, in some artisan locksmith's shop, was prowling, in a blue coat, around the Eiffel Tower.

One day, as I was coming back from Chartres, I fell out of the car at the exit of the Parc du Saint-Cloud and broke my leg. I was carried to the nearest hotel, the Hôtel du Palais, kept by Alexandre Dumas and his sons. I stayed there, in that hotel bed, for twenty-eight days, lying on my back with a weight pulling on my leg. I had had the bed pushed against the window. Thus, every morning, when the boy brought me my breakfast, threw open the shutters, and opened the window wide, I had the impression he was bringing me Paris on his tray. I could see, through the window, the Eiffel Tower like a clear flask of water, the domes of the Invalides and the Panthéon like a teapot and a sugar bowl, and Sacré-Cœur, white and pink, like a candy. Delaunay came almost every day to keep me company. He was always haunted by the Tower and the view from my window attracted him strongly. He would often sketch or bring his box of colors.

It was thus I was able to be present at an unforgettable drama: the struggle of an artist with a subject so new that he didn't know how to capture it, to subdue it. I have never seen a man struggle and defend himself so, except perhaps the mortally wounded men abandoned on the field of battle who, after two or three days of superhuman efforts, would finally quiet down and return to the night. But he, Delaunay, remained victor.

At that time, Delaunay, who had learned to paint from the Impressionists, had just completed a more or less short period with the Fauves. He had exhibited a series of extremely detailed landscapes and some ten, very highly colored portraits. He had encountered the first Cubists at the Salon des Indépendants, and all the young painters, faced with the loose construction of the Impressionist canvases, the Pointillistes' confettiwork, the disconnected quality of Divisionism, and the hysteria of the Fauves (their own youthful canvases), were experiencing more and more the need to return to more solid forms and to go back not to such and such an art form of the past, all of which seemed to them equally insufficient, but to the very sources of plastic forms, to question everything, to restudy all esthetic values, to mistrust inspiration, to suppress the subject, to reconsider all problems of technique, from the manufacture of colors to the use of lighting sources and the weaving of the canvas. During these six or seven years, from 1907–08 to 1914, storehouses of patience, analysis, and erudition were expended in the workshops of young Parisian painters, and never has there blazed such a fire of intelligence. The painters examined everything, their contemporaries' art, the style of all periods, the plastic expression of all peoples, theories from every age. Never had so many young painters gone to museums to examine minutely, to study, to compare the techniques of the great masters. They called upon the production of savages and primitive peoples and the esthetic remnants of prehistoric men. They were equally preoccupied with the latest scientific theories in electrochemistry, biology, experimental psychology, and applied physics. Two men, who were not even painters, had an enormous influence on the first wave of Cubist painters, the mathematician Princet, to whom they presented new plastic works and who immediately conceived a numerical formula for them, and the Hellenist scholar Chaudois, who controlled all the theories produced with the help of quotations drawn from Aristotle, from Anaximander, and the pre-Socratic philosophers. This intense critical and creative activity was called by Maurice Raynal "The Quest for the Fourth Dimension."

Delaunay was untutored but very sympathetic, tall, strong, possessed of enormous gusto for living, temperamental, a seeker after pleasure. All those brilliant aphorisms, all those superb theories made him dizzy. He reacted according to his temperament and, being a born painter, reacted through color as Apollinaire perceived so well that in his famous *Esthetic Meditations,* the book he devoted in 1913 to the Cubist painters, he doesn't talk about Delaunay, unsuccessful in placing him in that group of works and theories, waiting instead to find for him disciples and to speak of him in a second volume, for which he had found the charming title *The Orphic Painters;* unfortunately, the war and his death overtook him.

And this is how Delaunay worked.

He shut himself up in a dark room, the shutters fastened. After he had prepared his canvas and ground his colors, he bored a tiny hole in the shutter with a center bit. A ray of sunlight filtered into the dark room and he began to paint it, studying it, breaking it down, analyzing it in its elements of form and color. Without knowing it, he was devoting himself to spectrum analysis. He worked in this manner for some months, studying pure solar light, reaching sources of emotion beyond the limits of all subject matter. Then he enlarged the hole in the shutter a bit and began to paint the play of colors on a transparent, fragile material like the pane. Reflections, fragments of mica; his small canvases took on the synthetic look of jewels and Delaunay introduced into the ground colors precious stones, specially powdered lapis lazuli. Soon the hole made in the shutters became so large that Delaunay opened the leaves completely and let the abundant daylight penetrate into his room. The canvases of this period, which are already a little larger in format, represent closed windows where light plays in the panes and on white muslin curtains. Finally, he drew the curtains and opened the window so that you can see a yawning, luminous hole and the roof of the house opposite in shadow, hard and solid, a primeval form, heavy, angular, bent.

Delaunay is increasingly drawn by what is taking place, there, outside, and the infinitely minute play of light he studied in a sunray he now sees as gigantic, enormous in the luminous ocean welling over Paris. It's the same problem but in another proportion and on an immense scale.

He next paints those canvases of fifty-six meters, "La Ville," "Les Trois Grâces sur Paris," where he tries to reconcile the academic style and all the painterly novelties he has just discovered: the Seine, with the peak of Notre Dame, the Parisian suburbs, and Alfortville. At last he finds a new subject which allows him to apply all his discoveries and all his techniques: The Big City. A multitude of new problems appear, analogies, relationships, spiritual and physical contrasts, questions of perspective, matter, abstract questions, unanimism, and synthesis. And Paris' whole personality engulfs him.

More and more, he who spends months contemplating Paris from the top of towers, more and more his eyes turn toward the Eiffel Tower, that extraordinary form.

It was then I met him.

I talk to him about New York, Berlin, Moscow, about prodigious centers of industrial activity spread out over the whole surface of the earth, about the new life being formed, about universal lyricism, and that tall youth, who had never left Paris and was only interested in questions of form and color, had guessed all that while he was contemplating the Tower, deciphering the first colored billboards that were beginning to cover houses, watching the birth of mechanical life in the streets before his very eyes.

And now, think of my hotel window opening onto Paris. It was the subject of all his preoccupations, a ready-made painting which had to be interpreted, constructed, painted, created, expressed. And that was quite difficult. In that year, 1911, Delaunay painted, I believe, fifty-one canvases of the Eiffel Tower before succeeding.

As soon as I could go out, I went with Delaunay to see the Tower. Here is our trip around and in the Tower.

No art formula known until then could make the pretense of resolving plastically the problem of the Eiffel Tower. Realism made it smaller; the old laws of Italian perspective made it look thinner. The Tower rose above Paris, as slender as a hat pin. When we walked away from it, it dominated Paris, stiff and perpendicular; when we approached it, it bowed and leaned out over us. Seen from the first platform, it wound like a corkscrew, and seen from the top, it collapsed under its own weight, its legs spread out, its neck sunk in. Delaunay also wanted to depict Paris around it, to situate it. We tried all points of view, we looked at it from all angles, from all sides, and its sharpest profile is the one you can see from the Passy footbridge. And those thousands of tons of iron, those 35 million bolts, those 300 meters high of interlaced girders and beams, those four arcs with a spread of 100 meters, all that jellylike mass flirted with us. On certain spring days it was supple and laughing and opened its parasol of clouds under our very nose. On certain stormy days it sulked, sour and ungracious; it seemed cold. At midnight we ceased to exist, all its fires were for New York with whom it was already flirting then; and at noon it gave the time to ships on the high seas. It taught me the Morse code which allows me today to understand radio messages. And as we were prowling around it, we discovered that it exerted a singular attraction for a host of people. Lovers climbed a hundred, two hundred meters over Paris to be alone; couples on their honeymoon came from the provinces or from abroad to visit it; one day we met a boy of fifteen who had traveled from Dusseldorf to Paris, on foot, just to see it. The first planes turned about it and said hello, Santos-Dumont had already taken it for his destination at the time of his memorable dirigible flight, as the Germans were to take it for their target during the war, a symbolic and not a strategic target, and I assure you that he wouldn't have hit it because the Parisians would have killed themselves for it, and Gallieni had decided to blow it up, our own Tower!

So many points of view to treat the problem of the Eiffel Tower. But Delaunay wanted to interpret it plastically. He finally succeeded with the famous canvas that everybody knows. He took the Tower apart to make it fit into his frame, he truncated it, and bent it to give it 300 meters of dizzying height, he adopted 10 points of view, 15 perspectives, so that one part is seen from below, another from above, the houses surrounding it are taken from the right, from the left, bird's-eye view, level with the ground. . . .

One day I decided to pay a call on M. Eiffel himself. Besides it was an anniversary, the Tower's 25th birthday or M. Eiffel's 75th. I was led into a little hotel in Auteuil, crowded with a swarm of heteroclite works of art, all frightfully ugly and useless. On the wall of that famous engineer's study were hanging photographs of some of his finest creations, bridges, designs of railroads, stations. And as I was referring to all that immense labor and to the esthetic which developed from his work, and as I was particularly complimenting him on the Tower, I saw that old man's eyes open wide, and I had the very clear impression he thought I was making fun of him! Eiffel himself was a victim of Viollet-le-Duc and almost apologized for having dishonored Paris with the Tower. Now those misunderstandings no longer astonish me; but I state with pleasure all the same that the number of engineers capable of participating in today's esthetic is becoming more and more numerous.

Extract from a lecture delivered
June 12, 1924, at São Paulo, Brazil.

from **Modernities**

ADVERTISING = POETRY (1927)

Advertising is the flower of contemporary life; it is an affirmation of optimism and pleasure; it distracts the eye and the mind.

It is the warmest sign of the vigor of today's men, of their power, of their puerility, of their inventiveness and imagination, and the finest success of their will to modernize the world in all its aspects and in all areas.

Have you ever thought about the sadness that streets, squares, stations, subways, first class hotels, dance halls, movies, dining cars, trips, highways, nature would all exhibit without the innumerable billboards, without show windows (those beautiful, brand-new toys for thoughtful families), without luminous signboards, without the false blandishments of loudspeakers, and imagine the sadness and monotony of meals and wines without polychrome menus and fancy labels.

Yes, truly, advertising is the finest expression of our time, the greatest novelty of the day, an Art.

An art which appeals to internationalism, or the polyglot; to crowd psychology; upsetting all the static techniques by making an intensive use, endlessly renewed and workable, of new materials and untried techniques.

The chief characteristic of worldwide advertising is its lyricism.

And it is here that advertising impinges on poetry.

Lyricism is a way of being and feeling, language is the reflection of human awareness, poetry illuminates (as advertising does a product) the image of the mind that conceives it.

Now, in the whole of contemporary life, only today's poet has become aware of his time, is the conscience of that time.

That is why I appeal here to all poets: Friends, publicity is your domain.

It speaks your language.

It carries out your poetics.

Language is born of life, and life, after creating it, nourishes it.

There is in the spoken language a spontaneity which shrouds and colors the expression of thought and makes grammar unstable.

The sentence precedes the grammatical structure, the word precedes the syllable. And language is subordinate to life in its infinite development.

Industrialists, have your advertising done by poets as Moscow does its propaganda.

* * *

I have often been asked what were the seven marvels of the modern world.

The seven marvels of the modern world are:
1. the internal combustion motor;
2. the S.K.F. ball bearing;
3. the cut of a great tailor;
4. Satie's music that we can finally listen to without holding our head in our hands;
5. money;
6. the bare neck of a woman who has just had her hair cut;
7. advertising.
I know 700 or 800 more that die and are born every day.

Paris, February 26, 1927.

242

It is three o'clock in the afternoon — the 18th of June, 1880.
It is Sunday, and Congress is not even in session.
The terrified urchins take to their heels.

The hours pass upon the vast deserted square and as the sun sinks the giant shadow of the Capitol covers the body of the general as with a pall.

CHAPTER SEVENTEEN

Johann August Sutter was seventy-seven years old when he died.

Congress has never pronounced in his case.

His descendants have refrained from all intervention. They have abandoned the affair.

The succession is still open.

We are in 1926. For a few years to come those who have the right can intervene, act, file their claim.

Gold! Gold!

Who wants GOLD?

Translated by Henry Longan Stuart

CHAPTER SIXTEEN

IV

The Great Harlot who has given birth upon the Sea is Christopher Columbus, discovering America.

The Angels and the Stars of St. John are in the American flag. With California, a new star, the Star of Absinthe, has been added.

Anti-Christ is Gold.

The Beasts and Satans are the cannibal Indians, the Caribs and Kanakas. There are also black and yellow ones — the Negroes and Chinese.

The Three Riders are the three great tribes of Redskins.

Already a third of the peoples of Europe have been decimated in this land.

"I am one of the twenty-four Ancients, and it is because I have heard the Voice that I have descended among you . . . I was the richest man in the world. Gold has ruined me . . ."

A Russian woman falls down in ecstasy at Sutter's feet while he is expounding the visions of St. John the Evangelist and recounting the episodes of his own life.

V

But Sutter is not permitted to give himself up to his rapturous madness.

Johannes Christitsch is his evil genius. It is Johannes Christitsch who reopens the historic case, who conducts it personally, and is determined to win, cost what it may. Christitsch goes to Washington every week. There he solicits, intrigues, fills up reams of stamped paper, flourishes briefs, rummages archives, brings new facts to light, and by his feverish energy galvanizes the ancient process into new and spasmodic life. Often he brings Sutter with him, or sends him in alone. He exhibits him, makes him speak — becomes his manager, in a word. Somewhere or another he has unearthed a general's uniform. He insists that the old man shall put it on, and even pins decorations on his breast.

So the martyrdom of the general commences afresh. He is dragged from office to office, from department to department. High officials deplore the case of this aged victim, take voluminous notes, promise to intervene and obtain him full satisfaction. When he is alone, groups of idlers form around him and make him tell them the story of the Discovery of Gold. Sutter is quite willing. He mixes his beloved Apocalypse and the doctrines of the Herrenhutters into the story of his life. His wits are gone. All the urchins of Washington can tell you he is crazy and their amusement knows no bounds.

The old fool.

"The richest man in the world."

What a scream!

VIII

One day, upon the streets, he meets three orderlies who are taking a lunatic to the asylum. The man in their clutches is a ragged and filthy creature, an old man, who gesticulates, who fights with his guardians, and who shouts incoherently. Breaking for a moment from their hands, he flings himself in the gutter,

filling his mouth, his eyes and ears with garbage, and grasping handfuls of mud and manure between his skinny, yellow fingers. His pockets bulge with ordure and he has a sack filled with stones.

While the orderlies are binding their patient, the general looks at him closely. It is Marshall — Marshall the carpenter of Fort Sutter and Coloma. Marshall recognizes his old employer. "Master, master, didn't I tell you? There is gold everywhere — everywhere!"

IX

One warm afternoon in June the general is sitting on the bottom step of the great flight that leads to the Capitol. As with many aged men, his head is quite empty of thought. He is simply enjoying a rare moment of physical well-being as he warms his old carcass in the sun.

"I am the general, general, general.

"I am the gen-e-ral!"

A ragged street urchin of seven is running down the great steps, taking four at a stride. It is Dick Price, the little match seller, the old man's favorite.

"General! General!" he cries, flinging his arm round the drowsy old man's neck, "you've won! Congress has just settled it. A hundred million dollars — all for you, General!"

"You're sure . . . ? Sure . . . ?" cries Sutter, holding the wriggling boy tightly.

"Sure, General! It's in all the papers. Jim and Bob has gone to get them. I'm going to sell the papers tonight! You watch 'em go!"

Sutter does not see seven little rascals behind his back who are wriggling with laughter like so many malicious sprites under the lofty portico, and gesticulating delightedly at their confederate. He jumps to his feet, draws himself to his full height, says but one word:

"Thanks!"

Then he thrashes the air with his arms and falls like a log. General Johann August Sutter is dead.

PART I: HEDWIGA

(Selection)

A melody bellowing from a record player.

Set in motion by the ceiling fans, the phonograph sucked in the couples, threw them out again in profile, stumbling, dizzy. Voices from every country, hymns from every nation echoed. Fluorescent lights glittered in the mirrors and women whirled about like humming tops.

Champagne corks exploded on all sides.

Dominating the melee of waving flags and the blinking of electric wreaths, the four brass trumpets of the mechanical orchestra stood out, imposing, shining, and greedy.

In a single glide on his shoulder blades and to an immense burst of laughter, Dan Yack crossed the polished floor. There was a brief struggle; then, liveried valets removed him from the hall, closing tight the dazzling ballroom doors.

Then Dan Yack fixed his monocle in his eye and, holding on to the ramp with both hands, descended the club's grand staircase on his heels.

The golden rods holding the rug down stabbed at his head, as painful as darts, and each step gave way under him like a collapsing springboard. He felt as if he were performing a dangerous acrobatic feat, between heaven and earth, on a level with the sky images and searchlights turning upside down in the distance; he was hot and arrived at the bottom of the steps as if he were coming out of a cloud bank, his eyes filled with multicolored confetti, his temples ringing, his chest expanding with the din of the party, his entire body bathed in sweat.

He was trembling.

Footmen, in uniforms decorated with black braid and peacock feathers affixed to astrakhan bonnets, surrounded him. One handed him his cane, another his hat, a third his gloves. He thanked them, like a fool, with exaggerated gestures and, nodding his head repeatedly, softly applauded with the tips of his fingers. They smiled, winked in amusement, nudged him familiarly, pushed him toward the exit. His eye set, his gestures flabby, his legs rubbery, he pretended to resist. Carried backwards by their supporting arms, he sang in a falsetto voice:

> . . . et benedictus fructus ventris tui . . .
> A-a-a-men.

Suddenly, he broke loose. He threw himself at the door. An areca palm rose up from the mass of green plants like a heron on one leg. Dan Yack cut it down with his cane and left, bareheaded, a palm leaf in his hand. As he passed, he slapped the astonished doorman who dropped his staff so that its knob, as it hit the ground, burst like a peashooter. A cab horse set off at a gallop, while the laughter of the routed lackeys tore open, as in a rape, the morning's pure scarf.

Now Dan Yack was sitting pitifully in the middle of the road at the foot of the tall buildings of the darkened Arsenal. He was bathing in horse urine and both hands rolled balls of smoking manure.

The Neva was flowing in the corner of his eye.

Oblique, threatening, the wooden skiffs raced downstream and tore at the rushing waves that the harsh wind raised against the tide and pushed upstream. Sudden shudders raised the hackles on the river's damp fur, a river that stretched and arched its back. Norwegian steamers mewed furiously. The saw-toothed maw of the drawbridges opened silently, and tiny steamboats fled in disarray, leaping like dolphins terrified by the sight of a shark.

Suddenly, the sky billowed out like a sail.

At once everything bent down, tottered, expanded, drew nearer and began to run, then fired a broadside, turned about in place, shivered and took off again with the wind, withdrew, shedding buckets of water. In the squall everything darkens, sinks down, becomes muddy. Great tossing buoys pass dancing, while the city lurches in the spray.

Five minutes later, the river is like a great body covered with goose pimples, stretched out with its head hanging down, its legs in the air, its thighs spread apart and held up. An island leans over it helpfully and moves inside its long veils of smoke. The river is seized with convulsions, glittering tongs violate the water that fills with blood; finally the sun comes to the world, bright and ruddy. Clouds hurry forward, seize it, dip it in a tub of starch, and when it leaves their embrace, it is suddenly higher and brighter.

Dan Yack jumps up.

He feels as if he has been present at a remarkable performance. He is overcome by it. He takes aim with his hand against his cheek and the clouds fall, a bull's-eye.

Everything changes appearance again and is forever engraved in his memory. In a hard light. The deserted wharf. The humble wash drying on the deck of the royal yacht. Those three sailors singing in a boat.

Dan Yack bursts out laughing and hurls insults at them.

Then he takes off running. He sings, ". . . et benedictus fructus ventris tui . . ." to the tune of a popular song.

With his hand, he beats an uneven tempo.

The night cabs return from the Islands. Over by the Stock Exchange, 50,000 wooden shoes drum louder and louder on boat decks and the navy flags snap like castanets. A solitary automobile races by.

Leaping, Dan Yack passes through all this noise. He seems to be dancing to the rhythms of an awakening city. Everything delights his eyes — colors, light, life: the drunks sunk into the bellies of cabs, the enormous prostitute flanked by two slender officers of the guard, the cab decked out with pompons, the limousine smiling. He shouts ". . . A-a-a-amen!" while he is crossing this wave of vehicles that threatens to drag him toward Nevsky Prospect where the first trolley shivers in the morning.

And, ending up behind the Winter Palace, Dan Yack suddenly shuts up. He turns around uneasily. His legs give way. Fatigue overwhelms him. An infinite melancholy deflates him, bloats him, weights him down. Staggering he reaches the Bridge of Sighs. He sits down in the gutter unmindful of the carts brushing past him. A watchman rushes up then withdraws discreetly as he recognizes this famous roisterer whom all of Saint Petersburg envies.

Dan Yack has the feeling he's rising into the air like an observation balloon. A straining cable holds him back as if it were anchored to his marrow. A weight. A steam windlass screeches. His nerves stretch to the breaking point. His heels leave the ground, then fall back, and rise up again, gently.

Little by little, this movement becomes more pronounced. The muscles of his calves join in, his tendons, knees, finally his thighs.

Now Dan Yack, without changing position, is stomping his feet, moving his arms. Even his head dangles, seems to separate from his body and swell.

He bursts out laughing again.

And all the city noises rush upon him once more. Amplified, excited, they arrive at full speed. They pour out of every street, at every crossing, without putting on their brakes. A carriage swept along on a current of air, a cab thrown forward, a machine sliding along, a wheel turning. Above the roofs, the wind is a turbine.

GENOA

(Selection)

In Naples, we lived on an immense estate shaped like a right-angle triangle whose summit, occupied by our large dwelling, windows, balconies, terrace framing from above the narrow streets, dark alleyways, tiny passages filled with drying laundry all sloping to the lower port, was located right at the foot of the steep ramparts of Saint Elmo's Fort (when the cannon marked noon its hot breath swelled the dining-room curtains, making Mother start every time), whose base was the rectilinear outline of the Victor Emmanuel II Boulevard, and whose two sides were clearly marked, the left by the funicular's railway track, bordered by a row of prickly thorned and bladed cacti, Barbary fig trees, agaves, aloes bearing their flower at the end of an often-broken mast; the right side by an old wall, and in places very high, full of ferns, iris, maidenhair, swarming with lizards that ran quickly and hid in crevices under those clumps of little blue flowers so delicate you might think them of porcelain and that the common people call "ruins of Rome," crested with bottle fragments and following all the turnings and windings, the convolutions of the

Salita de San Martino, a very busy ramp that climbed to the Vomero, reinforced by a bedrock of brambles, thorns, and brush, by streams of refuse, rubbish, pottery shards, and broken dishes, by used utensils that the poor people of the district threw over the wall, and by fallen rocks as befitted an old rampart. Mama wasn't happy there. She was afraid of thieves. But the children, my brother and sister, and the four Ricordi girls — my father had invited his friend to come live with us, a constant irritation to my mother: she thought the photographer too familiar and ill-mannered, and it was true that he was, but he was such a gay companion at the table, laughing in the Italian way, stuffing himself, drinking, his collar open, in shirt sleeves, and always telling stories about the court and the grand people he saw there, and to amuse his daughters, acting out the scenes, gesturing, gesturing! — but the children, especially Elena and I, who were the smallest, kept somewhat out of the way, I, because Mama was already getting extremely nervous and had too many worries, Elena, because her father would have preferred to have a boy like the King, his master, and the Crown Prince, his protector, the prince of Naples who claimed to have already assured his succession, the arrival of a daughter had disapointed him; the children lived in the enchantment of the marvelous garden whose enclosure Mama had formally forbidden us to enter, again because of the robbers who, according to her, were swarming about and on the lookout for children, and most particularly for the children of rich foreigners, to kidnap them for ransom. I can't imagine from whom she had these absurd ideas unless it was from Miss Sharp, our English governess, Lily, living in fear of the Black Hand. She collected newspapers that spoke of the Mafia, addressed warning letters to the *Times,* and fled at the sight of a tradesman coming into the garden. There was no better choice possible for twisting the mind of a child than that stupid governess, an old maid given to migraines, full of prejudices and ridiculous superstitions, and trembling like a leaf. Parents make those mistakes because they think they're doing the best thing or from snobbery. I don't know who had recommended Lily to us; she stayed with us for years.

But my father had given me a dog, a yellow and black cur who was called Leone, a lion in whose company I feared nothing or no one when I was hunting snails along the old wall that bordered the ill-reputed ramp of La Calade. Moreover, the lower gate, the carriage entrance, was watched by Ernest, our gateman; and the upper postern gate which led to the little Square of San Martino, at a hundred meters from the house on the right, and at which the tradesmen presented themselves — in the morning, it was Pascuali, our milkman, who rang first and who waited in the midst of his bleating goats, leading his cow, Caroline, who had been bought for me and whom he milked in front of the door, often accompanied by Bepino, his last born, a little boy of my age astraddle the beast, which made me envious, and I should have liked to have descended to the city to make their rounds with them — this postern was always triple-locked and outfitted with a peephole and only opened at the ringing of a large bell which could be heard in every corner of the house and after confirmation of the caller's identity.

In that immense garden, as bushy as a park and planted with native trees of various species and extended along the edge of the funicular by an orchard filled with all kinds of fruit trees whose sloping strata were marked by rows of centenary fig trees and whose embankments served as masonry for canals, gutters, small floodgates, fountains, terminating, at the very bottom of the property, in a large rectangular pond with, at the four corners, twisted medlar trees, situated in the middle of a quincunx shaded by white mulberry trees whose berries were as sweet as crushed strawberries, which made us linger there, stuffing ourselves, Elena and me, lulled by the frogs, and from which led a wretched path obstructed by large round stones leading to a forgotten bit of land, to a little house buried under the jasmine and heliotrope that hung down from the house, clinging to the always closed shutters, behind which a lamp burned at midday, where could be heard the music of a raging piano, from time to time a shadow passed between the disjointed louvres, a white jacket, a madras handkerchief, *zia* Regula, a madwoman who lived there, shut up, and whom nobody ever visited, and whom Elena and I, who were inseparable, came to watch at long intervals in the secret hope of surprising her one day when she would come out of her alcove to sit at her window and smoke her cigar, a long tuscan, or that she would silence her piano to take a walk outside as Benjamin, the old gardener, had told us she did sometimes, and we lay in wait in this loneliest part of the property, a real jungle, on the opposite side, on the extreme right, jeering, Benjamin cultivating there a vegetable garden, separated from the mass of weeds by a rotting, sagging gate whose lattices we would tear out to make swords and knives for ourselves and to cut down the thistles, the nettles, the tall gummy and sticky weeds we had trouble getting clear of when we were hiding there, Elena and I, on the other side of the gate, because that was forbidden — there was even a stake in this tangle with the word DANGER and, indeed, there was somewhere a cesspool in the morass of shaggy stems and great leaves wrinkled and slashed by the caterpillars from the gourd vines and pumpkins and dusty fans of the night-blooming Marvel of Peru whose papier-mâché-like flower has the odor of rancid butter in the sun — and also to infuriate the Englishwoman armed with an alpenstock who looked everywhere for us in the immense bushy garden and whom we could hear coming, rummaging in the laurel bushes, the camelia copses, the clumps of green, the curtains of ivy which were not lacking in the luckily uncared-for park, clucking, calling, getting unnerved, bringing on a crying jag because she was not succeeding in flushing us out, which made us laugh, Elena and I, who watched her through the luxuriant grass or from behind the sunflowers marking the limit of the vegetable garden and artichoke plants higher than our heads, and we slid furtively through the thick foliage and along paths known only to us, crawling in short spurts to come out, as if nothing had happened, on the pergola, in front of the house, where Alfred, my big brother, Elisabeth, our elder sister, Margarita, Iolanda, Malfalda, Elena's sisters, had already eaten their lunch and were doing their lessons, while my mother was sorting the plants in her herb garden (it was an attitude she had adopted once and for all to hide her inner anguish and sidetrack the nervous sickness that was undermining her) and Signora Rosa, Elena's mother, a gentle woman who was once again pregnant, was preparing a layette, hoping, this time, to deliver a male heir, which would give satisfaction to the court photographer, and we came forward with an innocent air, but our cheeks red from having run, holding hands, Miss Sharp, who had finally caught up with us, screeching, all out of breath, at our back and accusing us of all the crimes of Israel, Elena and me, and has palpitations of the heart and collapsed into an armchair, and swooned, letting fall the poker-work edelweiss alpenstock she could no longer hold on to and cried:

"Oh, my lord, my eyeglass!"

But the eyeglass was already on the ground, starred like a fat tear, and even two, when it had had the ill fortune to fall flat on a naughty rock, our gravel being studded with sharp flintstones, hard as iron, which give off sparks when you rub and hit them against one another, and which smell of ozone and loadstone. I had quite a collection of them, as well as a snail menagerie, and marbles, and tops, the Neapolitan kind with a long nail and shaped like multicolored mushrooms, large and small, and that you can spin on the palm of your hand, like God the world, or the King his people, the balance always uncertain. It's quite amusing. And it tickles. But you musn't be clumsy, especially when Leone was jumping after me, barking, and I had to raise my hand well over my head to put the top which was hypnotizing him out of his reach and without letting fall the whining toy that drove him crazy.

"Down, Leone, lie down, boy. You're too stupid, old fellow. You don't understand. This game is serious. Look. . . ."

But Leone would make me laugh. Then, for the fun of it, I would spin off a hundred tops right under his nose and Leone would throw himself on the gleaming, marble-embellished floor of the hall in the anteroom, as twenty years later, in 1915, I was to see Guynemer's plane, "Vieux Charles," rush roaring among the stars, bombs exploding in front of him. To catch what? Nothing! Unless Guynemer's little Spad foreshadowed, unknown to everybody, the ancestor of the airplane precursor, the flying fortress *Enola Gay* of Captain Paul W. Tibbets, who was to send up, a quarter of a century later, on exactly August 6, 1945, at 9:15 a.m., a monstrously real mushroom: lightning, clouds, smoke, wind, explosion, diluvian rain, flakes of fire, death by disintegration, radiation, irradiation, continuous death, slow death, leprosy and cancer, wounds, burns, gaping holes. That's what my dog makes me think of, today, fifty years later. I ought to have called him Bikini, if I had known. With a single hit 150,000 human beings were vaporized in a fraction of a second. Not even time to say Shit! . . . and all around the point of impact, for twenty kilometers, 150,000 others, lying like tops on their side. Pompeii, Hiroshima. What progress. You push a button . . . And for a trial run, that's not bad and, in fact, is even promising. It seems we'll do better the next time. Bravo! But did not Franklin D. Roosevelt, champion of Democracy and Peace, know that he would be damned and cursed by people for having ordered, encouraged, and financed "that"? It's certainly the act of a cripple who, his skull exploding, feels his head roll ahead of his wheelchair into his family tomb and who wants to cling to anything and who drags everything with him. (Like Hitler, who was paranoic, a raging madman who thought himself a prisoner of the outer world and kicked out at it between two sessions of morose delight in front of his mirrored wardrobe and who began to stamp with rage and howl, unable to free himself from his own reflection!) But what a crazy democracy the censer bearers extol in the peace of cemeteries, stock market candidates, successors to the President of the U.S.A., all failures and tools of the Brain Trust!

Leone died run over by a streetcar which was not even electric but drawn by mules. I was very upset. He still had the strength to cross the road, pulling himself by his forepaws, the hindquarters almost completely severed. He didn't understand what had happened to him. I patted his good head, he licked my hands, and there was a convulsion and a last jump, and a spongy dung ran from his rear and a clot of blood from his mouth. Poor beast! My dog was too happy, frisky.

The child came into the world, but was once again a girl, Monella, a nice little frog like those in the pond, and she was quickly forgotten because she only lived two or three days, and the morning after her funeral, while Signora Rosa, still languishing in her bed, was weeping bitterly, calling on the Holy Virgin, and with the professional mourners gone, filling the house with her despairing cries, Ricordi took the little family in a carriage to the Royal Palace, where all the old nobility that counted in the city, honorific renown, celebrity at any title, from the singers and tenors of the Teatro San Carlo to the court tradesmen, and even distinguished foreigners who had received an invitation, were filing past the empty cradle of the little Prince of Piedmont, son of the Crown Prince, the Prince of Naples, the future Victor Emmanuel III.

Waiting for our turn to go in, the carriage parked opposite the palace, Ricordi, who was in a good mood at the idea of approaching his protector and presenting his family to him, was joking and, to amuse his daughters, he showed them the statues which lined the façade and pointed out most particularly those, on a level with the entresol, of four generals from the time of Charles Albert, the nephew of the King of Sardinia, each one erect in his niche, in full uniform, head bare, bicorn hat under his arm or in his left hand, proudly puffing his chest out, pointing with the index finger of the right arm, gestures and poses that Ricordi commented on in the following manner:

The first general, who has his right arm held out in front of him and who is vaguely indicating something in the distance, is stating without fear of contradiction, "Somebody has farted!" The second, his chin in his right hand, his index finger at one side of his nose, his eye dreamy, seems to be reflecting and affirming, suspiciously, "That certainly stinks!" The third, rearing up, his right hand over his heart, his fingers spread out among his decorations, impetuous and proud, knowing that no one can doubt his word without having him put his hand to his sword, declares, challenging the whole world, his eyes burning, "I swear it's not I!" The fourth, his right arm raised in the air and pointing out the window of the queen's bedroom which is located just over his head, his eyelids closed, his nostrils dilated, his chest slightly drawn in as though he were asking forgiveness, his mouth half-opened, his face in ecstasy, is giving thanks, "Everything comes from the Almighty!"

After this jest of the talking statues, in the purest southern humor, always earthy, often scabrous, which borders on scatology and is only repeatable because it sets off a hearty pagan laugh without finesse or ambiguity or forethought, it was now our turn and the irreverent courtier and zealous photographer, suddenly impatient and extravagantly busy, pushing us, becoming expansive, greeting everyone in an officious manner, bowing and scraping incessantly in order not to go unnoticed, watching his daughters, retying the ribbons of one, smoothing another's skirt with the back of his hand, straightening the eldest's curls, fanning Elena with a perfumed handkerchief he took out of his jabot, pulling on my lace collar, strutting like a peacock, hurrying, hurrying my brother and sister, making us climb the great state stairway where valets in satin culottes and white stockings with fretted seams were lined up; file nimbly into the gallery between a double row of impassive guards in gala uniforms, high polished boots with gold spurs, leather breeches, plumed helmet, shoulder belt, cape straight or curved sword at eye level, fixed motionless; cross state drawing rooms filled with bedizened chamberlains, knights in embroidered capes, decorated aides-de-camp, lofty individuals covered with medals, crosses, diamond stars, suns on ribbons, a broad ribbon cutting in two their shirt front, grand ladies in dresses with trains, moving their fans, head heavy with ornaments, ears, shoulders, arms, wrists, fingers sparkling, gloves pulled up above the elbow or pulled down or folded like a perfumed lace handkerchief and their eyes extraordinarily severe or serious or dark or fixed or astonished or hard in their worried face, without makeup, between the diamond crests or sweeping plumes trembling in their hairdo and the rows of pearls or the heavy antique necklaces which gripped their neck, and the other family jewels taken out for twenty-four hours from the pawnbroker's, gold coronet, family colors, bangs worn over their forehead or the Parisian baubles they were wearing on this reception day; penetrate, considered a marked sign of favor, into the little red-and-gold drawing room, in Cordoba leather embossed with coats-of-arms and armorial bearings, reserved for the most intimate courtiers, and had us all bow together, like a general presenting an honor guard or a ballet mistress her pupils, prostrating ourselves before the Prince of Naples, his most serene highness, who condescended to interrupt a conversation to smile at us and dismiss us with a wave of his hand; then pass on tiptoe into an adjoining room, the porcelain bedchamber, and one after another bow low before him whom we children thought to be the Prince of Piedmont, a little sleeping baby that the Duchess of Caserta, disguised for the occasion as a classic children's nurse in the typical, sumptuous costume from some peasant province of the kingdom (and even perhaps of Savoy), was carrying in her arms, surrounded by other servants charmingly dressed in costumes from all the other provinces, from Tuscany, Venetia, Lombardy, Calabria, Sicily, from Pouille (but not from Romany or the Church States!) and who were all ladies-in-waiting, and the little prince of the blood slept, his fists tightly closed, *the thumbs inside,* the way little babies often do when you prevent them from sucking on them and as the great painter Vereshchagin removed the thumbs of all the corpses lying on the field of battle in his historical paintings of the wars of Holy Russia, of whom a large oblong canvas in which all the dead sleep like the little prince of the blood, their fists closed, *the thumbs inside,* and from which I couldn't take my eyes, filled a whole panel of the next drawing room where were seated the little baby's mother, the Crown Princess, and her grandmother, the Queen, wife of Umberto I, King of Italy, a red-and-blue drawing room that we only crossed single file, bobbing down and up repeatedly, as my little friend's father did before the august ladies while dragging us rapidly backwards, without giving us time to stop in front of the famous painting, for which my father's friend had the dishonesty to reproach us often afterwards, complaining of the lack of attention of children who didn't listen to what they were being taught; and, finally, we were able to satisfy our curiosity and admire the object for which we had come, the cradle that the people of Naples had offered to the son of their beloved Prince, and whose photograph all the newspapers had printed on the first page, and of which all society had been talking for a year as if it were the seventh wonder of the world, and Ricordi who had photographed it from all angles, that fragile royal cradle, ran around it, harangued, filled his eyes with it as if he had designed or executed it. Vanity of vanities, all photographers are like that who take themselves for creators, as the druggist for a scholar, the pharmacist for a doctor, the nurse for a surgeon, the paint merchant for a painter, the prompter for an artiste, the bookshop owner for a writer, the publisher for the immortal author of the works he publishes, and a Stokowski or a Toscanini for Beethoven himself! idiotic attitude that dates from the beginning of the nineteenth century, that Stendhal and Baudelaire were the first to denounce by jeering at Franklin and Americanism, bombast that takes on the proportions and virulence of a cancer and will stifle the modern world if mechanism and technicians haven't first brought it down by draining it from below.

The empty cradle was a masterpiece of the goldsmith's art, inset with mother-of-pearl, gold and silver, ornamented on two sides with shells detailing mythological events, invaluable cameos, and never since have I seen such richness of work and such a debauchery in the choice of precious materials used in any palace in the world, nor in any reproduction or description of famous cradles, nor later, in China, where I saw numerous pieces as baroque as they were curious, and not even at London, when Gaby Deslys's bed was put on sale after her death, an enormous courtesan's bed, all worked in heavy gold, absolutely round, where a number of people could lie down, the head in the center, the feet toward the periphery, and whose round mattresses, round pillows, round sheets, and covers were curiously laced to permit thirty-two positions. (It was the Marquis de Zuttes who bought this extraordinary bed to install it in one of his numerous castles in Spain or in Scotland, and the proceeds from the sale were disbursed to the poor in the Marseilles almshouses, following the express wishes of the testatrix, Alice Caire, called Gaby Deslys, native of that city.)

The visit to the Royal Palace had taken place in the morning. Toward noon we rejoined my father who was waiting for us at one of the most famous restaurants in the city and where the finest society was piling in; but we didn't even have time to do justice to that good lunch, Ricordi hurrying us along, so ill-timed was his love of mingling with the great, and, before dessert, he pulled us at a trot toward the official platforms which had been set up at the water's edge to review the flotilla, the first squadron of great warships, of which Italy could be justly proud; and at the défilé of troops that followed, the Abyssinian army—poor soldiers, it was the first time in my life I pitied soldiers—the Abyssinian army was wildly acclaimed by an enormous, delirious, and overexcited crowd. At nightfall a fantastic fireworks display exploded, the fleet anchored in the gulf bombarding the illuminated city with thousands and tens of thousands of fire bursts and versicolored rockets and the forts replying with mortars and explosions from all the surrounding hills, then, toward midnight, there was a monstrous bouquet, a general conflagration in the sky and the sea, sufficient to put Vesuvius in the shadow, and that only the fireworks makers, the Ruggieri brothers of Venice, who have done it from father to son for several generations, having proved themselves in all the festivals and public celebrations across Europe since the sixteenth century, could allow themselves and risk hinting at a catastrophe which turned into an apotheosis . . . But I was asleep on my feet.

Personally, I don't remember it; but to our little group, it seems that I was hero of the day. They told it to me when I was small in the same way I am repeating it today.

Ricordi had settled us in the Crispi box, the famous Italian statesman, founder of the Triple Alliance, that first model of the steel axle, but an elastic model (elastic that wasn't even synthetic!) and the first Council president to put Parliament on that slippery slope from which Italy began to slide into Germany's arms, the King held against the Kaiser's chest, falling into disgrace, the Duce fearfully embracing the Führer and dragging him into the abyss, just the other year, the Dynasty strangled as if by a monstrous hernia, all the characters in the tragedy entangled like Laocoön and his sons in the rings, the coils of the serpent.

Crispi, who was an elderly gentleman, with a large nose all pockmarked and heavily veined and with the somewhat pitiful eyes of a faithful dog, and who knew my father, had taken me on his knees, and, suddenly, I peed on his knees, not that the terrible mustaches, the thick eyebrows, the restless expression of King Umberto, sitting in the box at our side and who turned around often to see who the little boy was astraddle his Prime Minister's knee, had particularly impressed me or that the incessantly renewed cheers of the crowd massed at the foot of the royal tribune, raising a cloud of dust that burned our eyes and dried our throat had moved me, but simply because I had eaten too many sherbets during the afternoon, I felt like it, I didn't know how to hold back, I was tired, so I relieved myself and went to sleep.

It appears that Crispi had laughed at it, like a grandfather at his grandson's innocence; but on the way home, everyone made fun of me in the carriage, and once home, the way in which Ricordi could tell the thing while exaggerating it, embellishing it, mimicking it in the Neapolitan fashion, coloring it with raw expressions to make of it an improvised comedy in which he played the role of several persons, Crispi, me, the King, the crowd, with such shocked verve and such a funny accent that he finally made even Signora Rosa burst out laughing! Only Miss Sharp and Mama didn't laugh, Lily because she had not been invited to the celebration and was sulking and moping, Mama, Mama who had spent the day at home to keep poor Signora Rosa company, Mama . . . Mama . . .

I could never find out how Mama had taken the thing which subsequently so shamed the governess, when Ricordi and my father, at every opportunity, and especially when there were visitors to the house, made me submit to the retelling of that misadventure, to the point that it became a kind of glory eventually, as if it were a fine farce they were boasting about, Mama, Mama never flinched, didn't wince, even though that night recalled to her the first night she had spent waiting for my father who had not come back from the celebration . . . the first night of feverish waiting which was to repeat itself so often after that . . . and the celebration was over.

I won't insist. Shakespeare said it:

> Life's but a walking shadow, a poor player
> That struts and frets his hour upon the stage
> And then is heard no more: it is a tale
> Told by an idiot full of sound and fury,
> Signifying nothing . . .

Life is a farce, a comedy, a universal tragedy, and the fate that moves about all the characters in the drama without their knowing it, which shakes them like a goblet and throws them willy-nilly on the rug like dice in a poker game: Elena who was to be killed by an anonymous bullet one sunny, calm Sunday afternoon; the old King assassinated the following year (and it's perhaps because he was waiting for his assassin that he turned around continually in his gilded armchair that holiday); Mama dead in less than ten years in extreme solitude; and my father, after twenty-five years, remarried and completely ruined, farmer's son that he was, a self-made man; Victor Emmanuel the Younger who, like Max Jacob who was just as short in his slippers, stuffed a deck of cards in his boots and for good measure stuck an enormous plume on his cap to put himself on a level with a Mussolini, that bloated, pasty-faced "Carnival Caesar," a coward, an erotomaniac, and a liar, who was ignobly strung up by one foot, his head down, bleeding like a pig, while the little King was given the sack and Max was getting a martyr-poet's halo; the delicate little prince whom I had seen sleeping *his thumbs turned in* become Umberto II for one week, kicked out, and obliged to go into exile after having been kept out of the way for years, becoming bored, aging, prematurely bald, jaundiced, discouraged, frightened, soft, having done nothing, given nothing, he whom the people had received with so much love and welcomed with so much hope and good wishes; my brother a diplomat, my sister married in Italy, the Ricordi family scattered, and the old court photographer still living today, honored and almost a hundred years old, while I'm writing these childhood memories, typing, besmearing myself with printer's ink, a writer no less! for writing is a kind of abdication . . . who would have said it and how not to admit that the destiny that had played poker with all of us was only a drunken barman who had made us drink devilish cocktails, more numerous and of a less palatable mixture than the sherbet that circulated on a silver and gilt platter in the royal box, that day of the Great Celebration, and which had such a deplorable effect on me?

Another peepee story put us on the track of the difference between the sexes, and it was Elena — the little girls having their eyes opened wide earlier than little boys to those facts — who formulated the equation, a short time before the poor dear was killed, as I have said, by an unfortunate shot.

As short as it was and apparently free of all significance, I can date from the coming of Monella to the house all the changes wrought in our routine after her disappearance.

I have already noted how my father failed to return after the celebration. His absences became more and more frequent at the evening meal and even lasted whole days, and under the pretext of business trips, Ricordi began soon to accompany him, and he too was absent more often. For their part, my brother and sister and Elena's sisters who called us scornfully, she and me, *I promessi Sposi* when they came upon us arm in arm or with one arm tenderly around the other's neck on the long cypress-bordered path, where they passed in a carriage making fun of us, "the kids," who were not part of the group, going down two or three times a week to the city to have a treat, to go to receptions at friends of their age who had also found places in the official boxes the day of the celebration and whose parents, tradesmen at the court, high officials, upper-class bourgeois, officials, now formed a separate band, inviting one another back and forth and spending Sunday on such and such a neighboring family's estate, in the country or at the seashore. Naturally, Miss Sharp accompanied them everywhere, chaperoning the "young ladies" (I counted Alfred in their number), and the immense bushy garden was at our disposal and we never played finer games, Elena and I, wandering into the farthest corners; but on Sunday, by dint of insisting and making a scene in front of Mama — and also because Mama and Signora Rosa preferred their solitude, on Sunday, Mama to cherish her taciturn sorrow and pamper her nerves, Signora Rosa to prepare the justified reproaches she would heap up on her husband when he should reappear, each one shut up in her bedchamber at the opposite ends of the great empty houses — on Sunday I had permission for Maria, a good Neapolitan maid, covered with holy medals, badges, and scapulars, to accompany us to the Vomero enclosure, just a short walk away, where we spent the afternoon, playing around Virgil's tomb, picnicking on the grave, hiding to watch the little birds in their migratory season, old Maria taking a nap or counting her beads on the lawn of the abandoned cottage, and never had we been so happy, Elena and I, as during that period when we were left to ourselves and to our own inspiration.

My greatest passion was the training of snails. Bepino, son of our farmer Pascuali, had shown me how to keep them awake by tickling their belly with the end of a toothpick. We collected them everywhere, big ones, little ones, brown, white, yellow, others whose shell is like speckled coral and still others, dark or transparent and fragile, bordered in blue, in black, or whose median furrow is hard like mother-of-pearl, and others, stuck together in couples, drooling, foaming. While Elena, armed with the toothpick, tickled them conscientiously under the belly, I stretched threads in the air, from one twig to another, in a straight line, diagonally, zigzag, in a circle, in the shape of a star, and when the snails were wide awake, we would put them single file on these threads, hundreds of them one after the other, and their slow, amusing processions unrolled in all directions, on different, superimposed levels, like penitents, each little animal in his monk's cloak and each one carrying for a lighted candle his tentacular eyes which telescope so amusingly and are tactile. When we had had them perform the exercise a dozen times, we would stretch the same threads to the ground and the snails would follow all the complicated turns of the threads as an interminable train follows the rails of a train track, the long silver thread of Ariadne twisting back several times on itself in the turns and windings of a labyrinth before leading to the exit, and the exit was marked by a pile of fresh lettuce leaves where the well-trained creatures rested and feasted, but saddled, harnessed, caparisoned like circus horses in the stable, ready for a new performance. And we had them go through the specialty again and Elena clapped her hands.

Every Sunday I presented her with a well-trained menagerie that Elena would tie up in Maria's big headkerchief or that old Maria brought back to the house in her tucked-up apron, fretting and fuming all the way at our fancy, and crossing herself numerous times.

I don't know what Elena could have done with all those circus snails I gave her, I never saw a one of them again; I supposed that she played with them in the privacy of her room, showing them to no one and especially not to her sisters who would have uttered cries of horror, playing in secret and putting on shows, and I was proud and pleased with myself, and every day I looked for others, my principal hunting ground being the old wall of the Salita de San Martino, whose fissures contained specimens of phenomenal size and great variety, those from Virgil's tomb being rather runty and common; so every day of the week she and I would explore the old wall.

One morning, it was in the week preceding the day of her death, we were at the bottom of La Calade, near the dangerous part of the property, behind Benjamin's vegetable garden. The hunt had been good. Elena had tied up her short skirt into a game bag to carry the snails we collected and I had my pockets filled with fat slobberers.

"What about going to see *zia* Regula?" Elena said to me.

"Let's go," I replied.

We glided into the tall grass at the edge of the ravaged gate.

Now that we went every Sunday to Virgil's enclosure and put snares there, it had been a long time since we had come to this deserted spot.

That day there was nobody about. Benjamin was not in his cabbage patch. The little garden behind the cottage was deserted, and the piano was silent. The lamp was out and we could only see the dark between the sagging panels of the drawn shutters. But the door yawned open.

A half hour passed.

"Could she be dead?" Elena whispered.

We had sat down in the grass. We couldn't leave, the house seemed so mysterious to us with the creeping jasmine and the network of heliotrope that ran right up to the door, trailing on the ground.

We didn't take our eyes off the door.

Had the aunt seen us and was she not spying on us from the back of the hall? That could very well be and we were beginning to be afraid, slightly afraid. A breeze, less than a breath, moved like a trembling or a slight shiver the curtain of odiferous plants.

Who was *zia* Regula and whose aunt was she? We had often wondered and we knew nothing of it. Mama no more than Signora Rosa had ever breathed a word to us and when I questioned my brother and sister or Elena her sisters, they laughed in our face. "Aunt is aunt," they replied. And *zia* Regula couldn't be Benjamin's aunt since she played the piano like a lady. "She's a madwoman," answered Benjamin when we questioned the old gardener. "She smokes like a man but she's not wicked. I look after her and watch her so that she won't run away. She's always lived here. She's a woman who's had disappointments in love." Was she perhaps the former mistress of the estate? . . . Was she perhaps a fairy? . . .

And all of a sudden the aunt pops out of the house. She's a tall, fleshy woman, swarthy as a gypsy and dressed like those nomads in a flowered jacket and a long, pleated skirt dragging behind her on the ground. A red handkerchief encircles her head. She takes several steps forward and stops in the middle of the path. We were ready to jump up and run away, Elena and I. But the *zia* stands in the middle of the path without looking about her, without turning her head to the right or to the left, she stays there a good minute without budging, then whirls around and withdraws into the house. She stops a second on the sill to light a cigar and disappears without turning around. Then we began to run until we were out of breath.

"Did you see?" Elena asked me when we stopped, gasping, in the big cypress-lined avenue, near our parents' house. "Did you see, she peed like a man!"

Indeed, I had certainly seen the water flowing and making a puddle between *zia* Regula's legs when she had stopped still in the middle of the path, but I had not been aware of it.

"How stupid you boys are," Elena said to me, "you never notice anything."

And she explained to me, "We girls have to stop to do our business. Horses, cows dirty themselves running but have to stop to pee. On the other hand, boys stop to dirty themselves but pee while they're running. Do you think there are beings in this world capable of doing both without having to stop, walking or running? It's impossible. Even birds come to rest to leave their doo-doo, the little dears, who never pee. But the aunt can pee standing up, just like a man, without squatting. I'll never be able to do it."

"How do you know?" I said to her. "Try it!"

Then Elena spread her legs, stood in the middle of the

avenue, but after a minute the little girl dropped the snails she was holding in her knotted skirt, smoothed out her little dress, stared at me, her eyes filled with tears, and said, "I'm not a boy. I'm ashamed!"

And she turned around and ran away.

"Elena," I shouted behind her, "don't run away! . . . What's the matter? Don't be afraid!"

But the little girl was running without turning and dashed into the house.

"How silly girls are!" I said to myself.

I didn't understand. I stayed there, sulking. And I began to crush the snails Elena had dropped and I emptied my pockets in disgust for many of those I had put there had been crushed in our mad dash while we were running away, and I turned out my pockets, gooey and sticky with froth and full of soft objects. Then I went back to the cottage of the *zia* to prove to myself that I was not afraid like a girl.

The lamp was burning, and a senseless music burst forth behind the shutters.

Old Maria was grieving, and the funeral cries of Mediterranean women are like no others. Pagan curses, cries, threats addressed to the saints, appeals to the Holy Virgin and to the Infant Jesus who is called to witness, infernal, raucous bellowings and sobs and moans so protracted and nuanced they never end, ardent prayers belched out, consternation make up this funeral lament and there's something stagy in this public explosion of grief. Already a few isolated neighbors, some strollers, Sunday promenaders, hunters were entering the enclosure. The old servant's rage doubled. I shot out like an arrow to the Solfatare farm to find Pascuali.

"Pascuali, Pascuali! Come quick! We have to take her down to the house, it's already filled with people."

"Oh, lord, what a terrible thing! But do you think she's really dead?"

"Alas, Pascuali."

"But how did it happen?"

"It was a hunter. An ill-aimed shot. She's not moving anymore. But do hurry, Pascuali!"

"Wait until I change my shirt, today's Sunday, and I'll slip on a jacket."

"No, Pascuali, come as you are, there's no time to lose. We have to take her down to the house."

"Poor little kid . . ."

And Pascuali came, just as messy as I found him because he was busy raking up his compost heap, and we began to run, going down the path, with me in front, Pascuali behind, in his hand a strap that he had taken down as he went out of the stable, an old halter, Bepino running behind his father and behind Bepino came Carminella, Pascuali's wife, her hair disordered, beating her breast and already crying out, and behind her, frightened hens who were leaving by the gate that had been left open, and even the ass, who raised his head and stopped grazing to follow us with his eye, began to bray.

The enclosure was crowded. People were pressing up around the knoll, gossips, curiosity seekers that Pascuali had to shove aside, a circle of consternated hunters who were talking about the shot, and at the foot of the great umbrella pine, in the midst of a clump of good women kneeling and repeating in chorus the lamentations of old Maria leaning over her, lay the dear child, sheltered by the ancient roots, on a bed of pine needles, pretty as an angel, already in Paradise, her hands clasped, a spot of blood on her left ring finger, fallen from her left eye, in the corner of which, near the temple, a light foam made beads, like blood-colored sweat or dew. A bullet must have struck her in the corner of the eye and penetrated the brain, a bullet which must have ricocheted off the trunk of the centuries-old tree. Maria had closed her eyes. My little girl was resting, sweet and transfigured.

Pascuali went to work at once. He ran and tore off a board from the old door of the enclosure, like a lover tied Elena on this board with his halter, raised the dear burden onto his head and slowly set off, climbing up the hill, Bepino and I to his left and right, Maria, whose knees kept giving way, held up by Carminella, the other women behind those two, the hunters behind the women, sheepish as if each of them had been the guilty one, the other spectators forming a cortege with that innate sense of ceremony that Neapolitans show on every occasion, whether it's a question of the procession of Saint January or the festival of Piedigrotta, passersby joining us, their heads bare, people coming out of houses as we reached the top of the Vomero, so that there was a mysteriously forewarned crowd when we stepped out onto the little square of the Chartreuse de San Martino where the first steps of the Calade staircases descending to the house began, less than two hundred meters away, and that crowd kneeling through respect and love of death, wouldn't let us continue, but forced Pascuali to enter the chapel to put down his burden and display the little dead child before the altar, and candles were already being lighted, and prayers were being offered up, and the convent bell was sounding the death knell, and suddenly, beggars, cripples, and blind, as they are everywhere in Italy around churches and pilgrimage sites, poured out at top speed like a flock of birds of ill-omen, tumbled down the steps of the big stairs, overcome by an insane eagerness to see who could first bring the fatal news to the family . . . and in spite of my deep sorrow, excessively real and overpowering, I couldn't keep from smiling as I followed them with my eyes . . . those . . . those devils, Caladian tightrope walkers swarming at each landing, hunchbacks, the splayfoot, beggars, lepers, with thieving women and children, a veritable Court of Miracles.

. . . . .

I won't add a thing, except to say that on our return from Campo Santo where he had had his daughter's remains placed in the Ricordi family vault, the photographer went to the Vomero enclosure, nailed up the board Pascuali had torn down, and condemned the old door by putting another board across it that he had bought and stretching two or three sections of barbed wire at the entrance—and after that, none of us ever returned to Virgil's tomb.

. . . . .

And yet I'm there, hiding there by chance for a week without finding peace, and meditating and recreating and tormenting myself, evoking in my sleepless hours the unforgettable past and its deceiving optics, fallacious, lying, but yet miraculous because it is not only memory that awakens and begins to function automatically, but the eyes, the eyes of childhood that open, and for the first time, and in a harsh light that puts everything in relief, and when you have this impious vision of your own life, truly, it's because you don't hope for anything more. Everything runs out between your fingers, sand and soot, unlike the mystics who possess God and are possessed in return.

I still remember how, a month after Elena's death, a frightful odor spread throughout the house. It smelled of decaying flesh. They washed, soaped, scrubbed, scoured, disinfected, but in vain; then they had workmen come to take up flooring and tiling thinking to find dead rats, but there weren't any and the horrible stench, far from fading, grew so much stronger that one fine day it led directly to Elena's room from where, beyond a shadow of a doubt, it was infecting the whole house. By looking everywhere and sounding the walls, they finally discovered a cabinet hidden in the wall, filled from top to bottom with boxes and cartons piled on top of one another, all the packages Elena could lay her hands on or steal from her sisters, hatboxes, shoeboxes, glove cartons, painted horns that had contained candies or chocolates, tin cookie canisters, little multicolored baskets made of interwoven wood shavings, the kind you present on certain birthdays or feast days bulging with candied fruits, cardboard cartons little presents had come in, doll boxes, and all that was filled with hundreds and thousands of snails, carefully sorted and arranged according to size, shape, color, and that Elena's death had left to perish from hunger, from whence the abominable smell. Nobody understood what this strange collection could possibly mean, and I, my heart aching with joy and my soul poisoned by this discovery, said nothing. It was my secret . . .

272

. . . From that time — the winter of 1916–17 — I became eager
to pierce the mystery of Mary Magdalene, the lover of Jesus
Christ, the only woman who made Our Saviour weep . . . And
it is because the younger of my comrade Sawo's sisters had an
imperfection in her eye, what in medicine is called a coloboma, a
defect of the iris in the form of a keyhole fissure, that by putting
my mind to that hole I believe today I have penetrated into the
very soul of the Penitent of the Holy Ointment and am capable
of writing the story of her mystic wedding rites and of her contemplative life, if God so wills it and if the Anglo-Saxon bom-
bardiers leave me the time and the leisure, that secret book I've
been working at for more than a year, *La Carissima,* and from
which I will draw a film that I will produce in the very heavens
once the war is finished and I can obtain at a discount, by liqui-
dating my bonds, the marvelous planes, gliders, dirigibles, heli-
copters, and other machines indispensable for the ultramodern
techniques which alone will allow me to accompany, precede, and
circle about in order to film her at all camera angles according to

her uncertain flight when in her ecstasy Mary Magdalene is carried into the air by angels, as it is depicted on the rutted road of Saint Maximus, at the top of an ancient landmark four feet high, known as the Holy Pestle, for these machines of war, of murder, of destruction and nameless horror must be useful for something else, since aviators don't yet know how to use them to sanctify . . . But who has not deserved the heavenly fire? . . . Sanctus! Sanctus! these old stones cry out. . . . And what does the rivalry of opposing ideologies matter to us? It's all the same. And the economy, political or private, doesn't interest the human race. Bloated intellects. To live is to die . . . Sanctus! Sanctus! My squadron will sing like giant organs and will disappear into the host of angels transporting Mary Magdalene to heaven, naked under her adorable locks . . . Sanctus! . . . yes . . . into the very heavens . . . Shall I descend again or only, like a message, my parachuting film? . . . I think, I think I shall return . . . Yes . . . Live, first of all, live. I am of the earth.

New Directions Paperbooks

Henry Miller,
  Sunday After the War. NDP110.
  The Time of the Assassins. NDP115.
  The Wisdom of the Heart. NDP94.
Yukio Mishima, *Death in Midsummer.*
  NDP215.
Eugenio Montale, *Selected Poems.*† NDP193.
Vladimir Nabokov, *Nikolai Gogol.* NDP78.
New Directions 17. (Anthology) NDP103.
New Directions 18. (Anthology) NDP163.
New Directions 19. (Anthology) NDP214.
George Oppen,
  The Materials. (SFR) NDP122.
  This In Which. (SFR) NDP201.
Wilfred Owen, *Collected Poems.* NDP210.
Boris Pasternak, *Safe Conduct.* NDP77.
Kenneth Patchen, *Because It Is.* NDP83.
  Doubleheader. NDP211.
  The Journal of Albion Moonlight. NDP99.
  Memoirs of a Shy Pornographer. NDP205.
  Selected Poems. NDP160.
  Plays for a New Theater. (Anthology)
    NDP216.
Ezra Pound, *ABC of Reading.* NDP89.
  Classic Noh Theatre of Japan. NDP79,
  The Confucian Odes. NDP81.
  Confucius to Cummings. (Anthology)
    NDP126.
  Love Poems of Ancient Egypt. Gift Edition.
    NDP178.
  Selected Poems. NDP66.
  Translations.† (Enlarged Edition) NDP145.
Philip Rahv, *Image and Idea.* NDP67.
Herbert Read, *The Green Child.* NDP208.
Jesse Reichek, *Etcetera.* NDP196.
Kenneth Rexroth, *Assays.* NDP113.
  Bird in the Bush. NDP80.
  The Homestead Called Damascus. WPS3.
  Natural Numbers. (Selected Poems)
    NDP141.
  100 Poems from the Chinese. NDP192.
  100 Poems from the Japanese.† NDP147.
Charles Reznikoff,
  By the Waters of Manhattan. (SFR)
    NDP121.

Charles Reznikoff,
  Testimony: The United States 1885–1890.
    (SFR) NDP200.
Arthur Rimbaud, *Illuminations.*† NDP56.
  Season in Hell & Drunken Boat.† NDP97.
San Francisco Review Annual No. 1.
  (SFR) NDP138.
Jean-Paul Sartre, *Nausea.* NDP82.
Stevie Smith, *Selected Poems.* NDP159.
Stendhal, *Lucien Leuwen.*
  Book I: *The Green Huntsman.* NDP107.
  Book II: *The Telegraph.* NDP108.
Jules Supervielle, *Selected Writings.*† NDP209.
Dylan Thomas, *Adventures in the Skin Trade.*
  NDP183.
  A Child's Christmas in Wales. Gift Edition.
    NDP181.
  Portrait of the Artist as a Young Dog.
    NDP51.
  Quite Early One Morning. NDP90.
  Under Milk Wood. NDP73.
Norman Thomas, *Ask at the Unicorn.*
  NDP129.
Lionel Trilling, *E. M. Forster.* NDP189.
Paul Valéry, *Selected Writings.*† NDP184.
Nathanael West, *Miss Lonelyhearts &*
  Day of the Locust. NDP125.
George F. Whicher, tr.,
  The Goliard Poets.† NDP206.
Tennessee Williams,
  The Glass Menagerie. NDP218.
  In the Winter of Cities. NDP154.
  27 Wagons Full of Cotton. NDP217.
William Carlos Williams,
  In the American Grain. NDP53.
  The Farmers' Daughters. NDP106.
  Many Loves. NDP191.
  Paterson. Complete. NDP152.
  Pictures from Brueghel.
    (Pulitzer Prize) NDP118.
  Selected Poems. NDP131.
Curtis Zahn,
  American Contemporary. (SFR) NDP139.

* Paperbound over boards.   † Bilingual.
(SFR) A New Directions / San Francisco Review Book.

**Complete descriptive catalog available free on request from
New Directions, 333 Sixth Avenue, New York 10014.**

M.